DESPERATION ROAD

Other books by Michael Farris Smith

Rivers
The Hands of Strangers

DESPERATION
ROAD

MICHAEL FARRIS SMITH

NO EXIT PRESS

This edition published in 2017 by No Exit Press,
an imprint of Oldcastle Books Ltd, PO Box 394
Harpenden, AL5 1X
noexit.co.uk

ISBN
978-1-84344-987-4 (hardcover)
978-1-84344-986-7 (paperback)
978-1-84344-988-1 (epub)
978-1-84344-989-8 (kindle)
978-1-84344-990-4 (pdf)

2 4 6 8 10 9 7 5 3 1

Typeset in 12.75pt Garamond MT
by Avocet Typeset, Somerton, Somerset TA11 6RT
Printed and bound by CPI Group (UK) Ltd, Croydon, CR0 4YY

For more information about Crime Fiction go to @crimetimeuk

For Presley and Brooklyn, may your little lights shine

Acknowledgments

Thanks go to Birney Imes, Maridith Geuder, Matthew Guinn, Andrew Kelly, Erinn Holloway, Sean Doyle, Daniel Woodrell, Jason Richman, and Yuli Masinovsky. A special thank you to Lee Boudreaux and the team at Lee Boudreaux Books and Little, Brown. Another special thank you to Ellen Levine, who arrived at just the right time. A final thank you is for Sabrea, may you never grow tired of carrying me.

And if you spend yourselves in behalf of the hungry
and satisfy the needs of the oppressed,
then your light will rise in the darkness,
and your night will become like the noonday.
– Isaiah 58:10

The past is never dead.
– William Faulkner

1

THE OLD MAN WAS NEARLY TO the Louisiana line when he saw the woman and child walking on the other side of the interstate, the woman carrying a garbage bag tossed over her shoulder and the child lagging behind. He watched them as he passed and then he watched them in his rearview mirror and he watched the cars pass them as if they were road signs. The sun was high and the sky clear and if nothing else he knew they were hot, so he pulled off at the next exit and crossed the bridge over the interstate and headed back north on I-55. He'd seen them a few miles back and as he drove he hoped there would be a damn good excuse for what they were doing.

He slowed as he approached them and they walked in the grass, the girl slapping at her bare legs with her hands and the woman slumped with the weight of the garbage bag. He pulled onto the side of the interstate and stopped behind them but neither the woman nor the girl turned around. Then he shifted the car into park and got out.

'Hey!'

They stopped and looked at him and he walked over. Their cheeks red and sweaty from the heat and traces of a sunburn beneath the streaks of the blond, almost white hair of the child. The woman and the girl both wore shorts and tank tops and their shoulders were pink and their legs spotted with scratches and insect bites from walking in the rough grass on the side of the road. The woman dropped the garbage bag to the ground and it hit with a thud.

'What y'all doing out here?' the old man asked. He adjusted his hat and looked at the bag.

'Walking,' the woman said. She squinted as looking at the man meant facing the sun and the little girl folded her hands over her eyes and peeked between her fingers.

'You need some help? She don't look too good,' he said and he nodded toward the child.

'We're trying to get up to the truck stop. At Fernwood. You know it?'

'Yeah, I know it. Another ten miles or so. What you got there?'

'Gonna meet somebody.'

'Somebody with a car?'

'Yes sir.'

'Come on and get in. Y'all don't need to be out here like this,' he said and he reached down and picked up the garbage bag.

'It's heavy,' the woman said.

The old man grunted as he tossed it over his shoulder and the woman and child walked behind him to the long, silver Buick. He opened the trunk and set the bag in it and the woman followed the child into the backseat.

He watched the woman in the rearview mirror and tried to talk to her as they drove but she looked out the window or looked down at the child as he spoke, only giving one-word answers to questions about where they'd been or where they were going or what they were doing or what they needed or if she was sure there was gonna be somebody there to meet them at the truck stop. In the air-conditioning her face lost its color and he saw that there was a vacancy in her expression when she answered his questions and he knew that she didn't know any more about what they were doing or where they were going than he did. The woman's face was thin and he could only see the top of the girl's head in the mirror but she seemed to look down, maybe from exhaustion or hunger or boredom or maybe some of all of it. He hadn't been around children in a long time and he guessed she was five or six. She sat quietly next to the woman, like a wornout doll. The old man finally gave up talking to the woman and let her ride in peace, figuring she was happy to be sitting down.

In minutes the sign for the truck stop appeared above the trees on the left side of the interstate and he pulled off the exit and drove into the vast parking lot, where the big trucks moved in and out. Around to the right side of the truck stop were the diesel pumps and a row of motel rooms. The old man drove to the left of the truck stop, through the gas pumps and past the gift shop and truckers' showers and changing rooms and he stopped at the door of the café, which had its own separate entrance at the back.

'This all right?' he asked the woman and she nodded.

'C'mon, baby,' she said to the girl.

The old man walked around to the trunk and lifted out the garbage bag and set it down on the concrete. Then he reached into his back pocket and took out his wallet and he picked out forty dollars and he held it out to the woman.

She bowed her head and said thank you.

He nodded and said he wished he had more but the woman told him that was plenty. She hoisted the bag and took the girl's hand and thanked the man with a half smile and he held open the door of the café for them as they walked inside. He watched them through the glass door. A countertop and row of bar stools lined the right side of the café and the little girl tapped her fingers on top of each stool as they walked past and the woman dropped the bag on the floor and dragged it across the linoleum. He watched until a waitress took them to a table next to the window and he started to go in after them, to give them his phone number, to tell the woman to call him if her ride didn't show up and that he'd do what he could. But he didn't. Instead he got back into the Buick and he crossed over the interstate and drove along the highway, back toward home, where he parked underneath the shade of the carport and where he would then go inside and sit down with his wife at the kitchen table. He would tell her about the woman and the child and when she asked him what he'd been doing driving toward Louisiana in the first place he wouldn't be able to remember.

2

THE LITTLE GIRL ATE TWO GRILLED cheese sandwiches and a bowl of chocolate ice cream and the woman ate a plate of biscuits and gravy and they each drank several glasses of iced tea. It cost more than she wanted to spend but the way the child's face seemed to swell with each bite was satisfaction enough. If only for the moment.

After the bill was paid, they sat in the booth without talking, the girl using the crayons the waitress had given her to decorate the blank side of the paper menu. Maben counted her money and she had seventy-three dollars. She folded the bills neatly and stuck them into the front pocket of her shorts and she looked out the window across the parking lot at the row of motel rooms and she thought briefly of getting a room, taking long baths, watching television, and then sleeping with the girl next to her. Between clean sheets. With the air conditioner blowing and the door locked. The girl said look Momma and she held up the paper and showed her a blue *a* and a red something. Maybe a *b*. And either a green *c* or an *l*.

'That's good, Annalee,' Maben said. The child smiled and then she put the paper down and she drew a circle and began to create a face. The waitress walked by and asked if they needed something else.

'How much are those rooms?' Maben asked.

'About thirty-five, I think,' the waitress said. 'I'll find out for sure.'

'No,' Maben said. 'That's okay. You got a pay phone?'

'That way,' the waitress said, pointing at the door. 'Through there at the bathrooms.'

She touched the top of the girl's hand and said I'll be right back and then she followed the directions to the pay phone. A phone book hung from a metal cord and she opened it and began to try to remember the names of the people she used to know. Tried to think of a friend or some down-the-line cousin. Something. Somebody. She looked at the names in the phone book as if one might reach up and poke a finger in her eye and say hey look it's me. But it didn't happen. Too much time in between. Too much stuff in between. The kind of stuff that was supposed to make you feel good and it did in the first instant but then it only confused you or rotted you away and tricked you into thinking you needed more. Too much of it. She gave up on names and then she turned to the Yellow Pages and it took her a couple of minutes but she found a shelter that looked like it might help. On Broad Street. She thought she remembered where that was. She ripped the page from the phone book and folded it and stuck it into her pocket and she walked back to the table. It was another five miles to McComb and another two or three miles at least from the interstate to downtown and Broad Street. She didn't know if the child could go any farther today or not. And there was no guarantee that the shelter would even be there. She had tracked them down before only to get to the front door and find a faded note taped across the top explaining that due to lack of funding we regret that we have closed. Please call the police in case of an emergency.

He had said he'd be right back but she had known by the sound of it that he was lying. But he'd at least left a hundred dollars on top of the television. And he'd left the bag filled with her clothes and the child's clothes outside the motel room door. It wasn't as bad as it'd been before. She had almost felt a small victory in being left sympathetically. But that didn't change the fact that the van was gone and he was gone and she had already forgotten his name and she and the girl had been left alone again in a room that didn't belong to them. So they'd started walking. Three days ago. Going back to Mississippi because there was nowhere else to go. New Orleans had been no good and Shreveport had been no good and all she got from Beaumont had been the creation of the little girl and she didn't know why she thought they should head for Mississippi other than that was where the trail had started. She had left with nothing and she was coming back with nothing but another mouth to feed. And now that she was back the heat rising off the asphalt didn't look any different from the heat rising off the asphalt anywhere else. She had half expected something magical to occur once they crossed the state line and maybe it had with the old man giving them a ride and forty bucks. And as she looked at the ice cream dried in the corners of the child's mouth she decided that was about as much as she could expect.

'Momma,' the girl said.

'Yes.'

'Are we in Mississippi yet?'

'Yeah, baby.'

'Can we stop walking now?'

'Almost.'

'Can we get one of those rooms?'

'Stop asking questions and come on.'

They had slept off the road, walking into clumps of forest that stood back from the interstate, their clothes spread out across the leaves and dirt, eating packages of crackers and potato chips and drinking Cokes and breathing more easily in the cover of the night. They smelled and she knew it and once the girl was finished coloring they walked out of the café and through the gift shop and back toward the truckers' quarters. They ignored the truckers only sign and went into the women's dressing room. Maben stood next to the shower stall while the child bathed herself and after the child was finished and dressed the woman took a shower and felt a relief in the filth that ran down her body and washed down the drain. They took turns drying their hair underneath the hand dryers and the woman found clean T-shirts and shorts for them in the garbage bag. She told the girl to wait in the dressing room and she walked into the convenience store and stole a small bottle of lotion and she returned and lathered the child's red arms and face and neck and then she did the same for herself. She then washed their socks in the sink and she wrung them and dried them under the hand dryer while Annalee lay stretched across the tile floor with her head resting on the garbage bag. By the time the socks were dry the girl had fallen asleep and Maben sat down next to her and leaned her head back against the wall and prayed that no one would come into the dressing room while the child rested.

She had discovered that once things started to go bad they gathered and spread like some wild, poisonous vine, a vine that stretched across the miles and the years from the shadowy faces she had known to the lines she had crossed to the things that had been put inside her by strangers. It spread and stretched until the vine had consumed and covered her, wrapping itself around her ankles and around her thighs and around her chest and around her throat and wrists and sliding between her legs and as she looked down at the girl with her sunburned forehead and her thin arms she realized that the child was her own dirty hand reaching out of the thicket in one last desperate attempt to grab on to something good. She stroked the child's hair. Admired her small hands folded underneath her cheek. And then she lay across the floor next to her. There were times when it was impossible to sleep as all the evil in the world seemed to gather in her thoughts and she couldn't figure out how to keep the child from it and there were other times when all the evil in the world gathered in her thoughts and exhausted her to the point where she couldn't fight it anymore and this was one of those times when she gave up and with her head across her arm and her arm against the cold tile floor, she slept.

3

THEY WERE AWAKENED BY A STOUT woman in black boots and
a Waylon Jennings T-shirt. They sat up and rubbed their
eyes and then they got to their feet and the woman asked them
what they were doing.

'Nothing,' Maben said and she brushed at the child's hair with
the palm of her hand and then she picked up the garbage bag.

'You need a ride or something? I'm going down toward New
Orleans after I get some food in me.'

'We're all right,' Maben said and she took the girl's hand and
they stepped out of the dressing room. They walked outside
and sat down on the curb. The afternoon was falling away as
they had managed to grab a couple of hours of sleep, polite or
indifferent bathroom patrons stepping over and around them
until the stout woman decided to ask. Maben wondered if they
had time to make it to the shelter or if they would be stranded
again in the night. If there would be a place for them. If they
could help her get a job. If they had coloring books. If they
could stay for a day or three days or a month. If.

She looked at the motel rooms across the parking lot. She
looked at the girl. They had been on the side of the road or in
the woods for three days.

'Come on,' she said to the girl and they walked back inside

and to the cash register in the café where the room keys hung on hooks on a wooden board nailed on the wall. The girl who had waited on them stood behind the register stacking receipts and she looked up and said I thought y'all were gone.

'Not yet,' Maben said. 'We want one of those rooms if you got it.'

'Sure,' the waitress said and she put down the receipts and she took a notebook from below the counter. She opened it and made a couple of marks and she said it looked like room 6 was free. Thirty-five dollars even.

Maben pulled the folded bills from her pocket and as she counted out the money the waitress looked down at the girl and asked her name.

'Annalee,' the girl said. Then the girl looked up at the woman and said my momma's name is Maben.

'She didn't ask that,' Maben said and she handed the money to the waitress.

The waitress turned and took a key from a hook and gave it to Maben and she smiled again at the girl. Then she said, 'Be sure and keep your door locked.'

'Why?' the girl asked but Maben told her to come on and they walked across the parking lot toward the room. They stopped to let a big rig pass in front of them and when they started again the child began to skip along, anticipating sitting on something soft and watching television.

They had watched cartoons and the weather. Sat on the bed with their shoes off and legs stretched out. Sipped cold drinks from the vending machine. And now the girl was asleep with the television screen flashing across her clean body in the dark room. Maben walked to the window and pulled back the curtain. The parking lot was lit with yellow ghoulish light and more trucks populated the lot, settling in for the night. She could see across the lot into the windows of the café and the waitresses outnumbered the customers. She had spent more than half the money and now she felt stupid. If for whatever reason she didn't find what she hoped to find tomorrow on Broad Street, if the place was full or closed or simply not the kind of place they needed, then she had made a big mistake. Seventy-three dollars was not much money but take away thirty-five and another eight for lunch and it really wasn't much.

She walked over to the television and changed the channel to a news station and looked at the time on the bottom right of the screen. Ten after eleven. She walked back over to the window and sat down in a chair and again pulled back the curtain.

At least we don't stink anymore, she thought. Keep your door locked, she remembered the waitress saying but she didn't understand the warning. It seemed as though people were doing what they were supposed to be doing.

It was then that she noticed two girls at the edge of the parking lot who hadn't been there only a second ago. As if they had shot up from holes in the ground. One white and one black. They were dressed alike. Short denim skirts and white tank tops and flip-flops. Each held a small purse. Maybe sixteen, Maben thought. The white girl had her dark hair cut short like a boy and the black girl wore a red bandanna tied around her head. They walked together into the middle of the parking lot and then the black girl pointed at the purple truck and the white girl pointed at the black truck and then they separated. Maben watched as each girl walked to her chosen truck cab and stepped up and held on to the sideview mirror and tapped on the window. The door of the purple cab opened first and the black girl crawled inside. The white girl tapped again and adjusted her skirt and then the door of the black cab opened and she also crawled inside. The curtains of each cab were then pulled closed.

Maben counted and there were nine more trucks in the lot.

Nine times thirty. Two hundred and seventy dollars.

Nine times fifty would be four hundred and fifty.

She looked across the room at the thirty dollars wadded up on the table next to the television.

She had done it before and she hadn't thought about it in a long time, forcing herself to remove it from her memory. And as she thought about it now she felt as if it had been someone else. She had done so well forgetting it that she couldn't remember when it had been done and where it had been done or how many times it had been done but only that it had been done in a time when she had been backed into some dark and desperate corner by the rabid dogs of life.

She watched the trucks and wondered if those girls were old enough to drive. Wondered where they came from. Wondered if those men had ever once considered that those girls hadn't long ago been children. Or still were. Or maybe they never had been because they'd never had the chance. She looked at Annalee and realized what might await her if things didn't turn around and then she took a deep breath and looked back across the lot and then there was the vision of that night so many years ago. And that boy. That beautiful boy. Them sitting together on the tailgate parked on Walker's Bridge. Underneath ran the water of Shimmer Creek and alongside the creek and surrounding the bridge stood thick forest, the trees holding the bridge close, almost protecting it. The truck filling up the width of the bridge, its wooden rails leaning and rotting. Declarations of love long gone carved into the wood with pocketknives and bottle openers. The moon full and its light giving shadows through the trees and creating the illusion of an army of still ghosts lying in wait. The stars were many and beneath the music coming from the radio the crickets and frogs formed an abstract chorus over the trickle of the running water and she knew it was right. Knew he was right. So she told him to crawl up into the truck bed and lay down. Don't ask just lay down and don't look up and he obeyed and then she stood and she moved away from the truck bed and walked to the edge of the bridge. Don't peek, she said. She looked up into the sky for reassurance then she took off her T-shirt and removed her bra and stepped out of her shorts and her panties. She knelt and piled her clothes in a loose stack on the edge of the bridge. She stood and a chill ran over her body but she opened her arms and felt the moonlight and it held her like a pair of warm hands. She looked into the truck bed at the boy who had been telling her that he loved her. And she started toward him but then the dark was interrupted by the hum of an approaching car and the glow of headlights appeared over the hill, headlights that came fast, exposing themselves in two bright bursts before she could call out to him, before she had time to pick up her clothes and the car never slowed down. And she heard herself scream out to him as she hurried off the narrow bridge and onto the side of the road and she turned around in time to see the car meet the front of the truck. She ducked with the roar of the crash and Jason's tall and lean body was shot out of the truck bed and into the night as if he were meant to fly. The sparks and the screech and sound of twisting metal and running down that rough road toward the nearest house light. Breathing hard and running harder but feeling as if she were going nowhere, as if the house light were moving away from her as she ran toward it with her clothes tucked under her arm and forgetting she was naked until she finally ran into the yard and she stopped to put on her shorts and shirt. She left her bra and panties next to the front steps and she beat on the door and beat on the door, certain they would think they were being attacked or robbed and she began screaming out words like *bridge* and *cars* and *help* and *please God* until a light came on inside and the door opened and a man with gray hair peeked at her and believed that something was horribly wrong. And then getting in the car with him and driving down the road while his wife called somebody. Maben unable to answer his questions, only focusing ahead into the dark with anxious eyes and wanting Jason to be standing there as the headlights shined onto the bridge. She wanted to see him standing there wiping the dirt from his face and arms and saying damn that was close. But then seeing nothing and calling out and hearing nothing and then watching while the blue lights and the red lights topped the hill and then watching while the flashlights shined into the woods at the twisted and smoking heap of car and truck and then hearing them say we got a live one and telling herself it's him it's him it's got to be him and then it was the other one. The one that interrupted.

Through the haze of the years the night came back to her with clarity and punch as she stared with empty eyes across the parking lot. A car horn sounded and shook her loose and she turned and walked over and sat down at the edge of the bed and put her hand on the child's leg and watched her small chest rise and fall in a heavy sleep.

It wouldn't take long, she thought. It never had before. At least the way she remembered it. They never took long. Fifty dollars. No less. Maybe forty. The child was sleeping like the dead and would never know she was gone. She stood and put the room key in her pocket and she walked over to the sink and brushed her hair that hung limp against her head. She pushed it around with her fingers but nothing changed and then she wiped her eyes with a washrag and she kept telling herself that they didn't take long. They never take long.

4

'SON OF A BITCH,' NED SAID as he looked over the top of the glasses on the end of his nose. He sat at the end of the counter with a cup of coffee and the newspaper he had been waiting all day to read. The floor had been swept like he had asked and the dishes had all been washed like he had asked and there was only one table of customers. Three old women smoking and working crossword puzzles. He had only glanced at the front page headlines when he noticed the two girls walking across the parking lot. One white. One black. The same two he'd had to call in before.

He got up from the counter stool and walked over to the phone next to the cash register. He dialed the sheriff's office and when the woman answered he said, 'Hey. This is Ned over here at the truck stop. We got a couple of girls walking around knocking on doors again.'

'All right, Ned. They don't quit, do they?'

'Don't look like it. Don't y'all ever keep them?'

'For what?'

'I don't know. Scare them or something.'

'They don't scare too easy. We'll send somebody on over.'

'Fine.'

He hung up the phone. Watched the girls as they pointed at

the different trucks. He could have gone out himself and run them off but they would have walked down the road and come back as soon as he was inside. Don't get paid enough for that shit anyhow, he thought. He walked to the end of the counter and sat down with his eyes turned away from the window and he opened up the newspaper that would be today's for only another hour.

5

Maben opened and closed the door of the motel room quietly. She had already decided which truck she was going for and she walked directly to it, a blue truck with the rebel flag painted on its front grille. She climbed up onto the step of the driver's side. The curtains were pulled. Dark inside. She touched her fingertips to the glass. Caught her reflection. Her child slept less than fifty yards away. She felt nauseated already.

And then she pulled her hand away from the window. Bit her lip and told herself to trust that tomorrow would be better. That she would find something to help. This ain't no way to start over. And she stepped down off the truck and touched the room key in her pocket. She turned to walk back to the room and she saw the cruiser. It had pulled into the parking lot with its lights off and sat idling, the silhouette behind the steering wheel watching her.

Clint didn't mind this call and he didn't mind messing around with the girls because he liked what they would do with the cruiser parked off the road to keep from going to jail. He liked the free pie and coffee Ned gave him for running them off. He considered these perks of a job that didn't pay enough. He watched the woman in shorts stepping down off the rig and she wasn't what he was expecting. Not the black girl and the white girl who he wouldn't even have to say anything to. He'd just open the back door of the cruiser and wave them over and they'd say hey deputy and crawl in the back and an hour later after they had done what he wanted them to do he'd drop them off on the side of the road in front of the house where they said they lived and make them swear to give it a week before they headed back over there.

He was happy to see something new.

He got out of the cruiser. Hands propped on his gun belt and his face smooth and his hair parted. Too old was the first thing he thought.

'Hey,' he said.

Maben stopped.

'What you doing out here?' he asked. He spoke with the confidence of a man who knew that he had the power.

'Going to my room.'

'Not what I hear. Ain't legal to go in them trucks and do dirty things.'

'I didn't go in no truck. I said I'm going to my room,' she said. Then she reached into her pocket and took out the room key and showed it to him as if this were the evidence that would free her.

He moved on over to her and took the key from her fingers. He held it up to the light and inspected it. Then he gave it back to her.

'The manager called us. Supposed to be a family place.'

'I didn't do nothing.'

'I saw you up on that truck over there,' he said and then he looked at her legs. At her dirty shoes. He then studied her face. Haggard and worn but a pointed nose that seemed like it might have once been part of something pretty and gray eyes like slick dimes.

'How old are you?'

'I got a kid over there in my room. I got to get back.'

'Not right now. You gonna have to come along with me.'

'I told you I didn't do nothing.'

'That ain't what Ned said.'

'Who the hell is Ned?'

'Don't matter to you,' he said and he grabbed her skinny arm and she pulled back but she mostly pleaded I didn't do nothing. I got a kid in there I told you. He opened the back door of the cruiser and then he twisted her arm behind her and she couldn't fight it and she went face-first into the backseat, flopping over on her shoulder. He slammed the door before she could get up straight. He looked around the parking lot to see if Ned might be watching or if he might get an appreciative wave from somebody. But there was no one. She pleaded I didn't fucking do nothing and my baby is over there I done told you I didn't do nothing go knock on that truck and ask. I didn't do nothing. He got in and sat down behind the wheel and he turned around and told her to shut up and then he made a U-turn in the parking lot. Please officer I didn't do nothing. Please.

And that was the part he liked the most. When they started to beg. He stayed on Highway 48 between Magnolia and McComb. Nothing out there but a pool hall and a liquor store and then later on a bait shop. When she started to cry he told her to stop it. You ain't going to jail. If you were going to jail you'd be handcuffed already. Then he asked her name.

'Karen,' she said.

'Karen,' he repeated. 'I got a cousin named Karen. She ain't a whore like you, though.'

'Where we going?'

'Now, Karen. I'm the one driving.'

She stopped crying. She stopped talking. She sat with her arm resting on the door, staring out the window as the deputy drove along the two-lane highway. Clean white lines along the sides and reflectors dotting the middle that shined like diamonds in the headlights.

It was an easy one for her to figure out.

He turned off onto another road that was flanked by flatlands and after another mile he turned onto a bumpy, thin road that had been patched so lazily and so often that the radar and the radio on the dashboard rattled as the cruiser thumped along. Barbed-wire fence stretched along each side of the road and he soon slowed down and then he came to a stop and he turned off the headlights. Maben looked around and there was not a visible light in any direction. He reached above the dash and turned down the volume on the radio. The parking lights remained and an orange glow surrounded the cruiser as if to signal the demons from the dark.

'Look here,' he said and he tapped on the rearview mirror.

'I guess you know I'm about to come back there,' he said. Their eyes meeting in the mirror. 'Girl like you shouldn't care. Figure it this way. You're still getting paid but with a get-out-of-jail-free card instead.' He gave a small laugh and said something to himself she didn't understand. And then still with this low and brooding laugh he unbuckled his gun belt, the leather cracking as he slid it around his waist.

He held it up and said see here. We're gonna be friends. He set the gun belt on the front seat and then he opened the door and got out and he untucked his starched khaki shirt from his starched khaki pants. He opened the door slowly. Leaned his head down and told her to move over toward the other side. She scooted away from him and he sat down beside her on the seat. He told her to take off those dirty shoes and she did. He told her to take off her shirt and she did. And he kept on telling her things to do. And she kept on doing them. Keeping her eyes closed when he'd let her.

6

WHEN HE WAS DONE HE GOT out of the backseat and he
dressed standing next to the car. He saw her doing the
same and he said don't worry about that. We ain't done yet.

Maben pulled her shirt on over her head and ignored him.

He leaned down and with a smirk he said, 'You think I'm
playing?' She put on her shorts. And then he reached into the
backseat and snatched her by the back of her neck and pinned
her down on the seat and she let out a groan at the strength of
his grip.

'Take it back off. You hear me?' he said in a whisper with his
mouth against her ear. 'We ain't done.' He let go of her and she
sat up slowly. Wary of being slapped or worse. She pulled her
shirt back off and she said I thought that was what you wanted.

'It was.'

'I did everything you told me. I got a kid back there. I swear
to God.'

'If you got a kid back there then you'd damn sure better
do what I tell you. What you think would happen if that kid's
momma gets picked up for whoring herself out? Kid left alone
in a motel room. Guessing there ain't no food or nothing in
there either. What you think would happen? You'd better keep
on listening.'

She didn't answer. No reason to. She started praying that Annalee would stay asleep. Wouldn't wake up and believe her momma had left her. She hoped that like most nightmares this one would be over by daybreak and that she could be sitting in the bed next to Annalee as if nothing had happened when the child first opened her eyes.

Clint left the door open to the backseat. He was that sure. He got into the driver's seat and turned up the radio. Nothing going on. Then he took a phone out of the glove compartment and he dialed.

'Got us some new entertainment,' he said. 'Come on out and I'll show you. Yeah, same spot. Yeah, y'all can both come. Ain't nothing on the radio. Looks like we got all night. Same deal as always.'

He turned off the phone and set it on the seat next to the gun belt. He looked around at Maben through the safety glass and said me and you about to have some company. I'd suggest you be on your best behavior.

She held her shirt against her chest and he laughed at her modesty. She felt the wild, poisonous vine beginning to choke her. She looked at the door. Wide open. Wanting her to run or do something he could blame her for. She didn't know if it would be a few minutes or half an hour but soon there would be three of them. At least. And she didn't believe that she wasn't going to jail when it was over. She didn't believe that he thought she had a kid back there and even if he did he didn't seem to care. At some point Annalee would be discovered by a maid or leave the room and wander around looking for somebody and then there would be a phone call and that would be the end of the only thing she had left that mattered. She looked across the quiet, flat countryside. No lights and no answers.

'Want me to get out and wait for them?' she asked.

He looked around as if he were waiting for someone else to

answer. It'd be a good story he could tell one day if he had her sitting on the hood like some sexual ornament.

'Might as well. You gonna have to get out anyway. Don't put nothing on.'

'It's off already. Like you told me.'

'Then come on.'

She scooted across toward the open door, her skin sticking to the seat. He got out from behind the wheel and led her around to the front of the cruiser. She sat down on the hood and it was hot on her bare ass and she hopped up. She asked if she could get her shirt to sit on and he said okay and he turned and looked up the road and waited on their headlights. She noticed him looking away and she leaned across the front seat and unlatched the pistol from the belt and when he turned around she was standing there. Her naked body illuminated in the orange glow of the parking lights. Pointing his pistol at him.

'You gotta be kidding me,' he said and he was getting ready to laugh again but he didn't have the chance as she blew a hole in his throat. He went to his knees and she walked around to him and he squeezed his throat with both hands and the blood flowed black in the strange light and he lunged for her and she stepped back and he fell facedown. He rolled over, clutching at his throat. Tried to get back to his knees and she shot him twice more and he fell flat and still.

She lowered the pistol and then dropped the pistol and put her suddenly shaking hands on top of her head but she didn't have time for that so she grabbed her clothes and shoes from the backseat and hurried to get dressed, starting to cry in heaves but she stopped herself. You can't start that now and she went back to the front of the cruiser and he hadn't moved and wasn't going to and she picked up the pistol. His phone rang in the cruiser and she knew it was them and she looked into the backseat once more to see if there was anything of hers and then she started running down the road. Away from the cruiser she could hardly see her next step but it didn't slow her and she ran to the end of the road and she hoped she was turning the right way and she kept running as hard as she could run.

A curve lay ahead and she noticed the headlights shining from around the bend and she dived off the side of the road into the high grass, lying flat and wishing she could lie flatter. The car passed without noticing and she waited until the taillights were specks and then she began running again. She didn't know how far she had to go but she knew it was far. Her legs burned, the muscles already tired from walking in the heat for three days. But she ignored the pain and pushed and pushed. She ran with flailing arms and legs and she gasped for breath as the fear rose and came out of her in stuttered cries. Sweating and gasping and switching the pistol from hand to hand as if expecting one of them to know what to do with it. Her knee rose and knocked it from her grasp and the pistol bounced away in the dark. She screamed shit motherfucker and then dropped to her hands and knees. Feeling for it in the roadside gravel and calling out to it and then begging God to show it to her. The dust stirred and the rocks shuffled from her hurried hands and then she found it and she was up and running again. It was then that she heard the sirens.

She ran on until she could see the lights from the truck stop and as she ran closer she tried to think if anyone had seen her in the parking lot. If anyone had seen her get in the car with the deputy. He hadn't called it in. Hadn't talked to anyone when he picked her up. Had only used his phone to call his buddies to tell them to come on out and have at her. The first siren was joined by more sirens and she imagined the lights flashing around the dead man because she had seen them before. She imagined his open and dead eyes and the blood draining into the bends of the rough road and the crimson streams that the men in uniform would be careful to step around. The body slumped and folded as if it did not have bones and the open sky that gave no answers.

She stopped when she reached the edge of the truck stop parking lot. She didn't know how long she had been gone. All she knew was that she had made it back and that no one had seen her on the road. She paused before she walked into the lot. Fought to catch her breath and then she stuck the pistol in the back of her pants and tugged her shirt down over it. She stopped at the end of the motel rooms and leaned against the brick wall. Looked for anyone moving around. Looked for anyone in the café staring out the window. Across the lot a man stood at the front of his rig smoking a cigarette. When he was done he walked over to the café and went inside and she watched him sit down at a bar stool with his back to the window.

She waited until the man with glasses on his nose came over and handed him a menu and when the man walked away and into the kitchen Maben crossed hurriedly in front of the motel rooms. Room key in her hand. And when she got to number 6 she found Annalee standing in the window. Her eyes red and her hair tousled as if she had been trying to pull it out with her small hands. Maben unlocked the door and didn't speak but only knelt and hugged the child who was sweating and panting and crazyeyed. As she hugged her, out the window Maben saw the black girl and the white girl across the way. Standing next to the garbage bin behind the café and counting their money.

7

IN THE SOUTHERN MISSISSIPPI SWAMP YOU can watch the world awaken as the pale yellow sun edges itself between the trees and moss and widewinged cranes. Dragonflies buzz and raccoons come out of their dens and crawl along fallen trees. Turtles situate themselves onto stumps that will later become sunsoaked and hidden things slide beneath black water with murderous patience and skill. Limbs too old to hold themselves up any longer bend and break like old men accepting their marshy graves. Reptiles slither and blackbirds cry as the early light slashes and relieves the deep and quiet night.

This was the world that Russell thought of as he sat with his head leaning against the bus window. Getting up early and driving his daddy's truck out Highway 98 and turning toward the Bogue Chitto River and then driving onto a gravel road that ran alongside the thin river until the road simply ended. Getting out of the truck and taking the .22 rifle from behind the seat and walking half a mile until the ground became soft and then soggy and then stepping high to keep from bogging down and making it to the one-man boat tied to a willow tree. Muddy to his knees and climbing in and paddling out into the swamp and listening and watching and feeling like a part of what was happening. Sitting through the break of dawn and the light gaining strength and burning through the early haze and the air alive with the calls of birds and the hungry things searching for food. The .22 across his lap. Shot less and less with each visit as he had come to feel like a violator. The unnatural ring of his shot, which scattered the small and unknowing things and added blood to the water and he eventually only carried it with him in case of an alligator or some other fantastic creature rising from the black and starving for skin and bone. This was the world that filled his thoughts as the bus headed south on I-55. The world he remembered being part of as a younger man. As a boy.

It was a straight shot eighty miles south down the interstate and there had been enough rain during this last week of June to keep the countryside green but light shades of brown appeared in patches and suggested a drying out was in store if there wasn't some relief. Babies cried off and on and an old man snored in the seat behind him and the bus smelled of exhaust and he was taken away from thoughts of his youth and forced into thoughts of the man he had been when he was taken away. He had told himself he wasn't going to do it. Wasn't going to stare out the window and lament what he had lost, like some hapless guy in some hapless moment but he wasn't able to resist. There she was. Brown hair and filling her young woman body in young woman ways, excited about a wedding, dancing with him late into the night, lying close against him in the dark. He listened to the babies cry several seats behind him and he wondered about the kids they might have. About the house they might live in. About the backyard that might be at that house and about them sitting in wrought-iron chairs and drinking bottled beer and watching those kids run around the yard chasing fireflies. The bus charged on, a great rectangular mass of metal and glass and he imagined himself returning from a long trip to that woman and those kids who would be waiting on the front porch of that house and then the old man who had been snoring snapped awake with a shout and startled Russell and freed him from these images. He arched his back and stretched. Looked down at his hands and rubbed his thumbs across the small scars that were scattered across his knuckles and the tops of his hands. Scars that hadn't been there when he left.

He had spent his first week of freedom in a mandatory seminar for ex-cons that attempted to reacquaint them with the real world. He and six others wore street clothes without shackles and were driven in a van from the gates of the Mississippi State Penitentiary in the Delta to a Motel 6 on the back end of a truck stop off I-55 on the south side of Jackson. He had been unable to sleep. The room too quiet. The air conditioner too cold. Concern that the guy he was sharing a room with might do something. Anything. After doughnuts and coffee in the mornings they would go into a big room at the end of the hallway on the first floor and sit around a sprawling wooden table and listen to Mildred Day. She referred to herself as a reentry counselor. Somebody you only want to see once. Somebody you want to forget. A no-frills middle-aged woman with thick wrists and thick ankles and a thick waist. She educated them on finding work and maintaining contact with parole officers. She explained the differences in the price of living. What a gallon of milk cost. What car insurance cost. How much you make at minimum wage.

After three days of this, with the lure of the free world just outside their door and evidently too much to bear, two of the ex-cons skipped out around midnight and headed to Jimmy's, a south Jackson strip club with pink neon women shining over the front door and highdollar drinks inside. Mildred Day had warned them and the next morning when they didn't show up for breakfast she made a phone call and then went on about her business with her remaining students. At lunch she announced that the two stragglers had been picked up smoking cigarettes outside a convenience store and that they were currently on their way back to Parchman for another six months. She then said if any of you would like to join your buddies, Jimmy's has no cover charge until nine o'clock and drinks are half price until ten. Russell looked around at the other four men and they all shook their heads though visions of naked girls danced in their thoughts and one of the cons remarked to Mildred that those must have been some damn fine titties if they was worth another six months.

The remaining days passed with less excitement. She took them to the mall and the grocery store. She had them practice filling out job applications and identifying themselves as ex-cons. With certain eyes she stood in front of them and said out of the seven original members of the group, four of you will wind up back in prison. Two of you are already there. It's up to you. When the week was up each man had gate money and a manila folder tucked under his arm filled with everything the Mississippi Department of Corrections believed he needed to become a functioning member of society.

In the van on the way to the bus stop where the five men would go their separate ways three of them threw the folders out the window, a cloud of letter-size paper scattering across I-55. Busy people in their busy cars swerving and giving them the bird as they passed the laughing ex-cons. An hour later he was sitting on the bus. A free man. Staring out the window. Closing in on the place and people he hadn't seen in eleven years.

They arrived at the McComb exit and it didn't take long for him to see what he had missed. A cluster of new restaurants and hotels gathered just off the interstate and past those was a straight line of got-it-all superstores that stretched to the edges of the once sleepy neighborhoods where he had picked up a prom date or two. He noticed the parking lots filled with cars and women with children and strollers and he wondered where they had all come from. The bus moved past the slick part of town and wound through the place he had known – the rows of houses with porch swings, the elementary school with the rusted playground equipment, the magnolia trees on the lawn of the Methodist church. The quiet downtown and its brick buildings and bumpy streets. The bus rolled through downtown and stopped at the railroad tracks where the Greyhound and Amtrak stations shared the same square building. He stood up from his seat and threw his duffel bag over his shoulder and walked to the front of the bus. The driver opened the door and Russell looked out and twenty yards away two men leaned on the front of a white truck with their arms folded. Russell froze. Stared at the asphalt at the bottom of the steps.

'This is it,' the driver said.

Russell nodded. Moved down a step and paused again.

'I got a long road, buddy,' the driver said.

He took a deep breath and adjusted the bag and then he climbed down out of the bus. The door closed behind him and Russell stood still, the bus backing up and pulling away with a trail of blue smoke and the gears grinding as the driver shifted ahead. The two men began walking toward Russell and he didn't move. They stopped a few steps in front of him. The man on the left was taller and his shirt was untucked and the man on the right wore a white T-shirt that was a size too small. They shared the same sharp eyes and serious brow and they held their hands to their sides with their fingers wiggling in anticipation as if ready to draw.

'Welcome home, shithead,' the tall one said and they went for him. He hurried to get the bag off his shoulder but it was caught around his arm and it gave them time to get on him. The tall one hit him twice on the side of the head while the other man went low, grabbing Russell around the waist, pinning one of his hands and lifting him off his feet. He drove Russell to the ground, his back hitting the pavement with a whump that made him lose his breath and the tall one kicked Russell in the ribs while the other man punched at his face and stuck his knee into his groin. Finally Russell was able to roll his weight to the side but the man got to his feet and joined the other in kicking and then swinging at Russell as he struggled to get up. He made it to his knees when he was hit squarely in the eye by one of the four wild fists and he fell back, being kicked sharply in the ribs with the heel of a boot as he went limp. He lay there. Out of breath. Doubled over. The men paused and watched him crumble and the tall one spit and they were about to hurt him like they wanted to when a man in a red tie ran out of the station yelling, 'Hey! Hey!'

The men stopped and stood over Russell, panting like dogs.

The man in the tie hurried over and straddled Russell and threatened to call the cops and the two men backed away.

'Been waiting for that shit for a long time,' the tall one said.

'Hell yeah,' said the other.

'I mean it. Get the hell outta here. I saw it all.'

'You didn't see nothing.'

'Swear to God I did.'

'Don't worry. We'll see you again soon, Russell,' the tall one said. 'You hear me? Soon.'

The two men nodded in satisfaction and backed toward the truck. They climbed in and drove away, their heads turning and eyes locked on the fallen man like strangers staring at a car wreck.

The man extended his hand to Russell and said, 'Damn it to hell. Welcome to town.' He wore a short-sleeved shirt and his red tie was loosened. Russell took his hand and got to his feet with a grunt. He felt his eye and the place on his head where he figured there would be a knot. He bent over gingerly to pick up the duffel bag.

'I'm the station manager. You all right?'

He nodded. Wiped his mouth with the back of his hand. Felt his nose. Nothing broken. He put the bag on his shoulder and nodded to the station manager and started walking across the parking lot.

'You need a ride somewhere? I'm done here. Just got to lock up.' Russell turned around and said that'd be fine.

'Ain't far, is it?'

'Over there,' he said and pointed with his elbow tucked to his throbbing side.

'Then hold on. Won't take a second.'

The man hurried back into the building and Russell got down on one knee and took a cigarette from the duffel bag. He looked around. Up and down the tracks. At the sagging facade of a hardware store. At the empty parking spaces on the downtown streets. A few minutes later the door to the station opened again and the man came out and pointed at a two-door Toyota parked around the side of the building.

'Well. Come on,' he said.

Russell walked to the car. 'You mind the smoke?'

'Not if you got one for me. Been one of them damn days. I don't guess I'm telling you nothing.'

They got in the car and Russell gave him a cigarette. The man turned a vent toward Russell, the straight burst of air causing him to bat his eyes. He pushed the vent toward the ceiling and he rolled down his window. He sat with the bag in his lap and his knees bunched up in the compact space of the compact car.

'Where to?'

'Over there. Behind the fire station.'

'What fire station? Out by the mall?'

'The one downtown.'

'Shit. That station's been shut down five, six years. Don't reckon they care if we burn to the ground down here. Gotta sit next to all the new shit, I guess. Make sure some insurance man don't get all worked up. The station down here is apartments now. You believe that? Couple of gay dudes bought it and fancied it up. Think it was even on some TV show. You sure you in the right spot?'

'I'm sure. It's been a while. Over behind the place you're talking about. Michigan Avenue.'

'That's better. Street names are still the same far as I know,' the man said and he flicked his cigarette out the cracked window. 'So what was that back there? You get on that guy's wife or something?'

'Nah. Nothing like that.'

'Just old blood.'

'Old bad blood.'

'They seemed pretty damn serious. Weird looks on their faces. Especially that tall one.'

'Yeah. Especially,' Russell said.

The Toyota weaved through downtown. Women in heels leaving their bank jobs for the day and walking to their locked cars with black purses hanging from their arms. An open sign shined in a café window and a pack of grayhaired men stood outside its door smoking. They passed the old fire station and the flagpole was gone from the front yard and a dogwood stood in its place. A wrought-iron balcony stretched across the upstairs floor and plants hung from hooks and their vines leaned lazily across the balcony railing, swaying in the late afternoon breeze. The red brick had been painted dirty gold.

'Pretty, ain't it?' the man said. After the old station they left the downtown buildings and came upon a neighborhood. At a four-way stop Russell pointed right onto Michigan Avenue.

'About four down, I think. On the right. Or the left.'

'Yeah, I'd say it's one of them.'

It was five down on the right. Russell lifted his hand and said stop. 'Don't look like nobody lives here,' the man said.

'Nobody does.'

The man looked at the house and he looked at Russell. 'You sure you okay? I see a lot of weird shit get on and off that bus but I never seen a guy jumped before.'

'I'm fine.'

'Want me to run you over to the doctor or something?'

'Hell no.' He shook his head and then the man's hand and he opened the door and stepped out onto the sidewalk. He tossed away his cigarette and then he lit another one and he dropped the duffel bag to the ground. Stared at the house. Well, he thought. Home sweet fucking home.

8

THE HOUSE WAS LIKE THE OTHER houses on the street. A carport on the right, a porch in front, a porch in back, a thin walkway leading from the sidewalk to the door. Hedges under the front windows. An iron handrail up the front steps. Russell finished his cigarette and stood and opened the mailbox and took out an envelope. His name was scribbled on the front and he opened it and took out a house key.

Under the carport sat an old Ford pickup that was once red but only patches remained, as it had mostly faded to orange. He walked over to it and ran his hand along the truck bed. Patted her like she was a horse. A single crack spread across the width of the windshield and there was a small dent in the tailgate. The tires were worn and the truck bed was rusted in each of the four corners. A spare tire lying in the back. He opened the door and sat down behind the wheel. The bench seat was split here and there, slithers of foam sticking through the splits. A note was on the seat and he picked it up and read She's gonna need some love. He folded the note and tossed it down on the floorboard. The key hung from the ignition and he pushed in the clutch and gave it a turn and the engine strained but hit and he gave it the gas. It paused, gave a quick backfire like a popgun, then roared and in the rearview mirror he saw a gust of gray flow from the tailpipe and out across the driveway and he let it run for a couple of minutes.

He walked up the steps of the front porch and dropped the bag and he unlocked the door and walked in. The hardwood floors had been refinished dark like espresso and the fireplace in the living room had been bricked up. He walked from room to room and saw that all the walls had been painted a fresh coat of white. Random bits of mismatched furniture appeared in each room – a bed and a dresser in the bedroom and a coffee table and a beige couch and a bookshelf in the living room. In the kitchen he found a table with two chairs and on the counter sat a coffeemaker and a microwave. Next to the microwave was a new pack of cigarettes. Then he opened the refrigerator and found a six-pack of beer. Dear old Dad.

He took a beer and he opened the back door. The backyard grass was high and a wheelbarrow was overturned in the middle of the yard. An empty five-gallon paint bucket and some rollers and brushes were in one corner of the porch. A white plastic chair in another. He sat down on the steps and held the cold beer bottle to his eye and he tried to relax. Closed his eyes and breathed the heavy, free air. A bead of water trickled down the bottle and along his cheek and disappeared into the two-week-old beard he had begun as part of his new world. He then opened his eyes and opened the beer. Tiny insects danced across the tops of the high grass and oak trees kept out the lowering sun. On each side of the narrow yard the neighbors had erected six-foot-high fences to keep their cookouts to themselves. He rubbed his eye again. Felt the knot on his head. Felt his ribs. Then he lay back on the porch and stared at the cobwebs surrounding the porch light. A butterfly was trapped. Fighting but losing. A dog barked from somewhere and then another joined.

Eleven years, he thought.

Enough time for the people he had known to get married. Maybe more than once. Maybe more than twice. Time for them to have kids. To have jobs that they would now be doing well in, enough time for promotions and titles and offices with windows and maybe even company credit cards in their pockets. Enough time for the bookshelves in their living rooms to be filled with photo albums of snapshots from summer trips to Pensacola and Gulfport and when the kids were old enough a weekend at Six Flags or maybe even Disney World. Enough time to be in the second house because the first house wasn't big enough anymore. Enough time to have them driving vehicles they swore they'd never drive, vehicles with sliding doors and roof racks and enough cup holders for everybody. Enough time to forget about people who weren't there anymore. Enough time for their bodies to change and their faces to change and their hairlines to change and their personalities to change and enough time for the construction of the new stores and the new restaurants to cater to the needs of the new people.

He sat up and then stood and freed the butterfly from the cobweb while it still had a flutter in its wings. He held it between his fingertips, its wings veil-thin and chalky. Then he let it go and it tried to fly but instead swirled straight down and fell at the toe of his boot. He knew that if he left it there the ants would come and what a wicked way to die so he put his foot on the butterfly and ended it and he washed it away into a space between the boards with his beer. He walked over and sat down in the plastic chair and began to talk to himself.

She's one of them now. You know that.

Yeah, I know it. Known it for a while. Just seems different sitting here free instead of holed up. It all right with you if I pout about it for half a damn second?

Fine with me.

Good. Then leave me alone.

He sat and finished his beer and then he set the bottle down on the porch. He stood and walked back through the house, admiring the attention to detail of the paint trim. Noticed the consistency of the floor stain. Smiled at the notion of his dad who was too old to do it himself anymore but who was no doubt standing ten feet away from whoever was doing it and making sure they did it right. And he knew that his dad was sitting there. Waiting. And he didn't want to keep him waiting any longer.

9

HE REACHED DOWN INTO THE BAG of catfish food and grabbed a handful and threw it into the pond, the food spreading and floating and before the ripples had died the mouths came up from the bottom wide and eager and slapping at the surface of the water as the food disappeared. Mitchell Gaines watched for a minute with his hands in his pockets and then he sat down in his lawn chair on the pond bank. He opened up the can of crickets and baited his hook and with a flick of the wrist he sent the hook and sinker halfway across the pond. The pine trees on the other side of the pond gave a long shadow across the gentle swaying of the brown water. He leaned back in his chair though he knew this wouldn't take long with the catfish already stirred by the food. It was cheating but it was his pond and his fish so he was easy on his own rules. He wore a cowboy shirt with its sleeves rolled up over his elbows and he wiped his hands on the already filthy pants that he'd been wearing for the last three days.

He had two more lawn chairs and on the ground next to his chair was a Styrofoam cooler filled with ice and canned Cokes and a halfpint of whiskey on top of the ice. By the afternoon the drinks and whiskey would be gone and the healthiest of the catches would be nestled in the melting ice. He had figured he'd spend the late afternoon skinning and filleting the fish and by tomorrow they would be sitting around the kitchen table with fried fish and hushpuppies and he'd get the woman to make coleslaw and then they could sit on the back porch with coffee and look out across the land that always seemed more vast to him under the night sky. The line hit and he reeled it in and a catfish that needed a few more pounds flapped at the end of the line. He twisted the hook from its lip and walked to the edge of the water and he set the fish into the water gently and the fish squirmed and stirred up the mud and then disappeared. He sat down again and baited another hook with another cricket and let it fly.

It's finally come on, he thought. It's finally come on though it didn't seem like it ever would and I didn't think I'd be here to see it anyway. He looked at his watch and knew his son should be coming along any time now. If that truck cranked up.

He looked around the place. He spent most of his time sitting now after a lifetime of getting up and doing. Buying small houses nobody else wanted and painting them and replacing rotted floors and gutting kitchens and gutting moldy bathrooms and doing the roofing and tiling the floors and whatever else had to be done. Whatever he could do with his boy. Teaching Russell how to run wire and swap plumbing and how to measure twice so that you made damn sure you cut it right the first time. Making these little houses something he was proud of and then renting them to people who sometimes paid the rent and sometimes disappeared but no matter if it was good people or bad people living in them, there was always something to do. Always something dripping or an outlet not working or a dishwasher not running. Always something to do and if there wasn't something to do there was always another little rundown house somewhere that nobody wanted that was sitting there like a fallen tree in some forgotten forest and he would buy it and bring it back to life. There was hardly a neighborhood in town that hadn't been touched by him and Russell. Hardly a day had gone by since he had to give it all up that he didn't wish with the next sunrise that his back and legs would let him do the things he used to do. And not a day had gone by since his boy had been taken up into the Delta and put behind those walls that he hadn't prayed at night that God would keep him alive until Russell came back home.

And here it was.

He had prayed twice as hard after Liza passed. Hated like hell that she never got to see him again. Died with her boy locked up in that place. Paying for what he had done. Mitchell had come home one evening and found her lying down in the backyard next to her tomato garden. Work gloves on and sleeves rolled up and lying folded like an old doll. Eyes shut. A tranquil expression on her face. Gone. He hadn't thought much of death until then but after she was buried the thought of death seemed to follow him home from the grave site. It sat with him on the porch as he smoked a cigarette. Sat with him in the quiet of the house as he read the newspaper. Sat with him at the kitchen table as he drank coffee in the morning. Sat with him in his truck as he went about doing what he had always done and as his knees began to go as he knelt down to paint and as the strength in his arms began to go as he lifted ladders in and out of the back of the truck the thought of death seemed not only to sit with him and follow him around but also to take root in his mind and spread into his heart and his dreams. His muscles ached and his joints ached and his spirit ached and though he prayed that he would see Russell come down that driveway again he didn't much believe he would see it happen. Could tell by the way he felt. On several occasions he had written letters to Russell, trying to convey things to him that he didn't anticipate being able to say to him in person but he had never mailed any of those letters. Had ripped them into pieces and burned them on the dirt floor of the barn. Didn't want Russell to have to carry around any more than he was already carrying around.

His despair strengthened with time and with the emptiness of the place and with nothing to fill his hours and in his despair he had driven down to Bogalusa, Louisiana, to see his only brother. Hoping for some kind of reassurance. Some kind of revelation. And he found it. Found her there standing barefoot in front of the shack she lived in, which was in line with the long row of shacks they all lived in. Dark hair and caramel skin and dark eyes like the rest of them. The men and the women and the children and the babies. All of them there to work the fields and the machines for half of what Clive used to pay for the fields and the machines to be worked. She was standing there barefoot. Her skirt down to her ankles, made for a taller woman. Her arms folded across her chest and she followed him with her eyes as he walked with Clive past the row of shacks out toward the edge of the sugarcane where Clive aimed to show Mitchell the bright red tractor that had replaced the dull red tractor.

And after they had inspected the tractor and were walking back she was still there. Her arms still folded. Her eyes still following him. And he had nodded to her and she had smiled at him. As he and Clive sat on the back deck and finished their second cup of coffee, Mitchell asked if he could hire her. If she was willing.

'Hell. I don't know,' Clive said. 'You'll have to ask her yourself.' She was willing. Her husband dead before she had followed her sisters and their husbands to the sugarcane farm. A grown daughter somewhere back in Mexico. She had put all her belongings into a pillowcase and then she had gotten in the truck with Mitchell and they had driven back to Mississippi with the sun falling down a clear sky behind them, shades of soft pinks and reds seeming to push them toward home. A quiet between them. But a different kind of quiet. A shared quiet.

Not a damn thing wrong with it. That's what he'd come to after the first days and weeks of the strange woman in his house. It was something he had to come to so that he could fend off the guilt, the feeling that he was somehow being unfaithful to the life he had known with his wife. He'd finally shaken off the guilt as he and the woman came to figure each other out. He couldn't understand a word she said and she couldn't understand him. Not at first. They had pointed and nodded mostly until they began to figure it out and now if he wanted a glass of water or if she needed a blanket there were words. Larger pieces of something real that hadn't been there before.

He looked at his watch again. Something hit at his line but he ignored it.

He expected his son to understand but he didn't know and he'd soon find out. Not a damn thing wrong with it. Liza had passed and Russell was gone and a silence had fallen over the place that kept him awake at night and the woman had put an end to that silence. He looked at the house and Consuela walked toward him. She carried a basket and her wide hips swayed and he admired the shine of her black hair even from far away. She approached and sat down in the lawn chair beside him, stretching out her legs and crossing her bare feet. In the basket were purple hull peas and she began to snap and shell them. He had arrived at a point in his life when he could more clearly imagine the end than remember the past and it didn't matter where she came from because there wasn't a goddamn thing wrong with it. He smiled at her and she smiled back.

He heard the Ford when it turned into the driveway. He couldn't see the highway from the pond with the gravel road going up and then down between the highway and the house but he knew the sound from twentysomething years of driving it. From twentysomething years of fixing it. He watched the road and then the truck appeared and eased along the gravel. The truck had been so much a part of his life for so long that for a moment he felt as if he were watching himself drive toward the house. He smiled to himself and then the line hit again and he reeled in a big one. But he didn't want to mess with it right now and there was plenty more time and plenty more fish so he unhooked the fish and put it back and then he sat down in the chair. He set the rod and reel on the ground and he crossed his legs and waited on his son to get out of the truck and walk on over.

I made it, he thought. It finally come on.

The house was a modest one-story that Russell had helped his father paint the year before the wreck. It sat at the front of twelve acres that was wooded with patches of pines and oaks that had become less dense over the years with each passing hurricane or tornado. There had once been cows and a few horses and a couple of acres of corn but Mitchell had given all that up after Liza died. He'd sold everything but the tractor he used to bush hog and the two-man boat he used to sit in out in the middle of the pond when the sun was low and the sky was lavender and there was that particular kind of loneliness that came with a fading day. The small pond was a hundred yards behind the house and had been stocked with catfish when Russell was a kid and had spent summers sitting on the same bank that Mitchell sat on now, drinking orange sodas and eating oatmeal pies. And now there was a new roof and a different porch swing and he wondered how much of this Russell would notice.

He watched his boy stroll along, looking around at the house and the shed and the barn and out toward the pond as if it were the first time he had seen the place. Russell had always been tall and thin but Mitchell noticed that his shirt hung on him as if it had been borrowed from an older brother. Russell walked along the worn path between the house and pond and when he was halfway Mitchell stood. Russell came across the pond bank and said how you doing old man and the old man grinned with his lips held tight to keep it from getting away from him and he gave Russell a solid handshake as if he'd just sold him a calf. Then Russell looked at the darkhaired woman who looked back at him with brown eyes.

'This here is Consuela,' Mitchell said. Russell nodded to her.

'Es mi hijo,' Mitchell said and he waved his hand toward Russell.

'Yo se,' she said.

Russell looked at his father as if he were an impostor. His father scanned him from head to toe. 'You look all right,' he said.

'I feel all right.'

The woman dropped the peas into a pail. Russell pointed at her.

'That's Consuela.'

'You said that.'

'She helps out some. Come on and sit down.'

They sat down in the chairs and Mitchell opened the cooler and took out Cokes for both of them and he set the halfpint in his lap. He handed Russell the can.

'Nice day,' Russell said.

'Hot, though,' his father answered.

They sipped their Cokes and stared across the pond. Not speaking for several minutes with the years having separated them from the things they used to talk about. Things like the rental houses that Mitchell owned or the cows that he bought and sold or the dinner Russell's mother had just made. The dropped peas tapping the bottom of the pail was the only sound.

'She speak any English?' Russell asked.

'Sí,' she said.

'She picks it up here and there.'

'You too, sounds like.'

'Got to, I reckon.'

'I reckon,' Russell said and he grinned. 'You're a sly damn dog.'

'What you mean?'

'You know what I mean.'

'It ain't like that.'

'Where does she live?'

Mitchell didn't answer. Sipped at his Coke.

'You're a dog,' Russell said.

'She lives in your old room out there over the barn.'

'I bet.'

'Consuela,' Mitchell said. 'Duermes donde?'

She turned and pointed at the barn.

'Okay,' Russell said. 'You coulda told me.'

Mitchell shrugged his shoulders. 'I coulda.'

'How long she been out here?'

'About a year or so.'

'She just walked up the road one day?'

'Maybe she did.'

'Maybe she didn't.'

Mitchell shifted in his chair. 'If I tell you got to promise you can't tell nobody.'

'Who am I gonna tell?'

'I don't know. That's something I had to say.'

'Fine. I won't tell anybody.'

'She came from your uncle Clive's sugarcane farm down in Bogalusa. He's got a ton of them. Living in shacks and shit. Kinda rotten if you ask me. A modern-day plantation. I went down there to see him and we was looking around and I saw her. I asked her if she wanted to come up here and she said yeah.'

'You asked her?'

'In a manner of damn speaking. You know what I mean. I told somebody to ask her and they did and she came on with me.'

'So she's a slave,' Russell said.

'No. She was a slave. You should see how Clive has got them piled on top of one another. And pays change from his couch, seems like.'

'You pay her?'

'Some.'

'So you pay her to work and whatnot and she lives in the barn and I'm guessing she's not exactly a voter but she's not a slave.'

'If you don't shut the hell up I'm gonna call the damn sheriff and tell him to take you back.'

Consuela finished with the peas and she set down the basket and wiped her hands on her long denim skirt. She then stood up and said something quick and Mitchell nodded and she walked toward the house.

'It got quiet out here,' Mitchell said when she was out of earshot. 'I don't know what else to say about it. Your momma gone and all.'

'I know. You don't have to explain anything.'

'Some nights I'd sit out back and sounded like it might sound if the world came to end and there was nobody else walking around.'

Mitchell reached down and picked up the fishing rod and sent the hook across the pond. 'I didn't figure I'd have to explain it much to you. I tried to quit feeling bad about it. I don't know if your momma understands.'

'Mom's been gone awhile. I think she'd get it.'

'I hope so.'

'She would.'

'Cause Consuela sleeps in the house sometimes.'

'It's okay. You damn dog.'

A fish took the hook and the sinker bobbed and Mitchell let the fish run a little and then he reeled it in. This one was plenty big and he stood up to bring it on in and he unhooked it and Russell made room in the cooler. They sat back down and Mitchell handed his son the rod and told him to have a turn but Russell said no thanks. Mitchell set the rod on the ground.

Russell leaned back in his chair and said, 'I appreciate the truck.'

'I figured you could use her. Needs a tune-up, though,' Mitchell said and he opened the whiskey and took a sip and then he chased it with the cold Coke. He handed the bottle to his son.

'And the house,' Russell said and he took the bottle. 'You sure you don't need somebody living there who pays for it?'

'That little house has been bought and paid for twice. I don't need it.'

'Well. All right.'

Mitchell looked at him sideways. 'You growing a beard?'

'Yes sir.'

Mitchell felt at his own smooth face. The sun hung above the trees and he squinted as he looked across the water.

'Looks like it's still some big ones in here,' Russell said.

'Pretty big. Thought we'd get us a few and fry them up tomorrow evening. If that's all right with you.'

'Sounds good.'

'What happened to your eye?' Mitchell asked and he pointed at Russell's head.

Russell touched his fingertips to the redness and twisted his mouth. 'A going-away present from one of the boys.'

'Hope that's all you got.'

'It was. It's okay. Got worse than that a hundred times working on one of your houses.'

'Yeah. You didn't believe much in staying on ladders.'

Russell drank the Coke and then the whiskey and the Coke again and handed the bottle back to his father. But he felt better once it was down so he waved his hand and his father gave the bottle back to him. He drank again and then passed the bottle over and his dad put the top on and dropped it back into the cooler.

'It was them boys, wasn't it?' Mitchell said.

'Them boys what?'

'That smack on your eye. It was them boys.'

'Yes sir.'

'Don't guess they believe in waiting around.'

'Guess they figure they been waiting long enough. How'd you know?'

'There's a bunch of new buildings around here but that don't mean it ain't the same place. People talk like always. I was sitting at the café downtown and heard one of them old friends of their daddy running his mouth about coming to see you.'

'Their daddy there, too?'

'Naw. He's been dead a pretty good while. Since before your mother.'

Russell took a piece of ice out of the cooler. He rubbed it across the swelling eye and then tossed it into the pond. A mouth opened and closed around it and sank below.

'Were they at the house?' Mitchell asked.

'Better than that. In the parking lot when the bus rolled in.'

'I thought that eye looked like today's business. Anything else?'

'Nah.'

'What else you reckon they gonna do?' Mitchell asked.

'I'm not sure.'

Mitchell sat his can on the ground and he picked up the rod and reel and he took a cricket from the bucket. 'Come on out here and stay,' he said as he stuck the hook through the cricket. 'Long road. It's easier to see somebody coming.'

'I'm not bringing this out here to you. It'll be okay.'

Mitchell tossed the rod lightly this time, dropping the hook in the shallow water of the pond. The men watched the line until it ran and then Mitchell brought in a five-pounder.

'That's another good one,' Russell said.

'Won't take long like this,' Mitchell said. Russell opened the cooler and took out the whiskey bottle and two more Cokes. Mitchell took the hook from its mouth and laid it next to the other fish on top of the ice. The fish waved its body in its last attempts to be and then it fell still and Russell put the top back on the cooler.

The men returned to their chairs and they sat for a while. The sun falling. They kept the line in the water, holding on to a couple more fish, drinking from the bottle in small sips, talking in small bits about nothing. They got up and walked to the house where Mitchell sat on the back porch with a bucket and gutted the fish while Russell milled around in the shed and looked for the things he'd need to paint a house. Figured that was as good a task as any. It was all there. The ladders. Drop cloths. Brushes and scrapers. In the same spots he remembered them being in. He came out of the shed and over to the porch. Mitchell shook his head with his tongue sticking out of the corner of his mouth. Focused on the fish and his hands bloodied to the wrists.

'I'm gonna run on back to town,' Russell said. 'Feel weird being still.'

'That sounds right.'

'Seems I saw a café downtown. It any good?'

'Mostly. If you hit it right.'

'Well. I'm gonna try to hit it right.'

'And tomorrow night we'll fill you full of fish. Get some pounds back on you.'

'I'll come out tomorrow afternoon then.'

Mitchell looked up at Russell and nodded then said hold on

a second. He wiped his hands on a towel and then he walked in the back door and closed it behind him. Russell stood and waited and looked around the place. Just like he had done in a thousand dreams of home. He would go inside but he was saving that for later, not ready to see it all the same save for his mother in her apron with flour on her hands. The door opened again and his father came out with a shotgun tucked under his arm. He held a box of shells and he wiped the barrel of the gun with the end of his shirt and he walked over to his son and he held the shotgun out to him. Russell recognized it as his own 20-gauge, the one he used to walk the woods with looking for something to kill.

'What's that for?' Russell said and he hesitated to take the gun from his father.

'You know what it's for,' Mitchell said. 'Take it.'

Russell took the gun by the barrel and then he took the box of shells. 'I'm breaking about two dozen laws by having it.'

'I know it. I can't force it on you.'

'You're trying.'

'No. I ain't. But there's choices you gotta make.'

'It's not gonna be this bad,' Russell said and he tucked the barrel under his arm.

'You don't know how it's gonna be. I hope it ain't bad but you don't know.'

Russell nodded. Mitchell nodded. Then Russell said again that he'd be back tomorrow and he walked to the truck and drove off as Consuela watched from the kitchen window, standing at the sink where his mother used to be.

10

A GRAY LIGHT AS HE DROVE back to town. When he reached the house three boys were tossing around a football in the front yard of the house next door and a woman was on the front porch swing. He waved to her and she half waved back and then he went inside. He locked the door behind him and walked to the bedroom. It didn't take long to unpack as there were only the essentials – a handful of T-shirts and socks, a toothbrush and deodorant, and the folder filled with the supposedly helpful documents provided by Mildred Day. At the bottom of the bag was a wooden picture frame holding a photograph of Sarah. He took the frame and went to the living room mantel and placed her in the center. She sat on a bench in Jackson Square in the French Quarter, her hair pulled back, a pleasant smile on her face as if some reassuring memory had crossed her mind the moment the camera clicked. She had rested on a short bookshelf at the foot of his skinny, noisy bed for the last eleven years and as he set her on the mantel and stepped back he thought that somehow she looked younger removed from the confines of the square cell.

He spent another hour drinking and smoking on the back porch and then he was hungry and he remembered seeing the café on the ride from the bus station at the corner of Main Street.

He decided to leave the truck and walk. It took twenty minutes and he broke a solid sweat in the humid evening. He walked past houses with their television screens shining through the living room windows and three little girls, probably sisters, played hopscotch by the carport light in a driveway lined with rows of petunias. He crossed into downtown and spoke to a handful of men in suits standing together in front of a law office. They nodded and waved in the direction of the café when he asked.

When he got there the café was getting ready to close. But he looked tired enough for the waitress to stop wiping tables and stacking chairs and ask the cook if he had time for one more. Russell heard the cook swear but then agree and she told him it'd have to be something simple.

Russell sat down in a red vinyl booth and the front of the menu advertised a Big Breakfast. 'Is that simple enough?' he asked.

'Probably. Minus the grits,' she said. She took a pad out of her back pocket and reached for a pen that was supposed to be behind her ear. She felt her pockets and looked aggravated and he figured she had kids somewhere waiting on her. Hungry like he was.

'What to drink?'

'Still got coffee?'

She turned and looked behind the counter and half a pot remained. 'Probably ain't no good but we got it.'

'That's fine.'

She went into the kitchen and Russell heard the cook swear again and then she returned to his table with the coffee. He took a sip and it tasted like a slap in the face. The waitress went back to stacking and wiping and Russell fought with the coffee. The cook hollered for her and she returned to Russell with a plate loaded with scrambled eggs, sausage, bacon, hash browns, and toast. She went about her work and kept one eye on Russell, amazed at how fast he made the Big Breakfast disappear. When he was done he wiped his mouth and asked her how much. He left the money on the table and told her thanks and she followed him to the door and locked it behind him.

He spotted a gas station about a quarter of a mile away and he walked that way. He was still hungry so at the store he picked up some beef jerky and a couple of Honey Buns and a family-size bag of potato chips. He filled a giant Styrofoam cup with Coke and then walked to the cash register and motioned for the man with the ponytail to include a *Playboy* from the wire rack that sat tucked in the corner behind the counter. This is a good one the man said as he put the items into a bag and Russell said I never seen a bad one. He took the bag from the counter and then he walked back to the house, finishing the jerky and one of the Honey Buns before he got there.

He sat down on the living room floor and ate everything then felt sick. He thumbed through the *Playboy,* looking closely at the curves in the hips and breasts of the young, perfect women, trying to remember what one felt like. What one smelled like. He had long since forgotten and he had hoped that the fresh air would bring back the scent but he tossed the magazine aside and realized that only the real thing would make him remember. He kicked off his boots and walked through the house and turned off all the lights. Then he removed his clothes and lay on top of the bare mattress with the folded duffel bag serving as his pillow.

And that wasn't going to work.

He got up and put his clothes back on and he walked out in the backyard and lit a cigarette. He felt the tender spot over his eye and the tender spot in his ribs. Might as well call them up and get it over with. Come on over and let's finish it. Come on over here with whatever you got cause he's still dead and I'm not so come on over. I can take it. Took it all for eleven years.

Wasn't enough that I got held down and wasn't enough that I lost a couple of teeth. Then I gotta come home and they sit waiting on me. Come on over cause it can't be no worse. Hell no not any worse. Just come on and let me pay some more. Fuck. Damn near cut your head off, they said. Another inch that way and you'd have bled to death, they said. Another inch. Jesus.

He ran his fingers along the scar that stretched from ear to ear underneath his chin, camouflaged beneath the growing beard. Ripped wide open but alive. Ripped wide open but recovered. Ripped wide open but not wide enough. Lucky, they'd said. A miracle, they'd said. Bullshit, he'd said. The first week in prison he'd been beaten so badly that his eyes had swollen shut and as he lay on the nurse's table blind and throbbing he had called out for that extra inch. Give it to me now please God. You son of a bitch. Go ahead and give it to me. The nurse stuck him with a shot when he wouldn't shut up and then everything went black. When he woke he had picked up where he left off. Calling out for one more inch and then beginning to wonder about that one more inch and that was only the beginning of thinking about it. Of thinking about it and thinking about it. He had wondered about it a thousand times. A thousand times a year times eleven years came out to a lot of fucking wondering and it seemed to him now that there would be no end to it. Come on over. Bring whoever and whatever and come on over cause I ain't going nowhere. He imagined the brothers sitting in somebody's living room, drinking from cans, bragging about what they'd done. Got his ass right off the bus, they were saying. Stomped his ass, they were saying. Gonna do it again, they were saying. They don't know shit, Russell thought. They don't know.

A cricket hopped onto his arm and he watched it for a moment. Felt the tiny tentacles in the hairs of his arm. So gentle and unassuming. Like eyelashes batting against his skin. Then he tossed away the cigarette and smashed the cricket with the palm of his hand and he rubbed its guts up and down his forearm. Come on over, he thought and he felt the same rhythm in his pulse that he'd feel in the moments when there were three of them. Or four of them. A violent, pounding pulse that seemed to lift him up to some other level where he accepted the hurt and the pain. He wiped the bug guts on his jeans and he knelt down in the tall grass and he reared back his head and howled at the moon like some lunatic and he felt no end to it all.

When the howling died away he walked back inside and picked up the *Playboy* from the living room floor. He opened to the blonde with the green eyes. She lay on her back with her legs spread open, only a slither of satin concealing what she knew they wanted. He touched his fingers to the glossy page, eased them across the hard nipples, along the curve of the hip, up the inside of the thighs. And then he dropped the magazine on the floor and he got in the truck and drove downtown. He moved slowly between the old buildings, hoping to find anything with a neon sign that looked like it might be alive. Hoping to find others who could not be still in the night.

11

S HE HAD WASHED ANNALEE'S FACE WITH a washcloth and sat
next to her on the bed with her arms wrapped around her
until the child stopped crying and calmed down, promising
her over and over that she wasn't going to leave her. I swear to
God, Annalee. I swear it. The child eventually stopped huffing
and sniffing and then they moved back on the bed and pulled
the covers over them and Annalee rested her head on Maben's
chest and draped her arm across her mother's waist and she was
finally able to sleep again. Maben had slipped the pistol into
the bottom drawer of the dresser and she stared at the drawer
handle as she lay still until Annalee was thoroughly asleep and
she could move out from under her. When the tension left the
child's body and her breathing was slow and heavy, Maben eased
Annalee's arm from across her waist and then she gently moved
the child's head from her chest onto the pillow. She waited to
see if Annalee would wake and then Maben sat up in the bed.
Swung her legs off and stood.

She walked to the sink and took a plastic cup and filled it with
water and she drank it in one take. She did this twice more and
then took the wet cloth she had used to wipe the child's face
and she wiped her own. She sat down on top of the toilet and
closed the door to the bathroom and was still in the darkness.

Waiting for a knock on the door. Waiting for a siren. Waiting for something. Opening and closing her eyes. Unable to tell the difference. Listening and listening and listening.

She finally opened the bathroom door and she drank another cup of water. She looked in the mirror at the small mound on the bed under the sheets and blanket. I swear to God, Annalee. I swear it. She turned and walked to the edge of the bed. The sheet had pushed down around Annalee's waist and she lifted it and covered the child's sunburned arms. And then she took a chair and she sat down next to the window and pushed the curtain back half a foot, enough to see the parking lot from one side to the other.

This place, she thought. This road.

In her mind she began to trace her steps, to calculate what had gotten her here, into this night, with this sleeping child that she couldn't care for, with the wolves outside waiting to get her. But it was as if she were trying to fit together arbitrary pieces of different puzzles. No logical order or pattern or reason for one thing to fit together with the next. She had drifted for so long. Her mind was a cloud and her memories lost in the cloud and even if there were people and things worth remembering none of them would have done her any good right now. Would anyone or anything be able to save me from the shit I've fallen into?

Across the way a man and woman in matching denim shirts climbed out of a truck cab and walked hand in hand across the parking lot to the café. He opened the door for her and she slid her hand across his shoulder as she crossed inside.

Maben tried to think of someone else to blame but she couldn't. There was that one time, she thought. She was in the hospital bed and almost Christmas and the nurses wore antlers and the doctor carried candy canes in his coat pocket. Annalee came in the early morning and the nurse handed

Maben the tightly wrapped child and when Maben looked at her the expression in Annalee's eyes made Maben think that the child already knew her and in the moment of that first exchange she swore to God and the angels and the nurses in antlers that things were going to be different. I'm not going to let anything happen to you, Annalee. Not a damn thing. We'll be all right.

And they had been for a while. There had been a three-room apartment on the back side of a sliced-up antebellum with the nocturnal sounds all around – rats or maybe bigger animals crawling around underneath the slanting wooden floors and the loud television of the apartment next door and the banging around of the two drunk old men upstairs and the pill dealer in the other place upstairs and the constant comings and goings of those in need of him. A waterstained clawfoot tub and a waterstained sink and a refrigerator that dripped and left a tiny pinkish trail. A twin mattress that kept Annalee close to her as they lay together and a chair in the corner that wasn't meant to rock but Maben had cut holes in tin cans and slipped them onto the chair feet and then it rocked just right. The dropoff laundry three blocks away where Maben washed and folded clothes for people who didn't have to do it themselves and Annalee lying in a basket filled with clean, warm towels from the dryer and falling asleep to the electric lullabies of the washing machines. Getting paid in cash every Friday by the owner, a bent, whitehaired man with countless grandchildren. He had given her a stroller and a box of dolls and rattles and plastic blocks. A car seat if she ever got a car. Walking with Annalee, back and forth to work or to the Dollar General or to the grocery store or wherever they needed to go, the spring turning into summer and their walks together maybe out of necessity but always welcome to Maben as she wanted to wrap up the sun and the warmth and the child and the days together and put them somewhere safe so that one day she could get them back out and look at them and remember.

She stood from the chair and let the curtain fall across the motel room window. Shades of purple and gray across the bed. Across Annalee's exhausted little body. Maben knelt at the end of the bed. Sleep, she whispered. Sleep.

She moved her hand and turned and saw herself in the wide mirror covering the wall above the sink. She was draped in the dark. Faceless, almost shapeless. She stood still for a long moment and stared at her blank black figure. Then she slowly raised her arm to make certain she was real and the shadow in the mirror mimicked her movement and she knew that this was much more than a bad dream.

She let down her arm and crossed the room and sat on the floor with her back to the wall.

I didn't have to go up those stairs, she thought. Stay way the hell over there, bad habits. Stay your ass over there. I got a baby now and you're too sharp to play with.

She had started to listen for the steps, the fifteen steps of the staircase that split the middle of the big house and led up to the door of the pill guy. Late at night she listened and counted as they went up and counted as they went down. Rickety, horror-story-sounding steps and she created a phrase to match the fifteen steps, five words she whispered to herself in the dark, a word for each step, repeated three times. Don't go up the stairs. Don't go up the stairs. Don't go up the stairs.

Then she began to peek through the blinds and out at the street to see what they looked like. There was the Hispanic girl with the eagle or hawk or something with fabulous wings tattooed on her calf. The handful of young black guys in muscle shirts and sweatpants who looked fast and strong. The high school boys who arrived in an SUV that was worth a small house. The usual ragtag and wornout stragglers who ambled to the house from all sidewalk directions at any time of day or night.

During the day it wasn't difficult. She worked and then changed diapers or took Annalee for a walk or fed her or rocked them both to sleep. It was during the night after Annalee had woken her and Maben had given her a bottle and gotten her back to sleep that she imagined going up the steps herself and knocking on the door and getting a little something. Just a little something.

Stay way the hell over there. Back up. Keep going.

So then she began to watch for him and that became more difficult because she never saw him. Never caught him coming or going, only heard the muffled sound of his voice when someone was at his door and he became this strange, faceless thing that lived up the stairs and provided the magic beans.

Twice, both times in the middle of the night after Annalee was back asleep after a bottle, she had gone up. But both times she had won. Stopping at the door and her knuckles bending in preparation for a knock but she never raised her hand. The tension falling from her bent fingers. The voice inside backing her away and telling her you will not become what he wants you to become. She moved back down talking in rhythm with her steps. Don't go up the stairs. Don't go up the stairs. Don't go up the stairs. The second time she returned she closed her door and leaned against it and she was breathing hard as if she had been running from the bad guys and had slipped inside only an instant before they got her. She caught her breath and went to the bathroom and looked at herself and it was unfamiliar – health. They were eating. Didn't matter what or how much but they were eating. They were sleeping. She had stopped smoking two months before the baby was born and hadn't started back but for one at lunch and one at night. No beer. Beer had always led to nastier and happier things.

There is not one damn reason to go up there, she had said and pointed at herself in the mirror as if to add and I fucking mean it.

Several nights later he knocked on her door. She opened it and he was holding a small Ziploc bag containing a handful of pills. Some blue and some white. He held the bag out to her and said welcome to the neighborhood. He was wiry with deepset eyes and the distant look of the sleepless. He wore faded jeans and was barefoot and his blond hair was cut tight on his head. He held his mouth halfopen and his teeth were badly stained from cigarettes.

'I don't want them,' she had said and she closed the door. She waited and listened for him to walk away and then the Ziploc bag slid under the door.

'Then throw them away. I don't give a shit what you do with them,' he said and then he was gone.

Maben heard voices outside in the parking lot. Gruff voices and a couple of gruff laughs and then nothing. She slid her back along the wall and lay down on the floor with her arm folded under her head and she started to cry quietly. As she cried she could see the Ziploc bag sliding under the door. She could see the bad habits not listening to her demands to stay away. Not staying way the hell over there but inching closer and closer until they were right there with her and the child. The summer faded away and in early October the weather turned damp and cool and Annalee coughed and coughed and wouldn't sleep and her fever went up and down and because she had kept the Ziploc bag underneath the kitchen sink and not thrown it away, taking it out and opening the bag and sticking her fingers into it and raising them to her mouth was an easy thing to do. And by Christmas she was no longer paying the rent and by February she and Annalee were locked out of the apartment and that was where the clarity of what she remembered from the last four years ended. The fog settled in.

Maben sat up and wiped her eyes. She got off the floor and walked across the room and sat down again in the chair. She pulled back the curtain wide enough to see from one side of the parking lot to the other. Dawn was coming in a few hours and she knew that with the first light the world would begin to spin faster.

12

HE FOUND THE ARMADILLO, A CORNER bar on the bottom floor of a three-story building. He parked and went inside and sat down at the bar. Brick walls and a sticky wooden floor and a yellowstained ceiling. A dozen or so people sat at the tables and along the back wall was a small stage. Stacks of speakers were on each end of the stage and a drum kit set up in the middle. The chairs and tables were pushed back away from the stage, leaving room for dancing. A young man appeared from a door behind the bar. He carried a case of beer and he slid open the top of a cooler and stacked the bottles inside. His arms were covered with tattoos and his hair messed up in the right places. Russell sat alone at the bar and when he finished stacking the beers he gave Russell a nod and Russell asked for one of them. For the next hour or so this was the game. The bartender came and went in preparation for the night ahead and Russell sat quietly, smoking and watching, trying to decipher where one tattoo ended and another began. He occasionally asked for a beer and the bartender gave it to him.

In the next hour the door to the Armadillo opened and closed more frequently as the tables began to fill up. Russell moved to the end of the bar where he could watch the door. Most everyone who came in looked either too young to be in there or too old. A burly, bearded man came in the door and stepped into the middle of the floor. He looked around. Stuck two fingers in his mouth and whistled. Another bearded man wearing a black bandanna around his neck pushed open the door and then guitar cases and amps were walked in and through the maze of tables. Once the equipment was in place the band plugged in cords and tapped microphones and tuned guitars. It was the ugliest band Russell had ever seen.

Another bartender showed up to help with the crowd. A young woman, equally tattooed. Her shirt bared her belly and a sun flared around her belly button and Russell happily watched it move behind the bar. Jesus or Elvis could have walked in the door and he wouldn't have known or cared as he was magnetized by the black sun and the way its rays bent and twisted as she reached for bottles and poured strong drinks.

The bar stools filled up next with those who had come without friends and after the burly band drank a few beers and smoked a few cigarettes the lights went down and a row of moody, yellowish bulbs illuminated the stage and dance area. A guitarist struck a wiry chord and then on the count of four the night jumped to a new level as the burly band played Skynyrd as tight and crisp as Skynyrd themselves. Heads began bouncing and shoulders began swaying and there was no more talking, only yelling, and the band never slowed between the first three or four songs and a couple made its way to the space in front of the stage. Clutching and clinging more than dancing but damn sure not caring what anyone thought about it. Russell's knee bounced in rhythm and he noticed the tattooed bartenders pouring the drinks heavier than they had been pouring them before the music began. People kept coming in and it wasn't long before it was hot inside and in another handful of songs there were more sweaty faces than dry faces. Russell had to go to the bathroom but knew if he left his bar stool he wouldn't get it back so he tried to ignore it by watching the sun that was now glistening with sweat in the neon light of the beer signs hanging behind the bar.

The band decided to take a break and the bodies returned to their seats and the crowd seemed to take a collective breath. The noise and the energy falling and the bartenders hustling to get everyone filled up before the second set. The bar stool next to Russell opened up but was quickly taken by a blond man. A man Russell thought was much too pretty to be in a place like this. He asked for a drink and when it was delivered he tried to pay with a hundred but the woman bartender shook her head and said no damn way. She picked up the drink and handed it to someone else who wanted the same thing. The man asked Russell if he had change and Russell shook his head and the man returned to his table and explained to the three women he sat with that his money was no good here. One of the women reached into her purse and gave him a twenty and he returned to the spot next to Russell. Russell noticed his smooth hands as he held them folded on the bar and waited for another chance. And he noticed the starch in his shirt and the watch on his wrist and if it wasn't his first visit to the Armadillo Russell had a hunch it'd be his last. This time the man ordered two drinks and the exchange was made and Russell watched him walk back to his table. The woman who gave him the money leaned over and whispered into his ear and then she licked it and he pulled away and looked around as if his name had been called. She laughed and the other two women laughed but he didn't and he sipped his drink cautiously while the women continued to have a good time.

Russell couldn't hold it anymore so he had no choice but to vacate the stool. He left his beer on the bar hoping to mark his seat. Neither of the bathroom doors was marked but a line of women stood outside one of them. He was lucky to get in and out of the men's room but when he returned to the bar stool it was taken. His beer had been pushed to the side and a woman sat in his place, her shoulders covered only by the shoestring straps of her dress, her hair reaching her sunfreckled shoulders. Russell walked up behind her and started to reach around for his beer but as he reached the stool next to her came free as a couple all wound up together made their way out of the bar and toward somewhere that offered more privacy. He sat down and with less of a reach he slid his beer in front of him.

She looked at him and halfgrinned. 'Was that yours?'

He nodded.

'And I bet this was your seat,' she said.

'You'd win that bet.'

She started to get up but he said, 'Sit back down. We're good.'

She grinned again and held her drink with both hands. He didn't recognize her and he hoped she didn't recognize him. Her nails were long and pink like ten delicate daggers and bracelets dangled from each wrist. She sat with her legs crossed and sipped her drink as if she had all night.

The band decided the break was over and they started out with Hank Junior and it took less than a verse for the mood to rise again. Dancing replaced sitting. Yelling replaced talking. Russell had finished off his pack of cigarettes and he noticed a pack sitting on the bar in front of the woman. He pointed to them and asked for one.

She obliged and lit it for him with a lighter she pulled from a tiny purse that he hadn't noticed in her lap. She put it away then she folded her arms across her healthy chest and squeezed like she had missed herself. Russell watched her breasts push together but looked away quickly when she turned to him.

'You like to dance?' she asked.

'Probably not the way you do,' he said. 'I got a feeling you can shake it.'

'Few more of those and you'll be ready.'

'Few more of these and I'll be ready for anything,' he answered, surprising himself with how easily the remark came out.

She cut her eyes at him and then held out her hand. 'I'm Caroline.'

'Russell,' he said and he held her fingers and shook them.

He hadn't noticed but she had turned on her seat and was now facing him with her legs uncrossed and almost touching his hip. He was a man who had not seen the legs or shoulders of a real live woman in too damn long so he thought what the hell and he started at her ankles and followed up her calves and over her knees and up to her thighs to where the dress began. And then he trailed up her stomach and stopped a moment at her breasts and those freckled shoulders and then he made it to her chin and unsmiling mouth and nose and eyes and she stared back.

'So should I hike it up or pull it down?'

He shook his head.

'Want me to stand up and turn around?'

'No. Maybe.'

'Least you could do is dance with me first.'

'You don't want to see that.'

'God knows you owe me a drink after giving me such a look.'

'I can do that,' he said and he waved to the bartender.

They got their beers and clinked bottles.

'Damn it to hell. That was the best compliment I've had in about half a dozen years.'

The interview began. She asked if he was married and he said no. She asked if he had kids and he said no again.

'Are you sure?' she said.

'I think I'd know.'

'Shit. I heard that one before.'

He didn't think she believed him and he was right. He tried to sit up straight. Look at her when answering. He liked the way she leered at him with playful, suspicious eyes and when she asked what he did for a living he lied and said painted houses. He tried to keep his face forward so that she wouldn't notice the beginnings of the scar at the edge of the beard. Because she would ask about it. There was no doubt she would ask about it and then he would have to lie and that might blow the whole thing. He kept waiting for some Armadillo regular to stick his head in and try to drag her away.

He bought her another beer and she said don't you want to ask me the same questions but he didn't. He hadn't even bothered to look at her ring finger though she made it a point to drink with that hand and to play with her necklace with that hand.

The band kept on and Russell asked if they played here often. 'Don't know. I don't come here much,' she said.

You look like you own that bar stool, he thought to say. But he was hiding things so he let her lie. Russell then turned and watched the four rugged rockers, unable to decide if their better days were behind or ahead.

'They're not bad,' Caroline said. 'For this place.'

'Nope,' he answered, turning back. He waved for two more. He promised himself that he'd drink more slowly though he realized that it was a flimsy promise.

'Let's make a deal,' she said. 'I go to the bathroom and you keep my seat. You go and I keep yours. That's also the other's chance to make a run for it. No questions asked.'

'That's a damn good deal,' he said.

'Fine. Me first.'

She left her cigarettes on the bar and took her tiny purse in her hand and went to the ladies' room. Russell kept one hand on his drink and the other palm down on top of her bar stool. He wondered what kind of woman would make a deal like that.

How often she played and how often she came back to find the man gone. She didn't look like the kind of woman any man would run from. Not in the Armadillo. As he waited he watched the band and watched the bartenders and begged himself not to say or do anything stupid.

13

'YOU SURE HEATHER IS IN THERE?' Walt asked. They sat in the parked truck in the shadows of the parking lot on the other side of the railroad tracks. A clear view of the lighted door of the Armadillo. They had been sitting for an hour, first with the windows down but then the mosquitoes floated in and out and Larry had cranked the truck and rolled up the windows and turned on the air conditioner. The clock on the dash read half past midnight.

'That's what Jimmy said when he called.'

'Want me to go in and look?'

'Nah. I don't want them to know we're here. Want her and him to have a good damn time. Think the world is roses.'

'Did he say if it's the same guy?'

'Same one. Little blond shit she's been running down to New Orleans with.'

Only a few people had left while they had been parked. They had both been in the Armadillo enough to know that it didn't begin to break up until after one when the band stopped playing. Walt held a beer between his legs and he slapped his hand on his knee to the rhythm of the muffled drumbeat coming from the bar. Two more minutes passed. Larry sat motionless with his eyes fixed on the bar door with the stare of a dead man.

The band slowed it down with a George Jones and the bodies piled onto the dance floor anxious to be against one another. As the song drained on hands fell lower and mouths opened and those left behind sat alone at their tables with dejected, anguished looks on their faces as they stared at the swaying crowd that seemed to grow together and form some drunken and sweaty mass. Midway through the song Caroline moved her hand onto Russell's leg and she rubbed her fingers back and forth across the soft, worn denim. Rubbing in a way that let him know she was his. And it had been a long time but his instinct was not dead and he waved to the barebellied bartender for the tab and he was paid up before Caroline had the notion to move her hand away. He got off the bar stool and took her hand and she stood and moved her shoulders to the music. You want to drive or you want me to he asked and she pointed to him. Then they stepped around the deserted tables and out into the warm night.

'I'll be damned,' Walt said and he leaned toward the windshield. Russell and Caroline stood on the sidewalk holding hands.

'Sit tight,' Larry said.

'Are you serious?'

'Sit tight.'

'Son of a bitch. Our boy moves fast.'

'Right now he does.'

'First goddamn night home.'

'He must be used to getting his ass kicked. Don't look like it bothered him much.'

'Don't look like it,' Walt said and he slumped back against his seat. 'Gonna have to hit him harder.'

'We will. But not right now,' Larry said. 'I got my mind on the other one about to come out.' He rolled down the windows again. The music stopped inside the bar. Russell and Caroline both looked up and down the street and then Russell pointed. Minutes passed and the music never started back and Walt said that must be it and Larry said it's about damn time.

14

THE BLOND MAN HADN'T LIKED BEING there and was anxious to leave and as soon as the music stopped and the guitars were unplugged he said goodbye to Heather without ceremony and made his way for the door. He couldn't understand what was wrong with the Gulf Coast or with New Orleans or with Hattiesburg or with any of the million other places that a man and a married woman could meet and do what they wanted to do. But Heather had said don't be a coward. Let's keep it local tonight and let me show the girls what I got. This town was too small and he didn't like it and he had wondered all night why the hell he had agreed to it.

He walked out past a man and a woman holding hands. The man nodded to him and then the blond man put his hand into the pocket of his creased pants and took out his car keys. He turned the corner and walked a block to the parking lot that was next to the railroad tracks. It was darker there, no streetlight, only the faint glow floating over from the streets behind him. His shadow disappeared as he hurried to the car.

The footsteps came in a hurry and when he turned and saw the two men rushing toward him he wondered where they had come from. He tried to speak but didn't have time and they were on him like a storm. His nose broken with the first fist and he fell back across the hood of a car and they held him there and he took blow after blow to his head and face. He tried to cover up but they were stronger and relentless and they held his arms with ease and the pain from his nose like a sword shoved into his brain and he felt himself losing consciousness. When he was nearly gone one man pinned his arms to the hood of the car while the other spread his legs and punched him over and over and over in the dick as if to make sure it understood that you do not go into another man's wife. The blood ran over his face and neck and the four fists that had been pounding him were covered in the same blood. He couldn't move and he was at the edge of consciousness flat on the hood of a car.

The brothers stepped back and looked around and a handful more people had left the bar and were walking toward the parking lot. Larry wiped his nose on the back of his hand and checked for his own blood where he had gotten in the way of the fist of his brother. Let's go, Walt said. Here comes somebody.

Larry reached into his back pocket and pulled out an envelope that held the photographs of the bleeding man having a good time with Heather. He shoved the envelope down the front of the man's pants. Leaned close to his face and listened to him reaching for breath and he squeezed the man's bloody cheeks into a pucker and said that's what you get when you fuck with me.

The men hurried away across the blackest end of the parking lot. They climbed in the truck and drove a block and a half and stopped. Watched. Two women going to their car saw the busted blond man and a faint scream came out of the dark. The women hurried back to the Armadillo and Larry and Walt waited until Heather came out to see what was going on. She was out first and her friends followed her to the corner and across the street and they turned into shadows as they passed between the parked cars. Larry imagined them gathering around the punished man and none of them knowing what to do and the errant look in her eyes as she found her toy broken across the hood of a car. He smirked at himself in the rearview mirror and then turned his eyes back toward the parking lot where he could not hear Heather telling her friends to help him up and get him in the car. Could not see them struggling with his limp body and asking if they should call the cops and Heather saying are you deaf I said just get him in the damn car. He could not see them or hear them but he knew that when she finally got him somewhere and wiped the blond man's blood from her hands and from her dress and found the photographs down in the place she knew so well, she would then understand that it was her turn to crawl.

15

RUSSELL TURNED THE TRUCK RADIO TO an oldies station and the Temptations were playing and Caroline rolled her arms and clapped her hands like she'd seen them do on television. The windows were down and her hair spray wouldn't hold in the wind but she didn't complain. Russell enjoyed the show and considered clapping with her but didn't think he should let go of the steering wheel. She swayed front and back and side to side and her dress clung to her like Saran wrap and she tried to sing but didn't know the words so she stuck to the choreography. When the song was over she picked up a rubber band that she found on the floorboard and used it to pull her hair back in a ponytail. She kicked off her shoes and set them on the seat with her purse and cigarettes.

She's older out here, Russell thought. Thirty-five, maybe less, in the bar. Forty or more in the streetlight. At a red light he noticed the same freckles across her nose and under her eyes that were scattered across her shoulders. Some of the freckles were lost in the creases at the edges of her eyes. But her curves hadn't changed in the light and that was all he cared about.

She had asked to go to Russell's place but he said no and they were on the way to her house. They drove along Delaware Avenue. There was little traffic but for the fast food joints and the night air was lighter after a brief evening rain. They drove on until Delaware reached the interstate and then they passed over the bridge and made their way out of town, passing car dealerships and then wooded lots decorated with oversize for sale signs. Caroline calmed and watched out the window and Russell watched her as if she might disappear, unsure if God was actually going to let him be this lucky. In another half mile the house lights appeared back off the highway. Long driveways separating the houses from the bother of the passersby. Caroline pointed and said right up there and the truck slowed and turned right. Four small identical houses sat together at the corners of a flat square of new black asphalt. Each had the same white vinyl siding, the same green shutters, the same red front door, the same chimney sticking up from the same side of the roof. He stopped in the middle.

'Guess which one.'

Russell looked around. 'That one. With the pink flamingo.'

'Jackass,' she said.

'You look like a woman who would have a pink flamingo.'

'You ain't exactly home free, cowboy. Don't get smart.'

'It was a compliment.'

'Shit. I hate that thing. This one over here.'

He parked in front of the house in the back right corner. They got out and she stopped at the front door. She bent over and took a key from under the mat and when she bent Russell ran his hand across her ass knowing he could blame it on being drunk if it didn't come off the right way. But she straightened and turned and smiled and she grabbed him and kissed him. Then she pulled back and said I better get you inside.

She opened the door and Russell grabbed her again and she moved them to the middle of the room and Russell didn't know anything else to do but to go for it. He pushed the straps from her shoulders and thought please God and then he pushed her dress down to her waist and there was another please God and when she wiggled he knelt and pulled it to her ankles and she stepped out and then there was a thank you God. In another minute they were naked on the carpet and he forgot about God and he was on his back and she rocked on top of him holding his shoulders with her hands and then as she leaned forward on him and he held her waist and felt her breasts against his bare chest he bit his lip to keep from crying and the thought crossed his mind that if there was another man alive on the face of the earth who at that present moment was happier than he was then he didn't know how the son of a bitch could stand it.

16

THEY LAY NEXT TO ONE ANOTHER in the same spot in the middle of the floor where they had finished. Caroline had taken pillows and a blanket from a hall closet and covered them once they were done. Russell lay on his back with his eyes on the ceiling and Caroline slept with her head across his chest. Russell had tried to move her once but she had grunted and risen and then flopped back across him and so he had decided to ride it out. Go to sleep and face the music the next morning and see what she was really like. But the sleep part wouldn't come and he worked to build the courage to move her again and find his pants and leave. The night had been a gift and he wanted to remember things the way they had been – in low light, blurred by drink, happily irresponsible. The morning light would wipe that away. The beer had worn off and he could feel the headache coming on and he needed to get up and smoke the cigarette that would keep the pain away for a while.

He shifted some to his left and she made no sound. With his free hand he took the pillow from behind his head and stacked it on top of hers to keep her head from too much of a flop. Then as much as he could, he turned on his side and eased her off and onto her back and her head made an easy roll from his shoulder to the pillow. She made a mumble then tugged at the blanket and she turned on her side and faced him. He sat and looked at her, imagining her naked body beneath the blanket and the ways in which he knew her now.

He carefully picked himself up from the floor and he began to feel around in the dark for his clothes. He was relieved to find his pants first and he put them on and then he found his shirt and shoes and one sock. He held them in one arm while he crawled around and felt for the other sock and his underwear but when she sniffed and rolled over he thought the hell with it and he put on what he had. His wallet had stuck in the back pocket of his jeans and he remembered leaving the keys in the truck. He felt like there was something he should do. Leave a note. Kiss her cheek. Something. But the only thing he did was take another look at her shoulders. He then tiptoed to the front door and turned the handle with the care of a thief. He opened the door just enough to slide through, unaware that in the dark her eyes were wide open.

17

HE HAD STAYED OUT RIDING. WIDE-ASS awake with the adrenaline of the first day of freedom and he wanted it to go on and on. Three in the morning. Bought some more beer after he left her house. No reason to call it a night. Her smell on him and if he tried hard he could feel her on top of him as if she were straddling him now with her dress over her hips and her knees burying into his sides. He drove down to Fernwood and to the truck stop and he sat down with a roast beef poboy and when he was done he drove out onto Highway 48 and toward the lake. He heard the sirens and saw the flashes coming up behind him and he slowed and eased onto the side of the road and the cruisers roared past and he knew it had to be something bad. The highway ran straight and he saw them hit their brakes and turn off at a road about half a mile before the lake road and before he could get there an ambulance approached from the other direction and turned in behind the cruisers. Russell stopped and he didn't see what they were after but he saw the barrage of lights circling in the night sky so he followed after them.

In a mile or so he found them. The cars from the police department and the sheriff's department and the ambulance and a huddle of men standing around in the headlights talking to one another. Whatever had happened appeared to be over. Russell stopped the truck and one of the deputies saw his truck and pointed and then the other men looked and Russell felt like he shouldn't be there. He tried to back up and turn around but the road was too thin and it took a couple of tries and before he could get gone a deputy had called out for him to hold it right there. He carried a flashlight with him and he shined it into the truck cab and Russell didn't move. A man in street clothes accompanied the deputy.

'Get out of the truck and show your hands,' the deputy said.

Russell did as he was told and the deputy told him to walk around to the front of the truck and put his hands on the hood. Russell obeyed. The deputy gave the light to the other man and he walked behind Russell and patted him down and asked him what he was doing out here.

'Riding around,' Russell said.

'Riding around where?'

'Around here.'

'Doing what?'

'I told you. Riding.'

'You got ID?'

'In my wallet back there.'

The deputy took Russell's wallet from his back pocket and opened it. He pulled out Russell's driver's license which expired eight years earlier.

'I'll be damned,' the deputy said. 'Stand up and turn around. Didn't know you with that stuff on your face.'

'Boyd Wilson,' Russell said and he broke into a smile and they shook hands.

'Holy shit. You never know who you might find in the middle of the night.' Boyd was roundfaced and his forehead and hair seemed greasy slick in the flashing lights. His neck and cheeks had swollen with the years but Russell couldn't miss those squinty eyes and the crooked nose that had been broken twice during their senior football season. Russell shook his head at Boyd.

'When did you get home?' he asked.

'About noon.'

'Noon today?'

'Noon today.'

'Don't guess it's today no more but you know what I mean.'

'I do.'

'Well. Damn.'

'Damn,' Russell said.

'How was it?'

'About like you'd think.'

'Like in the movies?'

Russell forced a smile. 'Yeah. Except worse. In the movies somebody has a happy ending. I didn't see many of them.'

'You're out. That's a happy ending.'

'We'll see. How's Lacey doing?'

'Aw hell. Not bad.'

'She still turning backflips?'

'God no. She couldn't put her right leg in that old cheerleader outfit now. Two kids later and Jesus H. if shit don't change. Gotta love her, though.'

'How old are them boys?'

'Fifteen and thirteen. You wouldn't believe how much they eat. Oldest starts varsity ball this year.'

'He been running?'

'Running. Lifting. Both of them. They ain't like we used to be, running up and down the roads all summer and then getting ready a month ahead. They got them doing something year-round. Junior high and high school. Get pissed at them if they miss a workout in March, much less August.'

'That's good. They don't need to be like we used to be anyway,' Russell said.

'That's what Lacey keeps telling me. I just ain't sure they're having much fun. But it don't seem to bother them none.'

'They got a daddy with the department. They could get away with damn near anything.'

'They might figure that out before too much longer.'

Boyd slapped the other man in the chest and then pointed at Russell. 'This son of a bitch could fly back in the day. Couldn't catch for shit but if you threw it up he'd outrun you to it.'

'I caught a couple. You gotta catch it every now and then to get laid.'

'Speaking of, Lacey's sister split up with her husband not too long ago. She might be as hard up as you.'

'Tell her to grab a twelve-pack and come on over.'

The three men laughed and then Boyd gave Russell back the wallet. The other man walked back over to the scene.

'Hurry and get that thing renewed,' Boyd said.

'First thing.' Russell stuck it in his pocket and asked what happened. Boyd's face went straight and he blew out a big breath. 'Found a deputy out here shot dead. Shot a few times. Can't find his pistol, either. It ain't pretty.'

'Anybody I know?'

'Nah. Guy came down from Tupelo or somewhere a year or two back. He's been on thin ice ever since he got here. Wonder if something didn't catch up with him.'

'What was he doing out here?'

'That's the ten-dollar question,' Boyd said and shook his head. 'Don't nobody seem to know right now. I hate for Lacey to find out about this one. She hates it enough already. It ain't like it used to be when we were running the roads. Fighting in the parking lot or busting somebody's mailbox was about as bad as we got. These days you walk up to somebody's car and you might get your face blowed off. Any swinging dick can get a gun.'

A man from the crowd called out to Boyd and Boyd told him just a minute.

'I gotta run over there, Russell. Good to see you. Can't believe it's been that long.'

Russell nodded and they shook hands again and Boyd walked away. Russell waited a minute, mesmerized by the swirling lights. He then turned to get in the truck and Boyd hustled back over to him.

'Hold on,' he said. 'Don't get in yet. I'm told it don't matter if you're my momma I got to look in your truck. Stand over there.' Boyd pointed to a spot on the ground ten feet away from the truck and Russell stood on it. Boyd opened the glove compartment and looked under the seat and then he lifted the seat and found empty beer bottles and the shotgun and shells. He put the seat back and then he walked over to Russell and asked him if it was his.

'Used to be. Guess it is again.'

'Loaded?'

'Yep.'

Boyd scratched his chin. 'How's your daddy?'

'Still going.'

'Out there in the same spot?'

'The same.'

'You know you can't have a gun. Shit, Russell. You ain't even been home twenty-four hours.'

'I know.'

'Then why are you riding around with a loaded twenty-gauge?'

'It just worked out that way.'

'Not just a loaded shotgun but empty beer cans on the floorboard.' Russell gave a big exhale. Shrugged his shoulders.

'Do me a favor and unload it,' Boyd said.

'All right.'

'And don't drink no more right now.'

'Yes sir.'

'Look, between you and me plenty of those boys over there drive around looking to stick it to somebody. Might be why one is shot up. And don't none of them really give a shit about fellas who already been in once.'

'I gotcha.'

'Okay. Take off now. Go on home.'

Russell nodded. He cranked the truck and backed away from the scene and then he was again alone in the dark. But he did not think of going home. Instead he opened another beer and drove slow, looking for a good side road. The shifting shades of dark as he put miles between him and the flashing lights. He found a road between two fence posts where a rusted metal gate was bent out of shape and wedged open. The truck just fit through the opening and he followed the bumpy road until it ended in the middle of a pasture. He shut the headlights and got out.

But he didn't let down the tailgate. Didn't sit on the hood. Instead he paced around with the high grass brushing his legs. His arms folded and his lips pressed together. The beer can sweating in his hand.

He appreciated what Boyd said but he wasn't going to unload the shotgun.

There was a simplicity to Boyd that he admired. A wife and kids and a job with benefits and he couldn't help but think of Sarah. He had told himself that her picture wouldn't make it out of the box but she had made it to the mantel already. There had been no reason to bring her home with him. The memories of what had been had helped to sustain him while confined amid concrete and steel but there was no reason to bring her home.

But he had. He thought he knew where she lived. He had the address from the last letter she had sent him six years earlier. I have to move on, Russell. He's a good man, Russell. Nobody can help the way things turned out.

He wondered about the dead deputy. Wondered if his death had been merciful. Like the merciful death he had wished for so many nights as he lay awake, fearful of what might come the next day. To him or the man standing next to him.

Go on home, Boyd had said.

He shook his head. Figured Larry and Walt might be sitting on his front steps. Or the back steps. Or hiding in the closet. He kept pacing and drinking and thinking. Sometimes talked to the stars. Sometimes kicked at the grass.

He knew that sooner or later he was going to go to that address and find out if she was there and right now seemed like as good a time as any. He cranked the truck and swung around. Passed through the gate and lit a cigarette. And then he turned south on Highway 48 and made his way toward Magnolia.

18

IT WAS ONE OF THOSE SMALL and picturesque southern towns
that should have and might have been in the movies. Tall,
Victorian houses. Grand magnolias. Turn-of-the-century
streetlamps. Churches with steeples that reached into the
clouds. He passed a row of shotgun houses. One blue, the next
yellow, the next pink, the next white. He followed the highway
into downtown and turned left on Jefferson Street and passed
city hall. The courthouse stood at the end of the block and
then he turned right and drove three streets uphill to where the
road reached back around behind city hall and from your front
yard you could look out across the town. He had the address
memorized and he drove slowly along Washington Avenue
looking for 722. He found it on the corner, a fire hydrant painted
like a jockey at the edge of the sidewalk. He stopped the truck
on the opposite side of the street.

It was a two-story blue house with a steep roof. There was an
arched window on the second floor that looked like an upstairs
balcony. Burgundy shutters. There were two chimneys and a
porch that stretched the length of the front of the house and
turned the corner and reached down the right side toward the
backyard fence. A brick walkway from the sidewalk to the steps
and then brick steps and terracotta pots on each step. Yellow

and white petals hung over the edges of the pots. At the foot
of the steps a little red wagon was dumped over on its side.
Wicker furniture on the porch and empty glasses on the table.
Two cars were parked in the street along the side of the house.
Something big and black with four doors and something sleek
with round taillights. Alongside the house lay a soccer ball and
a baseball bat. A plastic slide perfect for somebody small.

All the appearances of happiness.

He put the truck in drive and he drove into the night
thinking about his life. With the effortlessness with which he
had arrived at this moment. I got drunk and killed somebody
with my car. That was it. He had marveled at the stories he
had heard from other inmates. At the complications they had
fallen into. At the opportunities they were given for things to
go right but then they went wrong and it seemed like it was
mostly the fault of others. He didn't have that story. I got drunk
and killed somebody with my car. It was as basic a story as you
could tell. He thought of her now like he had thought of her so
many times. Sleeping between soft sheets. Sleeping in a silent
peace or sometimes turning and reaching for him. Maybe it
had happened before but he couldn't imagine it now. Not after
seeing that house. Those toys in the yard. He saw her sleeping
and her dreams filled with sand castles and birthday cakes and
dinner parties while his dreams were filled with hand grenades.
Filled with things he didn't want to see any longer. Filled with
things he wished he could forget.

Back in McComb he drove along Delaware Avenue, serene
and illuminated by streetlights. Two police cars sat parked next
to one another in a pawn shop parking lot with the windows
down, the cops talking to one another. He drove on past grocery
stores and gas stations and he moved closer to downtown where
the streets were lined with churches and he slowed when he
came to the First Methodist Church with its high arches and

brick steps and wooden steeple that made a wonderful shadow into the street in the afternoons. He hadn't been a stranger to church or to God as he and his mother and father had gone every Sunday morning. His dad would drop him off at Sunday school and then he and Mom would sit on the seventh pew on the right side when his father joined them in the sanctuary for the service. Mom with her legs crossed and her Bible with liza gaines inscribed on the bottom right of the front cover on her lap. Dad next to her in a black suit that matched all his ties and when Russell would get restless Mitchell would reach around his wife and pinch his ear and look down at him with serious eyes. Russell would then move and sit between his mother and father. His mom would pull a pen out of her purse and let him draw on the bulletin. That would keep him through the message and then they'd stand up and sing and the preacher would stand in front of the pulpit and ask for souls and sometimes one would come but most of the time not and then they'd walk out the front and Dad would shake hands with the preacher and the old men and then they'd go home and eat something with gravy.

He slowed to a stop and parked on the street in front of those brick steps. Then he got out and walked around and leaned on the passenger-side door. He stared up at the steeple which lost its clarity against the backdrop of the night sky.

He had tried again in the pen. The prison chapel was filled with rows of metal folding chairs and the pulpit held a podium and more chairs for the brighteyed young man from a local church who led the singing and the preacher and two guards. The preacher changed by the month, visiting speakers from area churches, sometimes a traveling evangelist, sometimes a budding theologian fresh out of the New Orleans seminary. But he could never get used to sitting next to men who sang the hymns of love and forgiveness knowing what they'd done and knowing they were getting their redemption. Taking advantage of grace while those they had done it to were probably up at night walking back and forth across worn carpet or fumbling in the medicine cabinet searching for the pills to help them sleep. He didn't like the part of the service when these same men left their seats and stood at the pulpit and gave testimony. It was the same story over and over. Yes, I raped. Yes, I took another life. Yes, I stole. Yes, I raised a fist to my fellow man. But now I have found the love of God. Now I can see the light. Now I am found and on and on to a smattering of amens and hallelujahs and praise the Lords until Russell couldn't take it anymore and so he gave up. He didn't believe it worked that way and if it did then something didn't seem right.

Once he asked the preacher if he thought it was really possible that these men could inherit the kingdom if their repentance was legitimate.

'If I didn't think it was possible I wouldn't be here,' the preacher had said. He was a retired Baptist minister. He walked with a limp and he wore a white beard and blackrimmed glasses and something in the gravelly tone of his voice had told Russell that he had heard it all from the mouths of sinners.

'Do you think it's fair?' Russell demanded. He had been ready with the second question because he already knew what the preacher's answer would be to the first.

The preacher took off his glasses and wiped them with his tie. Then he held them to the light and put them back on.

'What do you mean by fair, son? What I think is fair or what you think is fair or what that prison guard over there thinks is fair?'

'You know what I mean,' Russell said.

'Yeah,' the preacher answered. 'I know what you mean.' And then he folded his arms and stared at Russell. Russell waited. The preacher took a deep breath.

'I don't think it's fair, either,' Russell said.

'But it doesn't matter what I think is fair or what you think is fair,' the preacher answered. 'The only thing that matters is what God thinks is fair. He leaves the door open. For everybody.'

Russell pointed to an inmate who was leaving the chapel. 'See that guy?' he said. The preacher turned and looked. 'That guy beat his grandma to death because she wouldn't tell him where the keys were to the car.'

'I know,' the preacher said.

Then Russell pointed at another guy. 'That one molested his little brother for about five years.'

The preacher nodded again.

'His little brother,' Russell repeated.

'I heard you.'

Russell pointed at another but before he could begin the preacher held up his hand and stopped him.

'And what did you do?'

'I made a big fucking mistake,' he answered. 'I didn't mean to. They meant to.'

'I'm not doubting you.'

'There's more gray than the way you make it sound.'

'There's gray to us. But only black and white where He's concerned. Says it in Matthew. You follow or you don't. I'll know you or I won't. It's a pretty straight line.'

'The way you put it there's ladders over the line. Or tunnels under it.'

'There's grace. If you want to call it a ladder or a tunnel then I suppose you can. But I don't know what you're trying to do. Trying to justify yourself by condemning them or trying to get me to say you and them are different. But it don't much matter what I say.'

When the guard blew the whistle Russell turned and followed his fellow inmates out of the chapel. He had never gone back. Many nights he had thought about what the preacher had said.

It's there if you want it. Don't matter what you've done. There was something odd about that. Seemed like there had to be a point of no return. Things you couldn't take back. He had seen the worst of men and he wanted there to be punishment for that so that he could feel like he was different from them.

He took his eyes off the steeple and he walked up the steps of the church. Wondered if the old preacher was still alive. If he was still helping those kinds of men find their way home.

On that night he had drunk more than usual for no particular reason other than it was one of those hot Mississippi Friday nights when you have a paycheck in your pocket and a good woman who loves you and clear reception on the radio station out of New Orleans that plays the old blues, aching voices that sing of mojo and insatiable women and red roosters and sneaking in and out the back door. One of those nights when the light stays until well into the evening and pushes the night out further and further and as long as there is gasoline being pumped at the gas stations then it seems a shame not to burn it up. Many times he had thought that it might have helped him if there had been some reason. Something that triggered him, shoved him, irritated him, violated him, motivated him to drink so much. Many times he had wished that there would have been something to point his finger at other than his own stupidity. But there wasn't.

Got off work early on Friday afternoon. Payday. Put some of his check in the bank and kept some of it in his pocket and he drove to a house on the east side of town where his father had asked him to see about something. Got there and knocked on the door and a woman with a baby on her hip and another little one holding on to her leg opened the front door and let him in and took him to the kitchen and showed him the leak. Went back out and got a toolbox from the truck and came back in and crawled underneath the sink and fixed it. Then she took him to the bathroom and flipped the light switch and no light came on and he asked if she had changed the bulb and she shifted the baby to her other hip and swatted at the kid on her leg and said do I look like a fool? Don't guess so he said and then he took a screwdriver and removed the switch plate and then pulled out the light switch and as in many of the dejected old houses his father had brought back to life there was a loose wire and it was the hot one and he tightened it and flipped the switch and the light came on.

He asked if there was anything else and she said no and he took his toolbox and left. Stopped at a gas station and filled up with gas and started to buy beer but then got that feeling. That Friday night, nothing to do tomorrow, damn it's a beautiful night feeling. And beer wouldn't do so he stopped at the liquor store and bought a fifth of bourbon. Old Charter. Aged eight years. The same kind of bottle that his dad had kept in the kitchen cabinet over the stove. Drove over to Sarah's apartment and she and her mother and her maid of honor were there. Planning. Always planning now. Only a handful of weeks away. He talked to them a minute and kissed her and she asked if he'd take her car and get the oil changed tomorrow and he said yeah. Got his bottle out of the truck and got in her car and slid the seat back all the way. Stopped at a convenience store and bought a giant Styrofoam cup filled with Coke and he poured out a third of the Coke and opened the Old Charter and started up. Drove out on the highway to JC's. A few trucks and a few motorcycles in the gravel parking lot. Door open to the pool hall and music coming out and he took his bottle in because JC only sold beer. Couple of guys with beards and tattoos at one table and a couple of guys in their work shirts at another and JC sitting behind the bar reading the newspaper. The small, wrinkled man looked up and said hey to Russell and saw the bottle in one of his hands and the giant cup in the other and he opened up the cooler and set two cans of Coke on the bar. He sat and talked with JC and watched them play pool. Some left and others came in and a couple of hours passed and it was closer to dark. A solid dent in the bottle now. Said goodbye to JC and nodded to some men he knew and walked out and got in her car. Head feeling about right and the night feeling about right and his life feeling about right. Drove on and felt good. Couldn't help but feel good. Stopped on the side of the road to piss and lightning bugs flashed across the field. Hundreds of them. Sat down on the hood of the car and watched them for a while.

Then he had to drive back to town for more ice and more Coke and he ran into an old girlfriend at the convenience store and she made a joke about him getting married and that being the end of it and he told her that he didn't hear many women talk like that but he knew she wasn't like many women. She said you damn right, Russell. You by yourself? I am except for half a bottle of Old Charter and she said you need some company? He said I thought you said that was the end of it. She said you ain't married yet and he smiled and said you don't need me. The night is young. It always is she said and she slapped him on the rear end and climbed in and they drank and drove through the neighborhoods a couple of blocks back from Delaware. She bit his ear and ran her hand under his shirt and he did the same to her while trying to keep it on the road. She grabbed at his belt and he said you better not and he drove back to the convenience store. She kissed his neck and got in her car and drove off and he did the same. Close to midnight now and back out to the desolate roads. Drinking more than he had planned on but driving and singing now and then with the voices on the radio and stopping at a stop sign and not sure which way to go. Then driving on and stopping at another and not sure which way to go. Eyes lagging behind if he moved his head from side to side. A deer cut across in front of him and he swerved and spilled his drink in his lap and he stopped the car. Got out and wiped his pants with napkins from the glove compartment. Poured another one and got back in and driving on and playing with the radio stations and coming over the hill and picking up speed coming down the hill and never seeing the truck with its lights off parked on the bridge.

The end, he thought. Then he corrected himself.

The beginning.

He walked down the church steps and the exhaustion grabbed him as the chimes in the steeple rang and announced 5:00 a.m. There was nothing to do but go and lie down. Several blocks later he turned onto his street and he saw the truck in his driveway.

Those sons of bitches, he whispered.

He parked the truck at the end of the street and grabbed the 20-gauge from behind the seat and walked toward the house. The light was on in the living room and Russell walked quietly to the front door and it was open, a foot wide. He nudged it fully open with the barrel of the shotgun and he saw Larry standing at the mantel and holding the picture of Sarah.

Larry looked at him and held the frame toward him. 'That's real sweet.'

Russell stepped through the doorway with the gun barrel toward the floor. 'Get out of here,' he said.

Larry set the frame down on the mantel. He adjusted the angle once. And then twice. 'I don't sleep much,' he said. He looked back at Russell.

'So what?'

'Just so you know. I don't sleep much. Ain't going to.'

'Me either.'

'I guess you know she's signed, sealed, delivered,' Larry said. He pointed his thumb at Sarah. 'Shame, too. She was a good ride. That's what I hear. Woman's got to cope somehow when her man is gone away.'

Russell raised the barrel and held it on Larry. 'I told you to get the hell out of here.'

'I saw her damn near strip naked downtown one night. Dancing and drunk and it was hot as hell. This ol' boy started grabbing at her on the dance floor and next thing we knew she was down to her bra. Skirt was up. He had his hands full of it.'

'Where's your stupid brother?'

'I think I might've even stuck a five in her panties. It was a good show.'

Larry picked up the picture frame again and rubbed her face on his zipper. 'Like that, honey. Like that,' he said. He grinned and winked at Russell.

'Come on out. I know you're here,' Russell said.

Walt moved into the living room from the kitchen. He was holding a beer he'd gotten from the refrigerator in one hand and he had a pamphlet he had taken from the manila folder in the other.

'Becoming a citizen again,' Walt read. 'How to become a model member of your community.' Walt held the brochure out to Larry and Larry laughed.

'I don't get the feeling it's gonna be that easy,' Larry said.

'He's got a whole file in there,' Walt said. 'Looks like they ain't expecting to see him again.'

'I would not count on that. You know he's gonna fuck up again.'

'Bound to.'

'Some stupid little slip and he'll be back.'

'Just one.'

'Like shooting somebody. That'd be real dumb.'

Russell raised the shotgun and held aim on Larry and then he spelled the word *trespassing* out loud. One slow letter at a time.

'It's got two *s*'s,' Walt said.

'It's got three *s*'s,' Larry said.

'No it don't.'

'Yeah it does.'

'No it don't.'

'You want him to do it again?'

'Shut the hell up and get your ass out of here,' Russell said.

'Here, Walt. You want some of this?' Larry handed the picture to his brother.

'Nah,' Walt said. 'I know where all that's been.'

'I said get the fuck out of here,' Russell said.

'That ain't exactly what you said,' Walt said.

'You look like a fag with that beard,' Larry said. 'Don't he, Walt?'

'Mostly.'

'Put the picture down.'

Larry dropped the frame on the floor and smashed it with his heel. Walt turned up the bottle and finished the beer and then he threw it at Russell but he was wild right and Russell didn't flinch as the bottle smashed on the wall behind him. He stuck the pamphlet in his back pocket.

'Our boy has a shotgun,' Larry said.

'That ain't fair,' Walt said.

'For now.'

'They do make more than one.'

'Where'd you get that?' Larry said. 'Part of your package when they showed you the door? Or Daddy give it to you?'

'I'm gonna count to three and then one of you is gonna lose a foot,' Russell said. He put the shotgun against his shoulder and aimed at Larry's feet.

'Fine,' Larry said. 'Come on, Walt. Guess we gonna have to come back tomorrow.'

'One,' Russell said.

'Where's your girl? The one you left the Armadillo with?'

'Two.'

'See? We're watching you, boy,' Larry said. 'Know where you are. Who you with.'

Walt grabbed Larry's arm and pulled him on, his eyes a little wider than Larry's at the sight of the gun. They moved away from the mantel and in front of the couch and toward the front door. Russell circled around them. Walt walked out first and Larry stopped in the doorway.

'You'd better keep that thing close.'

Larry stepped out the door and Russell held the gun pointed at the open door until the truck was cranked and gone. When he was sure he leaned the gun in the corner and he walked outside and down the street to his truck. He pulled it under the carport and he went inside and picked up the pieces of wood and glass from the frame. And then he took Sarah's picture and he ripped it twice and he walked into the bathroom and flushed it down the toilet. Looked at himself in the mirror. The gray hints in the beard. The scar. The eyes that seemed to belong to a stranger.

He glared and was quickly impatient with the image and he headbutted himself and the mirror shattered and cut a gash in his forehead.

He felt the blood run down the tip of his nose and across his lips and he leaned his head over the sink and let it drip among the shattered shards of mirror. He held his fingers to the gash and pulled a tiny piece of mirror from it. Then he wadded up some toilet paper and held it on the cut while he went to the truck and drove down to the all-night gas station where he bought Band-Aids. He sat in the truck and wiped the gash clean and covered it with a Band-Aid and then he went back inside and bought a pocket-size notebook and a pack of pens. The eastern sky had begun to change color and the sun would soon be on the horizon but he wasn't going to stop now.

Back down to Magnolia. He felt the bruises from the fight and a lag from the booze. He drove fast and hoped that the dawn would wait until he did what he had to do. In ten minutes he was idling in front of Sarah's house. He sat and stared and watched for lights. For movement. When he was certain the house was still he scribbled a note on the small notebook paper. He got out and hustled to the front door and slid it through the brass mail slot on the antique door. Then he got in the truck and left and regretted dropping the note through the slot but it was done now.

On one side he wrote his address.

On the other – Right or wrong I wanted to let you know I was back. Russell.

He drove back to the house and he walked into the bedroom and lay down on top of the covers with his clothes on. Just ahead of the rising sun. The shotgun next to him like a good friend. The bus ride and the fishing and the woman and the beer and the brothers all bunching together and taking over and pushing him to sleep though he hated the thought of closing his eyes. Knowing that the world still had him by the throat.

19

AT DAYBREAK MABEN WOKE ANNALEE AND told her to get dressed. Hours gone now. Enough time for the body to be taken away and examined. Enough time for men in uniforms to have combed the cruiser and the roadside. Enough time for word to have spread. Annalee asked why are we leaving and Maben said because we got to go and the girl moaned at walking again. Get up I said. We don't have time for this.

When they were dressed Maben put the few remaining bills in her pocket and said I'll be right back. She walked over to the café and stopped at the cash register. The same waitress from yesterday came over and said I bet you slept good.

Maben nodded and handed her the key and the girl said thanks but Maben didn't answer. She turned to walk out and noticed two men sitting at the counter, one with his glasses on top of his head and rubbing at his eyes while he waited on the other man in a black suit to finish talking on the phone. Maben hurried out and across the lot and Annalee was standing in the motel room door. Maben stepped around her and picked up the garbage bag containing all they owned and said let's go.

'I'm thirsty, Momma.'

'Come on. We'll get something down the road.'

'Why can't we get something here?'

'Because I said so.'

She had wrapped the deputy's pistol in a shirt and buried the shirt in the middle of the rest of the clothes. They walked out of the parking lot and to the interstate and turned north. Four miles to McComb. Not far after that. The morning sun met them without regard and they were both redfaced within a mile. Cars passed on their way to work. Or to wherever. She kept thinking of tossing the pistol into the weeds or into a ditch but there was too much traffic and she didn't want to stop, didn't want to be noticed or remembered. And she hadn't completely convinced herself that having a pistol was a bad idea no matter who it belonged to or how she got it. Maben and Annalee walked on and gusts brought the wind to them but it also brought dust and sometimes rocks with the wind. In a little more than an hour they saw the exit sign for McComb. One mile.

'Is that it?' the girl asked.

'That's it.'

'Where are we going when we get there?'

'Somewhere. Just keep on.'

She had lain awake the rest of the night wondering what to do. And she still didn't know. So they were heading toward the shelter. It was another two miles along a four-lane. They walked on past used car lots and hardware stores and liquor stores and Maben finally let them stop at a gas station that had a picnic table at the side of it. The table was in the shade of the building and mom and child sat down with cold drinks and powdered doughnuts. They finished up and walked on again, Maben promising the girl that it wasn't much farther. Another half hour and they could see the downtown buildings and Maben thought she remembered Broad Street being the street closest to the rails. The bag was getting heavier with each step and Maben's shirt was soaked through with sweat. The child's

114

forehead was red and wet and her face seemed stuck in a squint.

Maben hadn't noticed it but creeping up behind them in the southern sky had been thick gray clouds and still blocks away from the shelter they were startled with a snap of lightning and then came the thunder. The sunlight disappeared almost instantly and a moodiness fell around them and at a street corner Maben looked down to the left and she saw a pavilion and playground equipment and she pulled the child and said hurry on this way. They walked as fast as their tired legs would take them as the wind kicked up and then the first drops fell, fat drops that hit the pavement like nickels. They were nearly there when the bottom fell out and by the time they had made it under the pavilion they were as wet as if they had been dipped into a pool. Maben set the garbage bag on top of a picnic table and she shook her arms and head and the child did the same.

Gray hovered in every direction and it looked like they would be there for a while. Maben realized they were next to the cemetery. The rain washed the footprints from the playground slides and seesaws and puddles began to form in the holes that had been dug in the sandbox. Annalee walked over to the edge of the concrete where the drip from the roofline hit in tiny claps and held out her arms and let the water splash on her wrists. Maben sat down on top of a picnic table with her hand propped under her chin. She watched the rain bounce off the swing seats and then she turned and stared across the graveyard that sat next to the playground and she wondered whose bright idea it was to put the playground next to the graveyard. The gravestones looked slick in the rain and the red dirt of a fresh grave was turning to mud. The thunder roared and roared and there were quiet flashes of lightning and then the rain came harder and an unexpected gust of wind brought it to them. Annalee squealed and she ran over to her mother and Maben helped her up onto the table next to her and the rain beat on the pavilion roof and the sound of their desolation was even greater than it had been before.

The storm came on strong and then it left as quickly as it had arrived. They walked into downtown with steam rising off the sidewalks and streets. Shop owners set plants and sidewalk signs upright and at a café customers sat around tables eating toast and drinking coffee. Church bells rang from somewhere. Deep and resounding chimes that caused the child to look up into the sky. Maben switched the bag from shoulder to shoulder, both sides tired now. Curious eyes followed them. These wet and worn people. A big one and a little one. The blisters on Maben's heels burning and bleeding. At the end of Main Street they ran into the railroad tracks and she was right. Broad Street ran with the tracks. Maben set the bag on the sidewalk and bent over with her hands on her knees and the child patted her on the back and said it's okay Momma. Maben forced a smile at her and raised up and looked one way and then the other. No sign of Christian Ministries Family Shelter and she had forgotten the number. Only remembered Broad Street. There was nothing to do but keep walking. A police car eased up behind them and from the rolled-down window the officer asked if they needed anything and Maben said no. But then she asked about the shelter.

'Other way,' he said. 'Hop in and I'll take you down there.'

'That's okay,' Maben said. 'We're wet.'

'Don't matter.'

'We're okay.'

'You sure?'

'Yeah.'

'All right,' he said and he drove to the end of the block and turned right.

They retraced their steps back three blocks to where they started and crossed the street. Several more blocks and they moved out of downtown and walked past hundred-year-old houses. Some with boards across the windows and sagging porches and some rejuvenated with paint and new roofs and flower beds. Up ahead at a depot an engine pushed a railcar into another railcar and there was the sound of clashing steel and after that Annalee walked with her eyes on the train cars and she was still watching them when her mother said this is it.

It looked like it might have once been a church or a schoolhouse. It was brick and rectangular and behind the front desk was a row of partitions that stretched to the back of the building and between the partitions were cots and small dressers and nightstands. The woman at the front desk wore her gray hair pinned on top of her head and she was small but sure when she looked at Maben and Annalee and asked them what they needed.

'We need a place to stay,' Maben said and she dropped the garbage bag on the floor next to the girl. The woman came from around the counter and bent down to the child and asked her if she wanted something to drink. Annalee nodded and the woman called out and a teenage girl appeared from an office to the right.

'Bring us some water. Towels, too,' the woman said and the teenage girl went back into the office and returned with two bottles. The first thing both Maben and Annalee did was to press the cold bottles to their foreheads. The grayhaired woman pointed them to chairs lining the wall and the three of them sat down. Maben rubbed the towel over her head and then did the same for Annalee.

The woman said that her name was Brenda and then she began asking questions that Maben answered. Hardly any answers the truth. Annalee drank in silence, finishing her bottle before her mother. When Brenda seemed satisfied that the woman and child legitimately needed the place she explained that they had room but that it was only temporary. She didn't explain what that meant. Today is Friday and we'll start your clock. There is a small kitchen but if you mess it up you clean it up. We got the basics, so don't go looking for a menu. No men allowed into the building at any time. If that rule gets broke you'll be asked to leave immediately. We can put two cots in the same room so that you and the child won't be separated. There are showers and towels and soap. Washer and dryer. I'm here all day and somebody else comes in at night and the door locks at eight o'clock and you gotta have a password to be let back in. And if you want to work there's a café downtown that will let you wash dishes and work in the kitchen.

Then she asked what was in the bag.

'Everything,' Maben said.

The garbage bag had punctured and torn and clothes pushed out of the holes.

'Let me get you something else,' Brenda said.

'No,' she said and she pulled it toward her. 'This is fine. Can you show us our spot?'

'That's easy enough seeing as you're it right now. Had one woman run off God knows where over the weekend and another end back up with her boyfriend. Same one she ran from in the first place. It never ends. You can pick wherever you like. All the spots are about the same size. You might want to get toward the back, though, cause the train don't tiptoe when it comes through.'

They picked a spot in the back close to the kitchen and the bathrooms and underneath a tall window because Annalee wanted to see the moon when she lay down to go to sleep. Maben dug through the bag and pulled out dry clothes for both of them and they changed. She wanted to unpack the entire filthy wad but had nowhere to put the pistol so she shoved the bag underneath her cot. She went into the bathroom and washed her face and she wet a cloth to wipe Annalee's face but when she returned Annalee had fallen asleep. Maben touched the cloth to the child's forehead and then she put it down and she lay down on the cot next to the child and the walking and the worry caught her and she closed her eyes and dreamed of sirens and strange men doing whatever they wanted to do with her and she awoke with a quick shout. She looked around. Figured out where she was. Looked at the child who hadn't been bothered by her mother's shout and slept on.

Maben stood up and went into the bathroom and she sat down on the toilet. Buried her face in her hands. Began to breathe as if she'd climbed the stairs of a tall building. She felt herself beginning to sweat and she stood off the toilet and paced back and forth in front of the mirror. Tried to calm herself by humming and then singing but she couldn't think of a song so she turned on the faucet and splashed water on her face and told herself to breathe like a normal human but that was damn near impossible.

20

MABEN LEFT ANNALEE ASLEEP AND SHE walked back to the front to talk to Brenda who was sitting behind the counter reading the newspaper. Brenda lowered the paper and asked her if she needed something.

'That café,' Maben said. 'Something to do.'

'You gonna have to use sentences,' Brenda said and she folded the paper and set it aside.

'You said something about some work.'

'It ain't glamorous,' Brenda said. 'I can call down there and tell them you're coming. You out of money?'

'No. I got twenty dollars or so.'

'Then you're out of money.'

'Can you watch Annalee?'

Brenda turned up her nose. 'Not usually. But since ain't nobody else here I will.'

'She's sleeping right now.'

'Fine.'

Brenda picked up the telephone and called the café and told them she was sending someone down there to do whatever they need her to do. Maben thought that the woman put it perfectly. That it had long since been a theme. The woman hung up and gave her directions. Walk back down to Main. Turn right. Go one block. Turn right on Broadway. Two or three buildings down on the right. Maben thanked her and went on her way.

She found it easily and a man named Sims met her at the door. He wore an apron and he had a towel slung over his shoulder and a pen behind his ear. The café was empty in the midafternoon except for a man in overalls who sat at the counter drinking coffee. Sims asked her if she could wash dishes and she said yes and he took her into the kitchen. She spent the afternoon washing dishes and mopping the kitchen floor and taking out the garbage. Whichever way Sims pointed her. In a few hours she said she had to go see about her kid and he opened the register and took out an envelope and handed her a twenty-dollar bill and she had doubled her wealth.

'You did good,' he said. 'If you want to come back tomorrow, come on.'

She folded the twenty in her hand. 'You not open tonight?' she asked.

'It's Friday night. No reason not to be,' he said.

'Can I come back later then?'

He shrugged. 'I suppose. If you want.'

She said okay and then she walked back to the shelter and she found Annalee sitting on the floor with Brenda and the teenager who had brought them the water. Each of them with coloring books. She knelt and kissed the top of Annalee's head. She was hungry and she made a sandwich in the kitchen and she walked back to the front and sat down with them and noticed that the child had gotten better at staying between the lines.

Brenda looked at her watch. 'I got to go here in a minute. New girl comes in and stays from now 'til the morning.'

'She had anything to eat?' Maben asked as she nodded at Annalee.

'About two dozen Oreos.'

Brenda and the teenager stood up and went into the office

and Maben relaxed while the child colored a bear with blue fur and green eyes. Ten minutes later another woman came in the door. A young black woman with a big purse. Maben stretched her legs out straight and listened to the women trade thoughts about the day and the upcoming night. Then she slipped off her shoes and pressed her thumbs hard into the bottoms of her feet. Annalee sat with her legs crossed and Maben asked her if they hurt.

'Yes.'

'Then stretch them out for me.'

Annalee stuck her feet out straight and Maben began to massage the muscles in her small legs. She said not too hard and Maben eased up. Pressed her fingertips gently to the skin. Wanted to reach into the muscles and pull out the pain and tell her she would never have to run again because she was being chased but that would be a lie.

Brenda and the teenager walked past Maben and Annalee and said they'd see them tomorrow. The black woman stuck her head out of the office and said let me know if you need something. Got some paperwork to do.

Maben told the child she was going to get clean in the shower and Annalee followed her to the back. Sat on the cot with the coloring book.

'You still hungry?' Maben asked.

'Not really. My stomach hurts.'

'I guess so.'

Maben went into the shower and with the hot water on her neck she closed her eyes and mumbled to herself. It was a dream it was all a dream. A bad night like other bad nights and it was not real. Try and you can push it down. Way down. She nudged the hot water and made it hotter, almost scalding. And the steam rose and she begged it to be a dream. Her pleas as she sat in the backseat and he drove her into the dark and his hands in places they should not have been and the gunshots echoing across the vacant land and the harried face of the child in the motel room window. It was a dream. A nasty dream. The steam rose and the water spilled over her aching body and she felt it all and heard it all and it was not a dream but a nightmare and she felt it in the cloud of steam that shrouded her. The water so hot and her fears rising and with a quick twist she turned off the water and dropped her forehead against the slick tile of the shower wall.

She stood still. The water dripped from her body and tapped like tiny reminders. She lifted her forehead twice and let it fall both times and then she heard Annalee singing to herself and she raised her head. Half smiled. She stepped out of the shower and dried off. Dressed and sat down with Annalee.

'Got something I can color?'

The child flipped through the book. 'You want ducks or dogs?'

'Ducks. Dogs bite.'

'Not good dogs.'

'No,' Maben said. 'Not good dogs.'

21

BOYD GOT COFFEE IN A DRIVE-THROUGH and spent the morning riding and thinking about Russell. He didn't want to but he couldn't help it. There was no reason to think that Russell had been out on that dark road for any reason other than the one he had given. He probably felt like a rat out of a cage and he had seen the lights flashing and followed them and drove up on the scene by pure coincidence. No reason to believe anything else, Boyd kept thinking. He sipped the coffee and drove out on the highway down to the Louisiana line and back and he pulled into the truck stop for gas. As he filled the tank he leaned on the cruiser and took his sunglasses from his front pocket and put them on. He held his hand on his stomach and rubbed and pretended he had lost track of how much bigger he was now than he used to be.

When the tank was full he got back into the cruiser and drove to town and then made his way out toward Mr. Gaines's place. He hadn't been there since before Russell was sent away and he remembered being in the little pickup Mr. Gaines had given Russell and remembered smoking cigarettes and drinking tallboys and coming in a helluva lot later than they were supposed to. He remembered the night that Shawna Louise rode between them and they both pawed at her and she slapped them away wearing big silver rings on all her fingers and lime green eye shadow and she laughed big like a game show host and how they turned off onto a gravel road and took turns making out with her and trying like hell to do other stuff but she kept slapping and cackling until they both gave up. So many nights like that after football games and double-dating and for no good reason on summer nights. The sight and sound of Russell had conjured up a long list of memories and he wished to God he would have bumped into him at the downtown café. Or at the liquor store. Or at the gas station. Or anyfuckingwhere other than out on the scene last night.

He passed a flatbed stacked with hay bales and then slowed when he topped the hill and saw Mr. Gaines's place ahead on the right. The pond where it used to be. The house where it used to be. The sunlight falling across the water like it always had. He came to a stop in the driveway and stared. He watched himself and Russell fishing. He watched himself and Russell sneaking out the bedroom window on the back side of the house.

He sighed and ran his hand across his cleanshaven jaw. And then he put the cruiser in reverse and backed out of the driveway and drove into town. He had Russell's new address on a piece of scrap paper tucked in his shirt pocket.

Boyd thought he recognized the small house and was fairly certain he had helped Russell cut the grass or fix the fence or perform some other odd job Mr. Gaines had once given them. He got out of the cruiser and straightened himself. He walked across the small yard and up the front steps and as he reached out to knock the door opened. Russell stood there wearing only jeans that weren't buttoned with his hair tousled. He held a white coffee mug. Russell opened the door fully and nodded and turned and walked to the couch. Boyd nodded back and followed him inside.

'I been thinking,' Boyd said.

Russell sat down. He sipped the coffee. 'What's that?'

'I been thinking you're a son of a bitch. You didn't call me or nothing knowing you were getting out. Hell, I would've drove up there and got you.'

'It don't work like that,' Russell said.

Boyd tapped the badge on his shirt pocket and grinned. 'I got special privileges.'

'Then sit down with your special privileges. If you want some coffee it's in there.'

Boyd sat down in a wooden chair next to the television. 'You're skinny,' he said.

'You're fat. Your old lady must love the big rub.'

'Big rub? Never heard that one but I'll ask her about it later on. You get any sleep?'

'Not really.'

'Me neither,' Boyd said. 'We got us a situation and a half.'

Russell nodded. Drank from the coffee cup.

Say it, Boyd thought. Say you don't have nothing to do with it though I know you don't but say it just so I'll hear it again.

'Shotgun still loaded?' Boyd asked.

'Yep.'

'Who smacked you around? That face looks pretty new.'

'It ain't.'

'Just takes longer to heal when you get old, I guess.'

'Hurts longer, too.'

Boyd stood from the chair. He looked around the living room. Down the hallway. A mostly empty house and clothes lying here and there.

'You ride around much longer last night?' he asked.

Russell set the coffee mug on the floor and stretched out across the couch. 'Not really.'

'Bet it felt good.'

'Bet what felt good?'

'Riding around. Free air.'

Russell sat up. 'Somebody send you over here?'

'Hell no, Russell. Just trying to catch up. I'm still pissed you didn't let nobody know you were coming home.'

'Larry figured it out.'

'Who?'

'Don't give me that shit. You know who I'm talking about. The one who hates me. The ones who hate you are always waiting for you. So maybe you're the son of a bitch,' Russell said and he got up from the couch. 'I got to piss. Why don't we do this later?'

'Fine,' Boyd said. 'I got shit to do anyway. Hey, you know I'm glad to see you.'

'I know it. I don't mean nothing.'

They slapped hands and then Boyd walked outside. He stopped in the yard and looked back over his shoulder and through the open door he saw Russell go into the hallway and disappear behind the bathroom door. Quit being stupid, he told himself. Stupid is a bad way to start the day.

Russell spent the rest of the day on the couch sleeping off the long night before and then late in the afternoon he got up and showered. When he was dried and dressed he stuck another Band-Aid on the small cut on his forehead though it no longer bled. He got in the truck and put the 20-gauge behind the seat and drove to kill some time before going out to eat fish with his dad and Consuela.

He rode up and down Delaware like he used to do when he was a teenager and it didn't seem any different. Carloads of summertime kids with arms hanging out windows and ponytails flopping in the wind. Music with big bumps throbbing in the late afternoon. At a fast food joint the parking lot was filled with young bodies sitting on tailgates and on hoods. Some sipping drinks from giant plastic cups and some licking ice cream cones. He swung into the movie theater parking lot and only pickups were parked. Athletes wore letter jackets despite the heat and a couple of others wore cowboy hats and had their thumbs stuck in their front pockets. When he passed they stared and tried to place him and then one of them said what the hell you looking at?

When he pulled back onto Delaware a carload of girls in a momma's Cadillac moved alongside him and he kept their speed. They were singing along with the radio, sweet highpitched voices that were careless and off-key. He looked over and there were three in the front and three in the back. They didn't notice him at first but in the middle of a long note the driver looked over at him and screamed oh my God. She gave a wild laugh and the other girls stopped and saw him watching and they ducked and their squeals replaced the strained melody. Russell laughed back and the light turned green and the driver, cheeks sharp and eyes squinted, looked at him and called him a pervert and they all laughed harder and she gunned the Cadillac and it leaped like some prehistoric animal into the intersection.

That did it for the joyride.

He drove to his dad's place where he found his father and Consuela in the kitchen. Mitchell was dipping the fish in a bowl of milk and then into a bowl of flour and she stood next to him chopping cabbage and carrots.

Mitchell looked at his son's forehead. 'What happened?'

Russell reached up and pulled off the Band-Aid and dropped it in the garbage can and said nothing.

A wooden table for four in the middle. A dishrag draped over the edge of the sink. A row of brown coffee mugs hanging from hooks underneath the cabinet. The black and white tiles of the floor. The Coca-Cola bottle magnet stuck on the refrigerator. The framed picture hanging above the doorway of a handsome

Jesus with His hands folded on His lap and wearing a white robe and the light of heaven shining behind His head. Only Consuela was different. She was still barefoot.

'Come on a second,' Mitchell said. He washed his hands and wiped them on a towel and moved toward the back door.

'What is it?' Russell asked.

'Just come on. Need a hand.'

They walked out and across the yard toward the barn. Mitchell's truck was parked in front of the barn and he walked around and let down the tailgate.

'Couldn't get this out of here by myself.'

In the truck bed lay a concrete statue of the Virgin Mary with arms open and ready to catch anything that might fall from the sky.

'Jesus,' Russell said.

'It ain't Jesus. It's His momma.'

Mitchell grabbed the round bottom of the statue.

'Grab on. And be careful.'

They pulled the end off the tailgate until the Virgin tipped upright and when she did Russell barely ducked in time to dodge her left arm. She was eight feet tall with a sharp, pointed nose and a look of empathy.

'I figured it might make Consuela feel more at home,' Mitchell said as he looked at the Virgin with a sense of pride. 'You know how on TV you see those plazas and squares in other countries and there's always a statue in the middle? I know they got them in Mexico. Clive told me about it the first time he went down there. Said there were plazas with red dirt streets and Virgin Marys all over.'

'Where'd you find this thing?'

'Guy out on the highway with all those concrete angels and dogs. Had it put away for himself but I got it out of him. We were out riding around. Hitting junk stores here and there. She saw it and grinned and nodded and I took that for her wanting it, so here it is.'

'Here it is.'

'Or here she is.'

'Yes. It's a she.'

'Think I should move it closer to the house?'

The men looked toward the house and Consuela was standing at the edge of the yard watching them. She was wearing one of Liza's aprons.

Mitchell got a dolly from the barn. Russell got behind the Virgin and wrapped his arms around her waist and pulled back and Mitchell slid the dolly under her. She weighed as much as them together and her weight helped her roll across the slightly downward slope toward the house. Mitchell directed them to stop when they got to the middle of the yard where a blooming vine had run up and around an old metal post that was once the anchor of a clothesline. They wrestled her off the dolly and faced her toward the kitchen window. Mitchell looked at Consuela and she said something that he didn't understand and then she went back into the kitchen. Russell stepped back from her and admired her strong arms, her caring eyes, her open hands, as if news of the Christ child would flow from her lips any second.

'I ain't even gonna ask what you paid for her.'

'Good,' Mitchell said. 'Let's go eat.'

Back in the kitchen Mitchell put his hands back into the fish. The deep fryer sat on the porch just outside the kitchen door and he went back and forth from the fryer to the counter. Dropping fish in the fryer. Preparing more. Russell moved along with him, sipping at a beer, getting hungry. Soon there was a plate sitting in the middle of the table stacked high with crisp, golden fillets. While the men went back and forth Consuela had mixed the cabbage and carrots with some mayonnaise and oil and vinegar and pepper and a bowl of coleslaw sat next to the fish. When it was all ready Mitchell told Russell to open the fridge and get beers for everyone. He got the beers and then the ketchup and the hot sauce and then the three of them sat down around the table.

Russell reached for a piece of fish and Consuela folded her hands and bowed her head. Russell stopped and he and Mitchell waited while Consuela said her grace and then there was no more waiting.

Russell wanted to talk about his mother. About her last months and about the funeral but it didn't seem like the right time. So instead he talked about how hot it was and how good the place looked. When they were done Consuela cleaned up and Mitchell and Russell went outside and smoked cigarettes. When Consuela finished she met the men outside. Father and son sat down in rockers and Consuela stepped out into the yard and began walking toward the statue. She stopped in front and paused. Gazed at the concrete face. Then she began walking around again with her eyes toward the ground as if she were looking for something.

'What's she doing?' Russell asked.

'Walking around. Does it every night. Sometimes you can hear her singing to herself. Pretty songs. Sad sounding songs. Reminds me of your momma humming to herself when she was in the kitchen or working around in her flowers.'

The twilight surrounded them now. The first crickets chirped. An evening breeze. They watched Consuela. Her arms behind her back like a schoolchild in line. And then she started to sing and her voice blended with the coming night.

'Still think it'd be best if you stayed out here with us,' Mitchell said.

'Still think it's best I don't,' Russell said and he thought of Larry and Walt being there. Promising to come back. He knew they'd follow him wherever he went.

'What'd you do with the gun?'

'Sold it at the pawn shop.'

'Damn you, Russell.'

'Got thirty bucks.'

'Thirty bucks?'

'I'm kidding, old man.'

Consuela reached the pond and began making her way around it and she was only a silhouette in whatever light was left.

'How long does she do this for?' Russell asked.

'Don't know. Sometimes I'm back inside before she's done.'

Russell got them two more beers and they sat and rocked. Russell started to say something about finding a house to paint but he liked it better with nothing to say. Consuela finally came back and she went into the house and got a beer for herself and she sat down with the men.

'You know it. Don't you?' Mitchell said.

'Know what?'

His father drank. Paused.

'It's a pretty night,' he said.

'That ain't what you were about to say.'

'No. It ain't.'

'Then what?'

'Just that he's gonna come for you, Russell.'

'He already has.'

'He ain't all there. Never has been.'

'I'm aware.'

Mitchell raised from the chair and stood at the edge of the porch. He spit into the yard and looked out at the deepening night and said he's gonna come and keep on coming. Until he thinks he's done.

22

LARRY SAT IN THE TRUCK WITH his arm hanging out the open window. The truck was parked on the street in front of Russell's house and the windows were down and the radio was turned low. A crowbar and empty beer cans rested on the seat beside him. He started out simply riding. After a few he'd kept on riding. Now he was parked and trying to figure out the best way to put another scare into the man who killed his brother.

Larry was known as the tall one because he stood a head taller than any man in the Tisdale family, all of whom lined up nearly identical at six feet. Grandfathers, uncles, brothers, all of them. Six years separated him and his brothers, the youngest to the oldest. All of them had square foreheads and chins and kept their black hair cut short and parted on the left and their mouths were small and serious. He was the oldest. And the youngest had been in the dirt for eleven years.

His problem was that he was as loyal as a dog and he thought everyone else should be the same way. Over the years that had kept him in parking lot fights over girls and then later in bar fights over women. And it had kept him thinking about the day that Russell Gaines was going to be set free.

For his second wife he had married a woman who was ten years younger. Heather was Corvette curvy and she liked to dance until she was sweaty and she didn't seem scared of him in the moments when his temper revealed itself. He had met her at a bar in the Quarter after a Saints game. She was the daughter of a banker and she had that carefree swagger of the beautiful and the rich. She never went out into the night without being detailed from head to toe and she drank like a man. Her natural hair color had long been forgotten and she was well versed in using what she had to get whoever or whatever she wanted. She'd been surprised when Larry asked her to marry him and he'd been surprised she said yes. She shined on his arm when he walked into a room and he had at one time liked the envious and lusty stare that she commanded.

In the first years they had been sustained by a rough, physical energy, like two rival prizefighters. Heather had always liked that Larry could find something to hate. Liked it when he talked about his dead brother and how one day he was going to settle the score. Liked it when he talked about somebody who had screwed him on a job or tried to get the best of him in a barroom. Liked that he was raw, the fierceness that came into his eyes when he was rushing toward the edge. She stoked his temper and picked fights with him just to get the blood up so that they could tear into one another like starving animals. But like those prizefighters, they were also driven by wins and losses and their relationship was more like a competition and recently Heather seemed to be winning.

Larry had always known that sooner or later she would grow restless and drift toward the stares that followed her. Knew she'd look for something else to do. And though he had known it was coming, when it began he ignored it. Told himself that her excuses were legit. No I don't care if you spend the weekend shopping with your friends and no I don't care if you go down to the Panhandle with your friends and no I don't care if you go and gamble with your friends. And as she caroused he sat at home and raged. He drove around and raged. And then he recruited Walt, who had lost a marriage of his own, to ride around and rage with him. And he drank more and more and walked around with unfocused eyes, the same unfocused eyes that looked out the truck window now at the house where the man lived who had killed Jason.

The clouds had been gathering in him for a long time now and the storm had arrived. Snuck up on him the way that they sneak up in the summertime with the heavy gray clouds appearing in the western sky and then moving in like vultures and bringing lightning and wind and sometimes there isn't even time to close the windows. The clouds had been gathering and somebody was going to fucking pay.

He was there to do something but he hadn't decided what. It didn't look like anyone was home. Not a light on. Nothing parked in the driveway. He had taken a box of matches from the glove compartment and thought about a fire but instead he had lit a cigarette. He took the beer from between his legs and finished it and tossed the can into the yard.

He reached over to the glove compartment again and this time he pulled out an envelope. He opened it and took out a handful of photographs of Heather and a blond man sitting in a restaurant in the Quarter. They sat at a long table covered with a white tablecloth and the wineglasses glimmered in the light of the low chandelier. She smiled in every photograph. And so did he. The people leaning around the table with them all smiled. Even the goddamn waiter was smiling. Her dress was cut low and she wore a necklace he had given her two birthdays ago. Larry thumped the face of the blond man and knew the motherfucker wasn't smiling right now. There were more photographs of them leaving the restaurant. Going into the lobby of Hotel Monteleone. Sitting at the Carousel Bar with her hand between his legs. Holding hands as they waited on the elevator that had taken them up and into the room where the blond man had done thrilling things to Larry's wife. Or she had done thrilling things to the blond man, which is the way Larry figured it.

Copies of these photographs had been stuck into the blond man's pants as he lay halfconscious on the hood of the car. Larry held on to this set to take to his lawyer who had told him that if you don't want her to get your money you'd better get some proof. He'd been meaning to take them to the lawyer for a week but hadn't. His hate had been redirected with Russell's homecoming and he was pretty sure he was about to goddamn explode. He stuffed the photos back into the envelope and the envelope back into the glove compartment and he slammed it shut.

He grabbed the crowbar and got out of the truck. He walked to the front of the house and attacked the windows, spraying the glass and wood into the house and onto the ground and he felt the sting of shards on his arms and face as he moved from window to window, each one suffering a more violent death than the one before as his blood roared with the destruction. When he was done he walked back to the sidewalk and turned and admired his work as he breathed heavily and swung the crowbar at his side as if he were getting ready to go again. He caught his breath and lit another cigarette and waited to see if Russell might poke his head out of one of the holes but he didn't. He was for the moment satisfied and he tossed the crowbar over into the truck bed and climbed in the truck. He eased along the street at a walker's pace, hoping that the racket would rise the neighbors to look out their windows or come out of their doors to fear what he had done.

23

WHEN RUSSELL TURNED THE CORNER OF his street he saw the red taillights of the truck moving away from his house. Moving at a crawl. So he quickly turned off his headlights and waited for the truck to go away. Then he drove two blocks down and parked and walked to the house, leaving the shotgun in the truck. Passing someone's garbage he noticed a metal pipe in a pile of stripped plumbing and he picked it up and walked with it on his shoulder like a batter walking toward home plate.

He eased around the side of the house and went in the back door. He didn't turn on any lights and he walked into the living room, the glass crunching beneath his feet on the hardwood floor. He propped the metal pipe against the fireplace mantel. Put his hands on his hips. There was nothing to do but wait until the morning. He didn't want to turn on the lights. Didn't want the truck to come back and know he was inside. Didn't want to be there.

He sat down on the sofa but got up again when a piece of glass stuck into the back of his leg. He looked out the broken windows into the front yard and he felt a headache settling in. Figured it was too early in the night to give up on them coming back. It was sit and wait or get the hell out.

He got back in the truck and stopped and bought a Coke

and a couple of airplane bottles of Jim Beam and then he drove out to the lake. Boats filled the marina bays and lights gleamed on the slapping water at the boat ramp. He crossed over the dam and then there was only the dark and then the road led into forest that surrounded the back side of the lake, side roads here and there branching off into camping areas and another that led to the Bottom. It was unofficially accepted by the park rangers that the Bottom was the one spot where the kids could sit and do what they wanted as long as nobody was murdered and the trash was picked up. Russell drove into the Bottom and there they were. A circle of cars and a gathering of boys and girls standing around a fire, not too close, holding cans and cigarettes, the water behind them still and black. They watched him with firelit faces as he backed up and left.

Farther around the lake he found what he had been looking for. A dirt road that didn't stop until it hit water. Barely wide enough for the truck to squeeze between the trees. His headlights shot across the water and he watched for a moment and checked for alligators but saw no knobby heads and bulging eyes. He then carefully backed between the trees and maneuvered the truck until he was able to get the tailgate toward the water and he stopped close to the edge. He took the Coke and tiny bottles of liquor and dropped the tailgate and sat down with his feet dangling at the water's edge. Across the lake cabin lights spotted the bank.

The lake was always busiest leading up to the Fourth of July and then little by little the boats thinned out as the summer dragged on and the heat became tiresome. He remembered the Fourth of July two years ago when he had watched a gang of men stomp another man to death and call it fireworks. And then last year he had watched them do the same thing. The same men. He had watched because he needed to mark their faces. He had to know who they were and that was the best way to do it. To watch the evil so that you could stay away from the evil. As much as you could. Fireworks, they called it. It was an old man both times. Someone whose death wouldn't call for revenge. He wondered how they picked who it was going to be. He wondered how long they had known who would be their fireworks. Or if they thought that far ahead. You had to watch. You had to know. You couldn't look the other way.

He closed his eyes and tried to think of something else. Of Carly. Or Cameron. Or Caroline. Yeah, Caroline. That was it. Oh Caroline. Oh God yes Caroline. Got to find her again. Hope she'll let me again. Caroline. Try not to forget.

He shook his head when he thought about his father and the woman. Her dark skin and black hair and broad shoulders and wide hips but somehow fitting nicely alongside his father's straight frame. And he had noticed his father's movements, more careful and concentrated than before. Almost frail in the way he fought with the stubborn catfish fighting on the end of the line.

He took a drink and was glad that he wouldn't be around for the fireworks this year and he hoped that it wouldn't be anyone he had known. Sometimes he wondered if there would ever be a time when he wouldn't think of such things. Or perhaps maybe he'd grow to be an old man and those things would be gone out of his head like an old phone number or grocery list. But he looked at the sky and he listened to the night and he seemed to know the answer.

24

HE WOKE SATURDAY MORNING TO THE calls of birds and the low chugging murmur of a fishing boat. The sun rising and a mist across the lake. He crawled out of the truck cab and walked to the water's edge. Moved his head around in a stiff circle then stretched his arms wide and groaned. He could only think of coffee so he watched as a crane flew low across the water and then he headed for home.

When he pulled up to the house a man in a pair of slacks and a crisp blue shirt was standing in the driveway. He wore glasses and was balding in front and he had his hands on his hips as he looked at the broken windows.

Russell parked on the street and walked over to the man.

'Hey,' he said.

'Hey there,' Russell said.

'Everything okay over here?'

'Everything's all right. Just an accident.'

'Sounded like a few accidents.'

'I said everything is all right,' Russell said.

'You sure?' The man pulled at the end of his nose. He looked at the house again and then back at Russell. 'You know I got kids over there,' he said. 'You understand what I'm saying?'

'I speak English.'

'You know who did it?'

'What do you care?'

'I saw him. Saw the truck. Got the tag number.'

'I don't need it.'

'We've been living here eight years without a peep. I don't want nothing funny over here. It's quiet around here.'

'And it's gonna stay quiet,' Russell said.

The man shook his head some and then gave in. 'Fine,' he said and he started across the driveway. Then he stopped at the edge of the yard and turned back to Russell. 'I saw what happened. People don't do stuff like that without a reason. That guy meant business. Next time I'll be calling the cops.'

He walked to the minivan in his driveway. He climbed in and honked the horn and three boys and a woman came out of the house and joined him. The boys looked over at Russell as they skipped to the car but the woman never looked over, her eyes on her husband and then on her lap as she sat down in the passenger seat.

Russell went inside and cleaned up the broken glass and window frames and then he made a pot of coffee and sat down at the kitchen table. The phone rang and it was his father and he told him about the windows. Told him he'd be right out to get a tarp and a hammer and some nails and yeah it was them.

He drove out and his father had what he needed waiting on him, including a ten-foot ladder. They ate lunch and then they put it all in the back of the truck.

'Need some help?' Mitchell asked.

'I got it,' Russell said and he drove back to the house.

The ladder reached the top of the windows and Russell tacked the tarp at the top and bottom corners. It would be no use in calling on a Saturday about new windows and Monday before anyone could get there to replace them anyway and he hoped that the mosquitoes wouldn't carry him away before then. He also knew that anyone could get in whenever they wanted and he figured he'd be sleeping in his truck out at the lake again. When he was done he went back inside and drank some water and then the phone rang again. Damn it, he said. He picked it up and said yeah I got it. They're covered just fine. Yeah the ladder was tall enough.

They said goodbye and hung up and Russell went into the bathroom. He washed his hands and he looked closely at his beard. The gray strands here and there. As he was looking he heard a car door slam in front of his house and he tried to remember where he had set down the shotgun. He peeked out from around the corner of the bathroom and he could see out the diamond-shaped window of the front door. He walked across the living room and he seemed to recognize the vehicle from somewhere. A big black four-door thing. He opened the front door and there she stood at the foot of the steps.

'Hey,' Sarah said.

25

UP CLOSE HER HAIR HAD A reddish tint streaking through the brown. She wore black slacks and short black boots. A white shirt with the top four buttons open and forming a V.

They sat down together on the steps and stared ahead at the house across the street. She took her feet out of her boots and sighed. She wore no socks and Russell looked at her feet. At the flaking red polish of her toenails. He then looked at her hands and her nails were smooth and something was written and smeared on the top of her left hand. She wore her wedding ring and a watch.

'You look the same,' he said.

She smiled a little. 'Please.'

'You do.'

'Well,' she said. 'You look like you could use a few good meals.'

'I'm gonna catch up. Don't worry.'

She tilted her head as she studied his face. 'I like your disguise,' she said.

He touched the whiskers on his chin. 'It's been getting mixed reviews. But I think it keeps me hidden pretty good.'

'I might have walked right by you.'

'I might have stopped you.'

She patted her hands together. Looked at her feet. Stepped back into her boots.

'You all right?' she asked.

He leaned back on his elbows. 'Yeah. I'm fine.'

'I bet your daddy is happy.'

'He is.'

'I bet your momma is, too.'

'It would've been good for her to see me sitting here.'

'I bet she's smiling wherever she is.'

'I'd hope.'

Sarah held her hands together between her knees, fingers intertwined. She rubbed her thumbs together. 'So. What are you gonna do? Help out Mitchell?'

'Nah. Mitchell doesn't really have anything he needs help with anymore. He sold about everything except this one little house that I guess he hung on to for no other reason than me.'

He got up from the steps and walked to the truck and took out his cigarettes. He lit one as he walked back to her and sat down. He offered her one and she hesitated. Smiled and said I don't do that anymore. Then she said what the hell. For old times' sake. And she took one and he lit it and they sat together smoking.

'Nice house you got down there,' he said. 'Blue. Your idea, I'm guessing.'

'Ride through there in the daytime and you'll see all those big houses are white. Couldn't stand it.'

'Neighbors like it?'

'All but one old woman who walked over after we were about halfway done and said we didn't know how to respect a house like that.'

'What'd you say?'

'Nothing. Can't say nothing to people like that.'

'Chicken.'

'Not chicken. Mature.'

'Same thing.'

He flicked his cigarette into the bushes and he thought of the girl who had spray-painted stop signs and shotgunned beers and skinnydipped. He thought of her not telling the old woman what she wanted to tell her. Maybe her kids had been standing within earshot. Maybe her husband. Maybe it was simply who she had become.

'You still mad at me?' she asked.

He shook his head. 'No.'

'You sure?'

'I told you then and I tell you now. Nothing to be mad about. Seems like you told me the same thing.'

When it started she had made the four-hour drive twice a month to sit and talk with him for half an hour. Driving alone into the middle of God knows where, across the flat Delta lands and toward a concrete palace where the offenders survived one another. Frisked by men with guns. Touched in places where it would have been impossible to conceal anything. He had been embarrassed when she saw the kind of people he was living with and the kind of people who came to visit them. She had forced herself into smiling and forced herself into talking of the world outside the walls though her strained expression did little to conceal what she truly felt.

'I don't think I can come back, Russell,' she had said after two years of visits. Her voice wavering and her eyes glassy.

'I wouldn't if I was you. No sense in it.' He had known it was coming and in some ways was relieved to hear it but he answered staring at the tabletop between them.

'What do you mean no sense?'

'No sense in it. You know what I mean.'

'You don't have to put it that way,' she said.

'There's no other way to put it.'

'I know.'

'Good. I know, too. Go and don't come back.' He had practiced being harsh in the solace of his cell, talking to a cinder block as if it were the woman he loved. The woman he knew he had to persuade to get on with her life.

'I mean it,' he said. 'Don't come back.'

She looked around at the other people. Fought to keep from crying. Then he told her that there was nothing easy about it. It don't matter if we do it now or tomorrow or a year from now. There won't be anything easy about it ever and the only thing to do is just get up and go get in the car and go. Don't even look at me.

So she did. She pulled a tissue from her purse and wiped her nose and eyes and didn't look at him as she got up and didn't look as she walked to the door and as she drove across the Delta she reached up and snapped off her rearview mirror and threw it out the window.

There had only been one more letter three years later which explained her new life. He had flushed the letter down the toilet but he kept the envelope it came in so that maybe one day he could go to the address on it and try to get her to look at him again. Like she was now.

'You want a beer?' he asked.

'I'm already smoking when I shouldn't be.'

'Why shouldn't you be?'

'Because, Russell.'

'So. You want one or not?'

'I want one. But I'm not drinking one. I gotta pick up the kids.'

'Kids. Plural.'

'Plural.'

'How many?'

'Twin boys and a girl.'

'How old?'

'The boys are four and the girl is about a year and a half.'

'And who is our hero?'

'Don't say it like that.'

'I know. Sorry.'

'I thought you said you weren't mad.'

'I'm not mad at you. But there's a lot of shit I am mad at. Seems you'd understand that.'

She set her cigarette down on the step. 'I can.'

'Seems of all the people I know you'd understand it.'

'I do. Jesus. The doors don't close in my mind, either.'

He stood up from the steps and walked into the yard. Hands in his pockets. He faced her. Looked at the blue tarp. Looked at the old Ford.

'What happened to your windows?' she asked.

'Just replacing them. You know how windows get on older houses.' He then wanted them to be quiet. No more words. All he wanted was to walk over and sit down next to her and hold her hand. He thought that if he could do that then there would be something to hope for. That he could think he was really home.

So he walked over and sat down next to her and he held her hand. And she let him for a long, silent moment that reached back into the years. But then she took her hand from his and rubbed her palm down his back and she stood up and took a piece of paper from her pants pocket. She handed it to him and he looked at it. The note that he had dropped in the mail slot of her front door.

'Russell,' she said. 'You can't do this anymore.'

He wadded the note and held it in the palm of his hand.

'Okay,' he said.

'I'm not kidding.'

'Okay.'

'There's a lot between us now. A whole lot.'

'I know. But that doesn't mean I don't love you,' he said.

She folded her arms. Looked toward the sky. 'That doesn't mean I don't love you, either,' she said. 'Just means there's nothing to do.'

'It means that and a helluva lot more.'

'It's probably not even the same kind of love.'

'Maybe not for you.'

'I can't come back over here. You gotta promise you won't come around the house.'

'I promise.'

'You probably wouldn't even like me anyhow the way I am now.'

'I could say the same thing. But I bet I would.'

'Yeah,' she said. 'I bet I would, too.'

She then reached into her other pocket and she took out a ring. The ring he had given her. The ring she had said yes to. She placed it in the middle of her open hand and held her hand out to him.

He looked at it. 'I don't want that.'

She moved back to the steps and set it down beside him.

'I got to go,' she said.

'Sarah, take that back. It's yours.'

'It was. Once upon a time.'

He nodded. And she nodded. And she stood there waiting for him to get up. Waiting for him to say something else. But he didn't move and he didn't speak. So she walked to her car and got in. She looked at him as she drove away but she didn't wave. And neither did he.

26

SHE WASN'T TO THE END OF the block before she wanted it
back. God, she wanted it back. Couldn't understand now
why she had given it to him so forcibly. Without compassion.
Couldn't understand now why she had felt like she had to bring
it with her at all. She stopped at the stop sign and looked over
her shoulder. He was still sitting on the steps. Looking not at
her but ahead. She realized now that it was much more than a
ring. Much more than something she had kept buried in her
underwear drawer for eleven years. Much more than something
she had been careful to conceal when she moved in with a
husband and careful to conceal when they moved from the
smaller house to the larger house. More than white gold and a
small diamond. She realized now as she sat at the stop sign and
looked over her shoulder at him that the ring was much more.
Something magical. Never too far away. That led through a
doorway and to another life in another world with another man
and as long as she had the ring there would be that possibility in
her mind. That place to drift toward. Not a world that she could
cross into and not a world she was certain she would cross into
if given the choice but a world that was available to her to think
about sometimes when she was alone.

And now she had taken that small and magical thing and

delivered it to the man who was in the center of that other world and she knew that by leaving it with him this part of her life would disappear. She turned right and began to make her way toward her mother's house. Stopping at the end of each street and telling herself to go back though she damn well knew that she couldn't go back after she had only minutes ago declared to him that she couldn't come back. Not even to ask him to give her back that precious thing.

She moved across town. Driving and thinking about how she felt as she saw the note lying on the floor yesterday morning. Near the front door in the same place that the mortgage and the electric bill and the Christmas cards and other evidence of their existence fell every day except Sunday. How she had known who it was from and what it said before she knelt and picked it up and how she had read it once, twice, five, eight times as she stood in the quiet of the house in the earliest light. How she had read it over and over and how she had looked out the wide, rectangular window in the front door and imagined what he looked like in the night as he walked up her sidewalk and up her front steps and across her porch and to the door and how she had imagined what he looked like as he walked away from her door and down her steps and across her sidewalk, disappearing in the dark as he walked down the street with his hands in his pockets. And how as she stood there imagining him delivering the note, how she squeezed it between her fingers as if trying to get it to give one last drop and then hearing the first small voice of the day calling Mommy and then the other small voices following behind the first. Mommy, Mommy. And how she had felt as she smoothed the wrinkled paper on her thigh and then pulled out the waist of her pajama bottoms and stuck the note into the front of her panties as she heard the small feet hit the floor, preparing to come look for her. Helping to wash faces and brush teeth and then pouring cereal for the boys and sitting

with the girl and helping her learn with her spoon as she felt
the note flat against her skin as if it were his own warm hand
against her soft flesh reaching down and touching her in a place
that he knew. And how she was relieved when the big steps
came down the stairs and the big voice came into the kitchen,
giving good mornings and kissing heads and already prepped
for the day with the tie tied and the face shaved and the smell
of a freshly cleaned man. Your turn, he said. I'll finish them
up. She headed upstairs and she took the note from her panties
and read it again and then she folded it while she hurried to
get it together. In and out of the shower and hair and makeup
done quickly and dressed and shoes and then the note folded
an extra time and put into her pants pocket just as he called out.
They're ready. I gotta run. And how she sat down on the edge
of the bed and then it occurred to her to take the ring and keep
it with her until she found the courage to go and see him and
how she took it from the back of the drawer where it had sat
all those years and where it had allowed her to go through that
doorway and into that other world. And she thought now that
if she went back and asked for it then maybe he could somehow
understand all these things that she had felt.

Her mother and the children were on the front porch. The
boys tugged at each other and argued as they walked toward
the car. The girl stood next to her grandmother with her arms
up and ready to go. She said thanks for watching them and got
them all to the car and got them all buckled in and she drove
away quickly and knew she had to return. That having them in
the car would give her an excuse to keep it running. Just get out
and tell him it was a mistake and apologize and ask if he'll give
it to you and you know he will. Only make it quick. The boys
would ask who he was and later on they might bring it up with
their father in the room. Mommy stopped at some man's house,
one of them would say. And the other would say who was that

man, Mommy? And then he might ask the same and she would say I stopped by so-and-so's house to see if she wanted to go to a movie this weekend but she wasn't there and so-and-so's husband was pulling in and stopped and said hello before we drove off and so what are we going to do about supper tonight? She processed her answer and it felt fine so she drove toward Russell thinking of the best way to say it. She was nervous when she turned onto his street and defeated when she noticed that he wasn't on the steps any longer. She slowed in front of the house and she noticed that the truck wasn't under the carport. What are we doing? one of the boys asked and she didn't answer him. Then the other boy asked the same question. What are we doing?

She was quiet as she stared at the steps where he had been sitting. Where she had been sitting with him. Where he had held her hand.

Momma? What are we doing?

27

RUSSELL PUT THE SHOTGUN BEHIND THE truck seat and he drove downtown to the café. He sat at the counter and drank coffee as the Saturday evening crowd grew with each jingle of the bell on the door. The waitress kept topping off his coffee and he tore a napkin into tiny pieces and formed a tiny white hill.

At the table behind him a young girl knocked over her glass of tea and it caused her sister to jump and she knocked her glass and both fell to the floor and broke. The mother frowned at the guilty girl and the girl said it was an accident. Sims came over with a towel but it wasn't enough so he hurried back to the kitchen and then a woman returned with him. She held a bussing tray and her hair was in a ragged ponytail. The family stood back as she knelt and picked up the broken glass and then she cleared away the plates that had been covered in the spilled tea. Sims helped the family move to another table and the woman took the tray and set it on the counter and then she went into the kitchen and returned with a mop and bucket and cleaned the spill underneath the table and chairs.

Russell paid for the coffee and went outside. Lit a cigarette and looked up at the early moon and then he walked to the Armadillo and sat down at the bar. Two young men with greasy shirts and black under their fingernails sat at the other end. The bartender leaned on the bar and talked with them. No one else was in the bar and the music was off. Russell called out for a beer and the bartender took one from the cooler and brought it down and left it without a word and returned to his friends.

A group of women came in and sat at a table and two boys came in and left when the bartender asked for their IDs but other than that the place remained tranquil. Russell watched the clock over the bar move past eight and close to nine and he couldn't figure out why the place jumped on Thursday night but not Saturday. The group of women laughed big about something and Russell turned to look at them and then he noticed another woman standing in the doorway. She stepped inside and looked around with timidity. Scraped knees and bony shoulders. The group of women scanned her up and down and whispered as she walked over to the bar and sat down three stools away and she held a twenty-dollar bill tightly in her hand. She turned toward Russell and caught him looking and he recognized her from mopping the floor in the café. She asked how much a beer costs and the bartender said a dollar fifty and she thought about it a second and then said she'd take one. The back of her shirt was wet with sweat from the evening's work. The bartender gave her the beer and when she lifted it to her lips her hand shook slightly.

The place was different without the band and without the crowd and he wished now that he would have gotten a phone number from Caroline the night before last. That he wouldn't have snuck away in the middle of the night. He imagined how good it would feel to crawl into the bed with her now with the air conditioner turned low and the covers around his neck. He looked at the skinny woman and he noticed her squeezing the change the bartender had given her as if the bills were capable of taking flight. She no longer sat on the bar stool but stood next to it. When she finished the bottle she wiped her mouth on the back of her hand. Cut her eyes around the room and then walked out.

Russell motioned to the bartender and said one more.

28

LARRY CALLED WALT AND SAID HE was going to Buddy's and Walt said he'd meet him there. Buddy's sat on a wide curve along Delaware. A boxlike brick building with neon beer signs in the front window and it had once been a pet store and then a record store and then other things but the red brick had been painted a dark purple and the drunks staggered and shoved until the doors shut at 3:00 a.m. Larry walked inside and scanned the place. A bar lined the wall on the left and tables made from old wooden doors filled the front room. Televisions hung on the wall behind the bar and in the corners and the brick walls were decorated with photographs of football players in Ole Miss and Mississippi State and Saints jerseys. Something bluesy played over the speakers and two ceiling fans circulated the cigarette smoke and he didn't see anyone he knew.

Larry walked past the tables and through a hallway that opened onto a spacious back deck. There was another bar and plank floors and a couple more televisions. Mardi Gras beads hung from the exposed ceiling beams and a cigar store Indian stood at the end of the bar. The deck was screened and white Christmas lights hung around the top edges of the screen, all the way around. Two blondes sat at the bar with lipstick on their drink glasses but the tables were empty. Larry turned around and walked back and sat down at the bar in the front room.

A man with a shaved head and wearing an apron appeared from a door behind the bar and nodded at Larry. Sweat ran down his forehead and he looked irritated. He wiped his head on the back of his arm.

'Hey, Earl,' Larry said.

Earl shook his head. 'Damn help ain't nowhere to be found tonight. I never understand that shit. Guy walks in. Wants a job and I give it to him and then he don't show up for it. You know what I'm talking about?'

'Yep. About August they'll start dropping like flies on me.'

'What you want?'

'Beer. In a bottle. You seen Walt?'

'He ran in and out of here a minute ago. Said he had to go get smokes.'

Earl gave him a beer then one of the tables called him and he left. Larry drank the beer and looked at the front door as the day began to fade and night less than an hour away. The hour between dog and wolf.

Walt returned and sat down next to his brother and they nodded at each other. The Braves were on the television on the wall at the end of the bar and they watched the game mindlessly and moved only to look when the door opened or when they needed another drink. An hour passed and it was dark now and Earl ran back and forth between the tables and the bar and the kitchen and it was going to be a long night.

'You seen Heather yet?' Walt asked.

'Nope. I guess she waited around last night until somebody finally carted that son of a bitch away. I heard her go in another room when she got to the house. This morning I left out early and – big surprise – she wasn't there when I got home.'

'What you gonna say?'

'You mean what's she gonna say? I ain't saying shit.'

'I bet you won't have to wait long to find out,' Walt said.

'Why's that?'

'Cause she just walked in.'

She came their way and Walt grabbed his beer and headed for the back deck.

Heather propped her elbows on the bar. A strapless dress and fresh makeup and cleaned and shined. Larry shook his head and figured he should have expected her to be dolled up. It was the only way she worked.

'Buy me a drink?' she asked.

'You got money.'

'I left my purse in the car.'

'Then go get it.'

Earl stopped at the cash register and he waved to Heather.

'You got any white wine back there?'

Larry shook his head and huffed.

'What?' she asked.

'Nobody drinks wine in Buddy's.'

'Okay. What do you want me to drink?'

'I don't give a shit what you drink but you goddamn sure ain't sitting next to me with a wineglass.'

Earl waited and she asked for a beer. 'Happy now?' she asked and she nudged him but Larry didn't smile. And he didn't talk. She crossed her legs toward him, brushing his calf with her foot. He didn't take notice.

'Who's winning?' she asked.

'Winning what?' Larry said.

'That game up there.'

Larry raised his eyes to the television. 'The score is on the bottom of the screen.'

'I can't see that far.'

'Then get the hell up and go look.'

She had promised herself that she'd be more careful. That was three years ago and she had only become more reckless. Telling the blond man they didn't need to go out of town. Larry's head is up his ass. It'll be fun to go down to the Armadillo. But she had underestimated Larry and made him look like a fool and the blond man had paid for it. She needed to calm him down before she didn't have a place to sleep. Or a checking account. She wrapped a cocktail napkin around her beer and turned the bottle in her hands, her fingernails the same crimson as her lipstick.

'Are you gonna pout all night or talk to me?' she said.

He turned on the bar stool and faced her. He let his anger slide enough so that he could speak without yelling. 'I don't have anything to say to you, Heather. And you know why. How long you want us to sit here and play stupid?'

Larry had turned away again and she snuck a look at him in between the liquor bottles in the mirror.

'I'm sorry, Larry,' she said.

'Good for you.'

'I'm serious.'

'I know you are. That's why it's so pathetic.'

'Why is it pathetic?' Her face had changed now, losing its playfulness and becoming more aggressive.

'Why is it pathetic?' she asked again when he didn't answer.

'It's pathetic because you think you can walk in here all perfumed and shit and sit down next to me and I'll fall for it.'

'I'm not pretending. I screwed up. Okay?'

'No damn shit.'

'And I'm sorry.'

'The only reason you're sorry is cause you got caught which don't do much for your bullshit confession.'

'I swear to God, Larry. I'm sorry,' she said and she put her hand on his leg. He pushed it away and asked Earl for another beer. She stopped and let him mill for a minute. Thought that maybe she'd fake cry but she wasn't there yet.

She wrapped her hand around the inside of his thigh again and half smiled. 'I swear I'm sorry. And I'm done, Larry.'

'Done with what?'

'You know what.'

'I want you to say it.'

'Fine. I'm done messing around.'

'Messing around ain't what you do. Tell me what you're done doing. Gimme some detail.' His voice was louder now and several people from the tables took notice. Heather moved uncomfortably on her stool.

'I'm done sleeping around.'

'You ain't been sleeping, either. I want you to say it. Tell me what you're done doing or first thing Monday morning I'm going to take the same pictures I shoved down your boyfriend's pants to my lawyer and then I'm gonna come home and throw your shit out in the yard.'

She took a deep breath. He had her.

'I'm done having sex with other men,' she said.

'What else?'

'I'm done putting my mouth on them. I'm done bending over for anybody but you. I'm done, baby. I swear.'

She folded her hands in her lap and waited and she swore to herself that she'd never be careless again. That she'd make sure she kept it out of town. She wouldn't let him make her bow down again.

He pressed his lips together. Nodded. And then he told Earl he wanted two bourbons.

'On top of each other?' Earl asked.

'No, jackass. One for me and one for her.'

After Earl set down the drinks Larry slid her a glass.

'Here,' he said.

They drank in the strange silence that lingers around people who have gone through the motions but aren't sure if anything has been truly reconciled. Heather looked around the bar and ran her finger around the corners of her mouth to smooth her lipstick. There was one more thing to do to help him get over it.

'Let's run home for a while,' she said.

'I'm drinking,' he said.

'Come on, Larry. Let me make it up to you.'

He finished the bourbon and told Earl he wanted another. Then he said you go on home and I'll be there in a little while.

'Promise?'

'Just go on.'

She stood and kissed him on the cheek and then she walked toward the door. She glanced over her shoulder to see if he was watching her walk but he wasn't.

Walt waited until Larry was done with his drink and then he took her vacated seat and said I'm guessing you let her slide.

'Don't goddamn talk to me.'

'She's a broken record.'

'No shit.'

'She makes you look stupid.'

It was a hard right that Walt never saw coming but Larry was nice enough to give it to the side of his head and not his nose and once the two brothers got up off the floor and Earl pulled them apart they sat right back down to drink again.

For hours they drank and stared at the television and neither moved except to go to the bathroom and finally Larry left Walt with the tab and he drove to the end of Delaware Avenue where it ran into the interstate. He stopped at a gas station and bought a six-pack and then he turned onto the interstate toward

Louisiana. A full breadth of stars stretched across the summer sky and he smoked with the windows cracked and the warm wind whipped around him. He set his cruise control knowing that if anyone stopped him he'd go straight to jail. He leaned back in his seat with a beer between his legs. Swerving some. A strip of interstate that projected loneliness. He was two beers down when he reached the state line and the exit for Kentwood was less than a mile after that. He took the exit and turned to the right, away from the lights of the fast food joints and gas stations.

He drove a few miles until there was nothing but fences and the occasional mailbox and in this part of the country the night seemed to open its mouth and swallow the land and whatever moved across it. He came to a crossroads and turned left and the road thinned and led from the open pastures into the trees and it was darker then. He slowed down and watched for the turn. Around the second bend he turned up a driveway that was marked by a mailbox covered in a flowery vine and he turned off his headlights as he moved toward the house. He stopped the truck twenty yards away and he looked out the open window at the house. The red brick that she had wanted and the white columns that she had wanted and the two chimneys that he had wanted. There wasn't an inch of the house that he hadn't put his hands on while it was going up. The light was on over the front door and there were no other lights on in the house. He set his beer aside and got out of the truck and when he closed the door, a light came on in the window of her bedroom and her shadow appeared behind the curtain and she peeked out to see who it was.

He walked toward the front door and stopped. Don't scare her.

She opened the door and stepped out under the light, a kneehigh robe wrapped around her and her hair longer than the last time he had seen her. Down past her shoulders and a shade lighter. He put his hands in his pockets and tried to appear as harmless as possible.

'You're not supposed to be here,' she said.

'I know,' he said and he took a slow step toward her.

'I mean it, Larry. You need to go on.'

'I just thought I'd see how you were doing.'

'It's late.'

'He here?'

She looked around him and out into the dark as if something or someone else might be out there.

'Course he's here. He's sleeping. Like I was,' she said.

Off in the woods surrounding the house something howled as if it were hurt. His head turned and followed the sound.

'What do you want, Larry?' she said.

'You think I could just go in there and talk to him a minute?'

'No, Larry. God no.'

'Only a minute, Dana. I swear.'

'You been drinking?'

'Some.'

'You need to go on.'

He knew that every cop and court in Kentwood agreed with her and he knew that he had earned it. Even standing there drunk he knew it. He couldn't see his boy and he wasn't supposed to be within so many feet of her and he didn't argue that it was his own doing. It had been a long time since that had been decided and he hadn't forgotten. But he had driven down ignoring it and hoped she might do the same but he saw that she was as strong as ever.

'I heard you getting married,' he said.

She nodded.

'Think you really want to again?'

'You did.'

'That's why I'm asking. Just cause it's somebody new don't mean it's any good.'

'I'm gonna try anyway.'

'Can't be no worse, huh?' he said.

'If that's what you want to say.'

He swayed and had to catch himself from falling.

'I'm going inside and you need to go. Right now. Don't take this no further.'

'Is he playing Little League this summer?'

'He's too old for Little League now.'

'Already? Shit.'

Larry whispered something to himself. Made an X in the dirt with the heel of his boot.

'Can I go in and look? I won't say nothing. Just go look at him for a second.'

'Hell no.'

'Is he getting tall?'

'You wouldn't be able to tell it if he was. He lays down when he sleeps.'

'Goddamn it, Dana. I know that. Is he getting tall or not?'

She folded her arms tightly. 'Yes. He's tall. Now go home. I'm not saying it again. Go on home,' she said. She looked at him like she used to look at him when she wanted him to be better and then she went in the door. Locks clicked and the light went off over the door and then the light went off in her bedroom and he could feel her watching him. Waiting for him to go. That thing howled again. Sounded like it might be for the last time. He walked to his truck and backed out of the driveway and waited to turn on his headlights until he was out on the road.

He was often filled with a serenity as he drove alone on backcountry roads in the late recesses of the night, the empty roads and the feeling of being separated from the things that lived where the streetlights lived. But that serenity was just as often shattered and scattered into the darkest corners of the countryside as he was overpowered by the thoughts of the things that he hated – the wife that had been and the boy he couldn't see and the wife he had now and the men who tasted her and the dead who were gone and the living who would return. And then he would rage against the most striking object of his hate and he would look into the rearview mirror and see that object staring back at him and it was easy to hate the other things but it was always the most crippling to hate himself and it was in the most vile and the drunkest moments of self-inspection that he knew that one day he was going to kill Russell Gaines for killing Jason. And as time went on, the morning light had done less and less to rid him of this revelation.

He drove back into Mississippi, drifting from lane to lane without realizing it but making it home. He went into the house and stumbled and fell in the hallway and then he got up and he found the bedroom door locked. Open this goddamn door. He knocked loudly once and then she opened the door. He grabbed her in the dark and pulled at whatever she had on and then he fell on top of her on the bed and he tried as hard as he could to disgust her.

29

MABEN PUSHED ON THE FRONT DOOR of the shelter, expecting to find it locked and hoping that the woman didn't ask for a password as nobody had given her one. But it was open and she walked in tired but satisfied with the fortysomething dollars she had made and more satisfied that Sims had said she could come back and do it again. No one was at the front counter and the light was on in the office but the office door was shut. There was a glass window on the door with a mostly closed blind but between the slivers Maben could see the young black woman from the night before sitting at a desk talking on the telephone. She walked to the back of the building where she found Annalee sitting on her cot with her legs crossed Indian-style. *The Little Red Hen* was open across her lap and she was doing her best to read it.

'Hey, baby,' Maben said and the child looked up and smiled at her. Maben sat down next to her and asked her what she had been doing all night but before Annalee could answer Maben saw that the garbage bag was not under her cot where she had left it. She hopped up and looked under the child's cot and it was not there and it was not under the dresser. A duffel bag was tucked at the foot of the cot and Maben snatched it and shook it at the girl.

'Where's the bag, Annalee?' Maben asked.

'The woman said that one's better.'

'Where's the bag? I don't care if this one's better.'

The girl closed the book and walked over to the dresser and she began to open the drawers and show Maben that their clothes were nicely folded and put away. Maben took the child by the shoulders and said who told you to put those in there?

'I didn't do it,' she said. 'That woman did it.'

'What woman?'

'That woman that's here.'

Maben stood up straight and looked around as if she were dizzy and then she told Annalee to put her shoes on.

'Why?'

'Just do it.'

Maben walked back toward the front of the building to the office. She walked slowly, silently. She bent down when she reached the office door and kept her head below the glass pane. The woman remained at the desk. She remained on the telephone. Maben listened. I don't know what to do, she said. I found it unpacking her clothes. I told you. Should we call the cops? What do you think? I don't know. Maben raised her head so that she could see inside and the pistol lay on the desk immediately in front of the woman. Maben sank down after she saw it and she snuck back to the child and told her to get whatever she could carry and let's go.

'Why?' the child asked again and she started to cry. 'I don't wanna go no more.'

'Hush,' Maben said. 'You got to listen to me and hush.'

'I don't wanna go,' she yelled.

Maben yanked her and said I don't care what you want. Get what you need to bring and shut the hell up, Annalee. I ain't playing with you.

The girl quieted but whimpered as she grabbed a small stack

of books off the dresser that the woman had given her. Maben opened the drawers and pulled out clothes and stuffed them into the duffel bag but the bag was small and half the clothes stayed. She then turned and knelt to the child.

'Listen to me. Listen good. We're gonna go up here real quiet and go out real quiet. No talking. Go on out and wait for me on the sidewalk. You hear me?'

Annalee nodded. Looked away from her mother.

Maben grabbed her by the shoulders. 'I said listen. This is important. You hear me? Do what I say. You hear me?'

'Yes. I said yes.'

'Come on.'

Maben tucked the duffel bag under her arm and took the child by the hand and they walked toward the front. At the end of the partitions Maben stopped and gave Annalee the shush sign and then she peeked around the corner. The office door still closed and the light still on. The mumble of a voice. Bend down, she told the child. They hunched over beneath the level of the glass and moved quietly to the exit door and Maben held it open just wide enough for Annalee to pass through. Wait out there, she whispered. And take this. She handed the duffel bag to the child and gave her a small push. Then Maben crawled over to the office door. The woman wasn't talking much now but only saying yes ma'am or okay to the voice on the other end. Said I haven't yet I wanted to call you first. And Maben knew instructions were being given. Knew there was no way you find a pistol at a women's shelter and do nothing. Knew that as soon as she hung up the phone she would make another call.

She looked around. Then she crawled behind the counter and looked for something to throw. Looking for something she could throw far. Not a phone book and not a box of pens and not a paperback novel but on the middle shelf was a football and a baseball. She took the baseball and stood and she threw it toward the back of the building. It was a strong throw and it cleared the partitions and hit the wall above the bathroom doors. A solid whack. Maben ducked behind the counter and she heard the woman say hold on and the office door opened.

'Annalee?' she called out.

No answer. Footsteps past the front of the counter and then footsteps walking away and Maben got to her feet and she ran into the office and took the pistol from the desk and then she was out the front door and toward the child who was sitting on top of the duffel bag on the sidewalk. Get up get up get up and she lifted the child and grabbed the bag and then she set the child down and took off running. Come on I told you to come on and the girl ran behind her with the books held against her chest and calling out for her momma to slow down. Maben ran on, looking over her shoulder to make sure that the child was running behind her and when she got to the corner she stopped and waited for the child to catch up. She looked down the block toward the shelter and she thought she saw a figure standing on the sidewalk but she wasn't sure and she told Annalee to run baby run. She grabbed the child's hand and they started again and they raced up Main Street and at the end of the street a man came out of the bar and walked to his truck. She tucked the duffel bag under her arm. Squeezed the pistol with one hand and Annalee's arm with the other. Do exactly what I do, she told her. You hear me? Annalee grunted and Maben pulled her and they slid along the sidewalk. Crouched and creeping closer as the man got in and cranked the truck and they slipped right up to his open window. Maben stuck the pistol to the side of his face and told him to sit still and she told the girl to get in the other side. Hurry goddamn it she told the girl and when Annalee was sitting in the cab Maben hustled around the front of the truck with the pistol on him and she hopped in and slammed the door. Drive right now. I said drive. He didn't ask where. He only did what she said as the pistol shook nervously at the side of his head and he said he could drive a helluva lot better without that damn thing pointed at him.

She told him to go to the interstate. She kept the pistol down but pointed at him while they passed through the lights of Delaware Avenue. At the interstate he asked her which way and she looked left and then right and she said that way and pointed north. Russell turned north onto I-55 and she stayed turned on him with the child between them. No one spoke as they drove up past Brookhaven and he noticed the way she handled the pistol. Carelessly. A flimsy grip. And when he caught her looking away from him and out the window he reached over and snatched it out of her hand.

'Give that back,' Maben said.

'Sure thing,' he said and he held it in his left hand between his leg and the truck door.

She slumped back in her seat and then she leaned forward and put her head down on her arm on the dashboard.

'Don't worry,' he said. 'I'll take you wherever within reason.'

'Where we going?' the girl asked.

'Yeah,' he said. 'Where we going?'

Maben sat up and wiped at her eyes. 'I don't care,' she said.

'What the hell kind of trouble you in?'

She didn't answer.

'Pretty big stretch from mopping the floor to holding a gun on a stranger in the parking lot. All in the same night.'

She still didn't talk.

'Where we going, Momma?'

She didn't know what to say. She didn't know what to think. There had been years and years of this. Years of not knowing where she was going or what she was doing or the names of the people she was doing it with. Some of those years blacked out and some too fresh. The bruises and hungry days. The waking up naked in musty rooms with no lightbulb and no money and no idea of the name of the town. The man in Slidell with the convertible and the rehab in New Orleans where they strapped her to the bed for two days until the hallucinations were gone and the man in Mobile with the wad of cash and the strategy for beating blackjack. The man in Natchez with the cockfighting pit in the backyard and the good stuff from the guy with the piercings that led to the bad stuff from the guy with the piercings. Always believing the next step would be better. Always winding up in a tighter squeeze. And now the squeeze held two of them. She looked down at the child and she had opened a book across her lap though it was too dark to read.

Russell lit a cigarette and cracked his window. He offered Maben one and she took it.

'You want one?' he asked the girl but she turned up her nose. Then he asked her what her name was but the woman told her not to answer.

'Don't nobody need names,' she said.

'No names. No direction,' he said.

'We got a direction. We're going north.'

'No destination then.'

'You can let us out whenever you want,' she said. 'But you got to give me that pistol back. I didn't mean nothing. Just needed a ride right then. I can pay you for it.'

'How much?'

'Not much.'

'What you running from?'

'Yeah,' said Annalee. 'I liked it there.'

Maben took the book from Annalee's lap and closed it. The girl moaned and reached for it but Maben told her to wait a minute.

'You got to tell me something first,' she said.

'What?' the girl answered.

'When that woman put our clothes away what'd she say when she found the gun?'

'I don't know.'

'You got to think. Were you sitting there?'

'Yes'm.'

'Then think. What'd she say?'

The child put her finger to her chin and looked out the windshield. She bent her mouth.

'She said what the hell?'

'And what else?'

'Nothing. She asked where we got it and I said it was my momma's. But I ain't never seen it before.'

'You told her that?'

'I said I ain't never seen it before.'

'Then what?'

'Then she took it and went on. She looked funny.'

Russell listened. It wasn't difficult to figure out that something had come upon them that they hadn't been expecting. The woman had the look of someone who might have been used to it but there was concern in her voice. He had heard the sound from men who knew what tomorrow would bring and knew there was nothing they could do about it.

They came upon a rest area and Russell pulled off without asking and Maben didn't oppose. White streetlights lit the parking lot. A brick building of restrooms to the right. A pavilion and picnic tables to the left. A woman walked her dog in the grass around the pavilion and a group of motorcycles were parked in front of the restrooms and men and women in leather stood around the bikes smoking. Vending machines lined against the wall of the bathroom building and above the vending machines a round clock that read 10:05.

Russell parked close to the bikes. Killed the engine. Touched the cut on his forehead.

'I'm hungry,' the child said.

Maben opened her door and got out and the child climbed down after her. Maben gave her two dollars and told her to go get something. Then she sat back down in the truck with her leg swinging out.

Russell picked up the pistol and turned it in his hands. 'This is a nice piece,' he said.

'I didn't mean to have a kid,' she said. She stared at Annalee who stood in front of the vending machines trying to decide.

He started to tell her that she shouldn't say stuff like that but she rested her head back against the glass of the back window and continued.

'Can't feed her. Can't give her a place to sleep. I don't even know when it happened. Somebody just popped it in me. I was sitting around one day feeling like shit and I started throwing up and kept on until I figured it out. Then I wanted to do something but it'd get night and I couldn't bring myself to it the next day. Even sat in the clinic a couple of times. Sat there looking at some stupid magazine. Sweating. I'd sit there 'til they called me and I'd leave out. Then it'd get night again and I finally figured I'd keep it and see what happened.'

'Night always gets me,' he said. 'Makes me do stuff I shouldn't.'

'Something about it,' she agreed.

'You in some trouble?'

She nodded and watched the child.

'I'm gonna guess it's big trouble,' he said.

'Is there some other kind?' she said and she turned and looked at him. Her eyes seemed to be shrinking back into her head. She knew that telephone conversations were being had about her right now.

'This isn't your gun,' he said.

'No.'

There was a crack of lightning and then thunder and the men

and women around the bikes put out their cigarettes and put on their helmets and jackets. The bikes fired up and roared and snapped and each woman found her man and sat behind him. Maben looked at Annalee and the child held a drink can against one ear and a candy bar against the other. A man riding alone pulled ahead and the others followed him, the roar growing with the acceleration and then dying away as the bikes moved down the ramp and away into the night. When the bikes were gone the girl walked back toward the truck but Maben called out for her to go and sit down at a picnic table. For a minute. I got to talk to the man.

'What you supposed to do when you can't let nobody find you?' she asked and she tossed her cigarette onto the asphalt.

'That's a good one,' he said.

'And what you supposed to do when you got somebody you love and you know if they find you they're gonna take that somebody away with them?'

Russell shifted in his seat. Let out a breath. 'That's a better one,' he said.

Annalee sat on top of a wooden picnic table with her legs swinging over the edge. She ate the candy bar carefully as if she were wearing her best dress.

'She'd be better off anyhow.'

'You don't know that.'

'Yeah. I know it. Didn't know it 'til now. But I know it. Two hours ago I had some work and we had a safe place to sleep. Even if it was only gonna be a few days. Didn't know it then. If I knew it I didn't say it to myself. But I know it now.'

Russell lit another cigarette off the one that was dying. A car pulled into the rest area and a small boy got out of the backseat and raced toward the restrooms and his father got out and ran after him, telling him to hold it hold it.

'Maybe if you told me what was going on I could figure out a way to help,' Russell said.

'Maybe Jesus will come down from His high horse and cook us supper.'

'Maybe.'

'But probably not.'

'But maybe.'

'I did something that anybody else would've done and it's over and that's that.'

'Would you do it again?'

'I don't see why not.'

'Then stop worrying about it.'

'You and me both know it ain't like that.'

He unloaded the bullets from the chamber and he handed the pistol back to her. He put the bullets in his shirt pocket.

'The thing is you don't know what I can do and what I can't. Either I can help or I cannot. That's all there is. But you're not gonna find out like this. Don't seem like you got a whole lot to lose.'

The girl finished her candy bar and she hopped off the table and walked toward the truck. She looked at her feet and placed one foot in front of the other as if she were balancing on a high wire. Maben turned and looked at Russell. He was scratching at his beard.

'Where do you live?' she asked.

'About six blocks from where you stuck that thing in my ear.'

'I used to live in McComb.'

'I saw you mopping at the café. You must still live there.'

'We walked into town yesterday. Or the day before.'

'Walked?'

'Walked in. Ran out. Ain't been back in years. Since long before her.'

'What's your name?'

She leaned over and put the pistol in the duffel bag at her feet. 'All I want you to do is drive us. If you don't want to that's fine. We'll call it right here. But I'd appreciate it if you could take us on farther.'

Russell nodded. Annalee made it to the truck and Maben held her drink as she climbed over her mother and sat between them.

'I'm guilty of a lot of things, but leaving you and her out here ain't going to be one of them,' he said and he cranked the truck. 'I can go on a little farther.'

'Can I have that book back?' the girl asked. Maben handed it to her. Away from the lights of the rest area there was only dark ahead of them as the lightning from the coming storm flashed in the night sky behind.

30

THEY DROVE NORTH ON I-55. AROUND midnight they passed through Jackson and he turned east on I-20. Once they were out of the city lights and back into empty miles of interstate the child put her head in her mother's lap and went to sleep. Russell rolled the window down halfway and tossed out the bullets. After miles and miles of quiet and after she was sure the child wouldn't be listening Maben said you have to promise you won't tell nobody. Her voice was close to a whisper. Her eyes ahead on the headlights.

'Tell nobody what?'

'What I'm about to tell you.'

He had been thinking that he was glad she hadn't told him. He had been thinking that he was better off that way. That soon he would put them out somewhere and drive on back and forget about it. I got enough to think about already. Don't ask her anything else. Just drive. He had been thinking that he was glad he never had a kid. He looked at Annalee and wondered if she had ever been to school.

'There was a sheriff man killed,' she said.

Jesus Christ, he thought. Jesus Christ almighty. You were right, you son of a bitch. You could've shut her up but you let her keep talking and Jesus Christ almighty. Russell twisted the steering wheel in his hands as if to wrench what she had said back into her mouth but there wasn't a damn thing he could do about it now and still he wrenched harder and harder. She could have said anything. A crazyass boyfriend or money she owed or he would have even taken that she had kidnapped the little girl. Anything.

'I heard about it,' he said.

'This is his gun.'

She then stopped. More miles passed on.

'You can put us out wherever,' she said.

'I know.'

'It probably ain't gonna matter anyway.'

'I imagine there's a lot of people looking for that thing,' he said.

'Then I guess you see why I'm running off with it. I guess you see what somebody might think if they found me with it.'

'I can guess that.'

'And I bet you think you know something right now. But you don't.'

'I didn't say I knew anything. I'm driving.'

They came upon the exit for Forest and he said he had to get gas. He turned off and stopped at a gas station and filled up. Maben sat still and the girl didn't wake. When he was done he paid inside and he came out with a new pack of cigarettes and beer. He drove back onto the interstate and he opened a beer and set it between his legs. Then he opened another and handed it to her.

'You don't look like a killer to me,' he said.

'That's because I'm not.'

'I been around some. Killers, that is. And worse. Killers aren't even the worst. But I know what they look like. They look like they mean it. You don't look like you mean it.'

'I don't see how you can mean or not mean something you didn't do.'

'Yeah. I don't reckon you can.'

'And I don't see what's worse than being a killer.'

He looked over at her. 'You know what's worse,' he said. 'There's plenty worse.'

She brushed the child's hair away from her face. Stroked her pink cheek. She didn't answer him. She didn't have to. They drank their beers and drove on. They were close to Meridian when she began talking again. Explaining what had happened. How she and the girl had walked and walked to that truck stop and how they'd gotten a room and felt like people for a little while. How he'd found her in the parking lot and how he'd taken her off and what he'd made her do and that he'd called his buddies to come on and do it too and how it seemed like he was gonna make a few dollars from it and how he didn't believe her when she said that her kid was back there and how she believed that was gonna be the end of it. That they were going to do things to her that she didn't want them to do until dawn and then she was going to sit in jail and she didn't have any money to get out and the girl would be found and gone and even though I said I wish I woulda never had her I don't mean it. And how she didn't think about it much she just saw the pistol and she did it and that it seemed like something that hadn't really happened but that it had and she knew no matter what she explained to the people who mattered, no one would believe her over a dead man in a uniform. She kept her voice low while she talked but he could tell she wanted to scream.

'Bad shit happens to good people,' he said when she was done.

'Nah. I ain't a good person. Bad shit happens to everybody,' she said. 'I wish to God it'd take a break when you're trying, though.'

The lights of Meridian glowed ahead in the night sky. But before they reached the city limits sign, Russell turned south on I-59.

'You got to tell me one thing,' he said. 'Why are you holding on to that gun? That thing can bury you.'

She stared out into the faint highway light. 'If there was one thing that could do you in wouldn't you want to know where it is?'

He nodded. He understood her argument and thought to give the other side of it but decided to let her determine her own fate.

'You're making a square,' she said.

'You didn't tell me not to.'

'Don't take us back there.'

'We're still a long ways off. Sooner or later we got to stop.'

'I told you a while back you can let us out wherever.'

'You need a better plan than that.'

'You the one who said you could help. Now you know it ain't so simple. I bet you thought I was running away from some asshole who smacked me around.'

'Hoping is more like it.'

'No sense in that.'

'In what?'

'Hope.'

'I'd say where you and that girl are concerned that's the only damn thing that matters.'

They continued on in quiet until they approached a sign for a campground off the next exit. Russell looked over to ask Maben if she wanted to stop for the night but she was asleep, slumped against the door and her head against the window. Russell took the exit and turned right and followed the highway for half a mile and he turned at the plywood sign for the campground. The campground was a couple of acres that had been thinned out and the camping spots were bare patches of dirt within a scattering of trees and a circle of stones sat in the middle of each spot for a fire. He drove along and the campground was mostly deserted. He passed an old Volkswagen van and then he passed a truck with a camper on the back and an old man and woman sat around a fire. When he was clear of others he picked a spot and parked the truck. He turned off the headlights and got out. The sky was covered with clouds and the only light was that of the fire, an orange speck fifty yards away.

He flicked his cigarette lighter and walked around to the passenger side. Then he reached into the cab and he tapped her on the shoulder. She lifted her head and looked at him and he whispered we stopped. In the middle of nowhere. Lay down for a while. She opened her door and slid out from under the child and she walked around and climbed back in on the other side and lay alongside the child with her feet hanging off the end of the seat. Russell followed her and when he pushed the door half shut and bumped her foot she raised up.

'Sorry,' he said.

'Maben,' she said.

'What?'

'Maben. That's my name,' she said and she lay back down.

He came around to the back of the truck and climbed over into the bed. He had planned to lie down but instead he sat with his back against the tailgate. A faint breeze blew and he watched the fireflies blink across the woods. Watched the fire across the way. Watched the bodies sitting close to it. They looked gray.

He had only known one person named Maben. And he hadn't really known her. He had known who she was. He had watched her at the sentencing, crying and shaking as if she had understood something about the boy who died that no one else could understand. He thought about the Maben who was sleeping in his truck and he started to do the math but it wasn't necessary. She looked older than she probably was and that was about right. He laughed a little but not much. He had seen enough in his life to not be surprised by a damn thing.

31

IN HER DREAMS SHE STOOD ON a hillside and looked down across the meadow. The child stood in the midst of the waisthigh wild flowers that swayed with the wind and seemed to move in circles, her hair being lifted and let go and lifted again by the cool air. She stood with her arms folded as she watched the child who held her arms out and her hands were open and she traced her palms over the tips of the flowers and smiled as they tickled the tender center of her hands. Pinks and blues streaked across the horizon and the clouds moved across the sky like a slow train.

She saw it coming off in the distance, crawling or maybe slithering, only its tail visible. Rising high and waving in an S, thick and reptilian like something ancient. As it crept closer the wind gained strength and began to howl, blowing sharply into her face and she began to call out to the child. Come this way. Right now come this way but the child didn't hear her. The tail moved closer and she began to scream and when the child still didn't hear her she screamed louder and louder and she tried to move but her feet were buried in the ground and that thing was within striking distance now and the child never saw it coming and as it raised the top of its head from the wildflowers Maben woke with a shriek and she fell off the seat and onto the floorboard. The child woke up and began to cry when she saw that there was only the dark and another strange place and her mother held on to her and said I am here. I am here.

32

OYD HAD PUT IT OFF. WAITING to be told you have to go over
there and talk to him about it. A dead deputy on a desolate
road. The only vehicle to come upon the scene driven by a man
who had been out of prison for about five minutes. A loaded
shotgun in the vehicle. An expired driver's license. When asked
what he was doing out there he had said he was riding. It didn't
matter if he knew the man or not it was too much to ignore and
they had nothing else and were looking for a road to follow. He
couldn't dance around Russell any longer.

So Boyd checked in at the office and drank his coffee. He
made a couple of calls that weren't answered and he realized
it was Sunday morning. He then drank a second cup and
he figured he might as well get it over with and he told the
dispatcher he'd be back around lunch. It was an eight-mile drive
from the department office in Magnolia to McComb and he
didn't take the interstate but instead went along the highway
with its log trucks and flashing yellows at crossroads. Anything
to slow him down.

The first thing he noticed when he came to the house was
the blue tarp over the windows. Hard not to. The truck was
gone. He got out and walked around to the backyard. High
grass and weeds. Paint buckets and empty beer bottles filled

with cigarette butts on the back porch. A dog barking from the neighbor's yard behind the headhigh wooden fence. He walked around the side of the house and looked into the bedroom window which had no curtain. Clothes scattered on the floor. A sheet wadded on the bed. Boxes stacked in the corner. He moved around to the front and knocked on the door so he could say he'd done it and then he climbed back into the cruiser. He drove downtown to the café and he sat at the counter and ate biscuits and gravy and then he drove out toward the father's place. That was the only other place he figured to look for him.

He walked to the back door and saw Mr. Gaines sitting at the kitchen table with Consuela. She was eating pancakes and he leaned back in his chair with the Sunday paper held open. Boyd knocked and they looked up together and Mitchell got up reluctantly and walked over and opened the door.

'How you doing, Mr. Gaines?' Boyd said.

It took Mitchell a moment but then he recognized Boyd and he held out his hand to him.

'Come on in here,' Mitchell said and Boyd followed him into the kitchen. Mitchell asked him if he wanted coffee and ignored him when he said no. He poured a cup for himself and for Boyd and he told him to sit down. Mitchell moved the newspaper aside as he sat across from Boyd.

'Ain't seen you in quite a while,' Mitchell said. 'Looks like somebody's been feeding you.'

'Got that right,' Boyd said. 'Married a woman who don't cook very good but she cooks a lot of whatever it is.'

'There's worse.'

'Sure is. Got two boys who'll beat me to it if I don't watch it.'

Boyd looked at the woman and she listened as they talked and he waited on Mitchell to introduce her but he didn't so he got on with it.

'I don't guess you've seen Russell this morning?' he said.

Mitchell shook his head. 'Not this morning.'

'You wouldn't know where he is would you?'

'At the house would be my guess. You been by there?'

'Yes sir. Before I came out here.'

Mitchell sat up and rested his elbows on the table. 'He done something wrong?'

'No sir. Just need to talk to him for a minute.' Boyd pushed his coffee cup around. Took a sip.

'Sorry about your man. Went to get some catfish food yesterday down at the co-op and heard it mentioned,' Mitchell said. 'Crying damn shame.'

'Yeah. Wives don't like hearing about stuff like that.'

'I don't reckon they do.'

'Kids, neither. Even big ugly ones.'

'Your boys ballplayers?'

'Every chance they get. The oldest started summer workouts this year.'

'I bet he don't mind.'

'Hell no. He loves it. Probably gonna start him out at linebacker. He moves pretty good.'

Consuela finished her pancakes and she stood and rinsed her plate in the sink. Then she took the coffeepot and added to their cups though little had been sipped. She set down the pot and then she walked out of the kitchen and then there was the sound of a choir singing coming from the television.

'You ain't here cause of her are you?' Mitchell asked.

'No sir. Not at all.'

'Cause she don't do no harm.'

'You don't have nothing to worry about, Mr. Gaines.'

'Then what do I have to worry about?'

Boyd pushed his cup away. 'I got to talk to Russell about the other night. After we found our man out there, Russell came driving up. Way out there. Him and nobody else all night. So I got to talk to him about it. That's all.'

'That's all?'

'Swear it.'

'You know him better than that.'

'I know.'

'He wouldn't do nothing like that, Boyd.'

'I know that. Maybe he saw something. A car or truck or whatever. That's all. Just tell him I need to talk to him. Tell him to call me and only me. Soon as he can.'

'I will.'

'Thanks for the coffee,' Boyd said and he stood up.

'I tell you what you might do as long as you're talking about Russell.'

'What's that?'

'Watch them boys. Tisdale. Especially that tall one. He already broke out all the windows over at Russell's house. And Russell's got a mark on the side of his head where they met him down at the bus station.'

'He call the police?'

'For what?'

Boyd reached across the table and shook Mitchell's hand again. 'I'll keep my ears up,' he said. Mitchell didn't get up and he nodded at Boyd as he left. He then sipped at his coffee and he sat still and stared at the refrigerator door. From the other room Consuela clapped her hands to the gospel rhythm.

Boyd drove back to the office and when he walked in the door the dispatcher told him to call the sheriff. Boyd went to his desk and sat down and dialed. Yeah I went to see him. No I didn't cause I don't know where he is. His house and his dad's. Dad don't know either. Yeah it might mean something. I don't know. Yes sir, I'll keep on 'til I talk to him. He hung up the phone and he turned his chair around and looked out the window.

Across the street a teenager in an orange jumpsuit and chains was being put into the back of a van and being taken to a place where he would stay for a long time. He didn't like that Russell wasn't at home and wasn't at his dad's place. Didn't like that Mr. Gaines hadn't seen him. Didn't like that Larry was behind the corner waiting to jump out with guns blazing. He didn't like that back in high school all they had to do was play ball and drink tallboys in the summer nights and chase skirts and now they lived different lives, different from what any of them probably imagined. How could you imagine the complexities of what might come? The one thing Boyd did understand was that it was his job to catch the bad guys and he hoped like hell that Russell wasn't one of them.

33

HE WOKE WITH THE FIRST LIGHT of day, mosquito-bitten and barely able to stand straight from the few hours he had slept in the ridged bed of the truck. He walked around the campground, stretching his back and reaching toward the sky and twisting and trying to get himself right. The Volkswagen was gone and the old couple sat in the same chairs around the same circle of stones that they had been sitting around in the late hours of the night as if they had never moved. Russell waved to them and the elderly man raised his tin coffee cup in response. Maben and Annalee slept and he didn't wake them. He lit a cigarette and walked around. The air seemed smoky in the earliest light and he came upon a springfed creek no wider than a doorway and he knelt and stuck his hand into the cold, trickling water. The honeysuckle climbed into a thatch of pines and he smelled its sweetness and it caused him to lick his lips with a morning thirst. He cupped his hands and took a drink.

So. What if it is her? So what?

That's what he had been thinking all night. So what? I don't owe her anything. I don't owe Larry and Walt anything. I fucked up and I paid for it and that's that. The only person I still owe is the dead boy and I'll pay for that soon enough. It'll come for me like it comes for everybody. And when it comes I'll stand there and then I'll be judged again and I'll pay again if I still owe something. But I don't owe nobody down here. Nobody.

It was easy to think of the brothers in that way. Not so much Maben and the child. There was something about her. The way she looked, like she'd been picked up and put down time and time again and like she held on to the girl and shot a man because she couldn't take it anymore. At least that's what she had said and he found himself believing the story. Hoped it was true so that he wouldn't end up the dupe. But she had been shaky with the pistol, so shaky that he had been able to reach over and pick it from her hand like it was a straw. Didn't hold it like someone who wanted to shoot. He thought he understood the way she felt and no I don't owe her anything but goddamn it. She was right. They wouldn't believe her. They would take the child. She would end up in the same type of place that he had just left. She was right.

He had told her he could help her but he was wrong. He didn't see anything ahead that would be in her favor if that pistol was found. He didn't see anything ahead that would be in her favor if someone didn't hold out a hand to her and the child. He remembered himself in the first days and weeks of being put away, alone and scared and isolated and confused and waiting to be jumped on. He figured the look on his face was much like the look on her face now. By the time he stood up from the side of the creek and wiped his hands on his pants, he had resigned himself to the fact that he was going to play the fool and then he walked back toward the truck where he saw their heads in the window.

He tapped on the glass and opened the door. Each of them was sweaty on the side of the face that had been down. Annalee rubbed her eyes and said she had to go to the bathroom and she and Maben got out of the truck and walked into the woods. Russell sat down behind the wheel. The gas tank was close to full and would probably last until they could get back to McComb. All he had to do was get them rolling and if they wanted out they'd have to jump. He looked over at the man and woman and they had a fire going and the woman held a skillet. Russell walked over to them and said good morning and the old man tipped back the hat on his head. His neck was bumpy from a bad shave and he wore a long-sleeved shirt buttoned at the collar. The woman wore a sweatshirt and a hairnet held down her gray hair. She wore a work glove on the hand that held the skillet and she was cooking eggs over the fire.

'Smells good,' Russell said.

'I ain't got no money,' the old man said.

'We ain't got nothing,' the old woman said.

'I don't want nothing you got.'

'My wife can shoot.'

'Shoot what?'

'Anything. She don't miss.'

'If I wanted to do something to you don't you think I would've come over here in the middle of the night?'

'I was watching,' the old woman said.

'So was I,' he said.

'All I want is some food. For that little girl over there. She's gonna need something to eat before we start riding.'

'We ain't got enough,' the woman snapped. A loaf of bread and a tub of butter sat on an aluminum table next to their truck. Russell looked over at it. A pan of some kind of meat sat next to it and a band of flies buzzed around the pan. Paper towels and paper plates and a quart of beer.

'How about a few slices of that bread?' Russell asked.

'We ain't got enough,' she said again.

'You must be a kidnapper,' the old man said. 'That's what I told my wife last night. That must be a kidnapper. A woman and a girl and no food and no tent and no nothing. Kidnapping.'

'I'm not a kidnapper. I'm a man who wants a few pieces of buttered bread.'

'We ain't got enough.'

Russell took a five-dollar bill out of his back pocket and reached over to the table and set it down. Then he opened the loaf of bread and took out five pieces and he buttered them with a plastic knife while the woman stood at the fire yelling and pointing at Russell and then yelling and pointing at the old man to get up and do something but the old man didn't even turn around in his chair. Russell tore off a paper towel and wrapped the bread and then he told them that the meat smelled like shit and he walked back to the truck. Maben and Annalee were sitting in the cab again. Russell handed the buttered bread to Maben and she said what is that and he said breakfast. He cranked the truck and as they left the campground, the old woman shook a spatula and yelled at him in a gravelly, fading voice and Russell thought she might have a heart attack any second. The old man raised his tin coffee cup again and she smacked him in the back of the head.

At the interstate Russell turned south and Maben told him to let them out at the next town.

'I will,' Russell said. 'At the next town when I stop.'

'We need to get on.'

'I know you do.'

The child ate the bread and wiped the butter from the corners of her mouth on her shirt. She offered a slice to her mother and Maben took it. She offered a slice to Russell and he told her to eat it. At the next town Russell ignored the exit. And he did the same at the next and the next and Maben said I mean it. Stop.

'You might as well sit tight,' he said.

'I can't.'

'Yes you can.'

'No I can't.'

'You're gonna have to unless you want to drop and roll.'

Maben folded her arms like an unhappy child. Annalee asked if she could turn on the radio and Russell said yes. In an hour they were in Hattiesburg and he turned west on Highway 98 and in another hour they crossed the Pike County line.

'I can't believe this shit,' Maben said.

Russell didn't answer. He turned off the highway ten miles before town and took the back way to his dad's place. Tractors moved across fields leaving dusty trails and cows stood in ponds. A graveyard at the top of a hill amid mosscovered trees. A dead armadillo in the middle of the road. He came up the highway and turned right and in a quarter of a mile he turned into the driveway and the front end spun in the loose gravel. Maben didn't talk. Russell parked next to the house and the child pointed at the barn and said I thought barns were supposed to be red.

'Sit here a second,' Russell said, getting out and taking the keys with him. He walked around the house and found his father and Consuela sitting outside on the back porch eating tomato and bacon sandwiches.

'You want one?' Mitchell asked.

'I gotta talk to you.'

Mitchell put his sandwich down on the plate as if that would help him hear better. Then Russell said, 'I need the barn. My room. Consuela's room.'

'For you?'

'Not for me and I only need to hear yes or no. That's all. I can explain it later and if you don't like it I can do something else but right now I need yes or no.'

Mitchell looked at Consuela. It wasn't her room anymore.

'Boyd Wilson find you? He was out here looking this morning. You into something I need to know about?'

'I'll tell you one day but not today. Yes or no,' Russell said. 'That's all I want to hear.'

'Whatever you got to do,' Mitchell said.

Russell nodded and he walked back to the truck and he waved for them to get out.

'Bring your bag,' he said to Maben and she draped the duffel bag over her shoulder. She helped Annalee down from the truck and she held the child's hand as they walked toward Russell and he told them to follow him. They walked past the house and out across the backyard and to the barn. At the back of the barn was a door and then a flight of steps and at the top of the steps was one large room. In the room there was a double bed and a love seat and other odd bits of furniture. There was a refrigerator and a small cabinet and countertop and a sink. The floors were wide wooden planks and the ceiling was exposed and a ceiling fan hung in the middle of the room from a two-by-four that had been nailed across the beams. The room was hot and steamy and Russell began to sweat just standing there. He walked across the room and turned on the air conditioner that sat in the window and then he pulled the string on the ceiling fan. He pointed at a door in the corner and said that's the bathroom. There was nothing in the room that belonged to Consuela and he wondered if she had ever been out there at all.

'It's hot,' Annalee said.

'I'll have to get you some towels and sheets,' Russell said. 'It'll cool off in a little while.'

'I ain't staying here,' Maben said.

'Why not?'

She didn't have an answer.

'I'll be right back,' he said and he went down the stairs and to the house and Consuela met him halfway across the yard with a stack of towels and sheets and a bar of soap and shampoo. His dad remained in his chair on the porch and he watched Russell without expression. Russell returned to the room and the child was standing with her back against the air conditioner and it blew her hair across her face. Maben was sitting on the edge of the bed taking the clothes from the duffel bag and then she took out the pistol and she placed it on the mattress. Russell set the things on the bed next to her and he asked them if they wanted something to eat.

'I do,' the child said.

'I guess I do, too,' Maben said.

Russell returned to the house and he asked his father what they had to eat. Mitchell asked Consuela to make a plate of sandwiches and she went inside to the kitchen. Russell sat down on the porch steps and wiped the sweat from his forehead. He waited for what was coming but he didn't have to wait long as his father got up and walked into the yard and stood in front of him and said I suppose you're planning to tell me just what in God's name is going on.

34

'To tell you the God's honest truth, I don't know what the hell is going on,' Russell said. He rubbed the back of his neck. Looked out toward the barn and the pond. Shook his head. 'Ever since I got off that bus feels like there's something in the air around here. Something hanging around. Can't see it. But I can feel it.'

Russell reached down and picked the tip of a grass blade and he tossed it aside. 'You remember when I used to bring home a dog every now and then?'

'Them old strays. I remember. Your momma hated that.'

'Why'd she hate it?'

'She hated it cause they always run off after some days and you'd get all pissed off about it.'

'That's my point. The one I'm about to make. Those two out there are like that. Like those strays. Don't matter what hell they've been through. Don't matter how hungry. Give them food and a soft bed and they still got to run off sooner or later. That's what she's gonna do so just let them stay out there and I guarantee you she'll be gone one morning dragging that girl with her. And that's why I'm not gonna tell you nothing more other than I found them and they need somewhere and you know why they can't stay at the house with me.'

Mitchell stepped back onto the porch and sat down again. Consuela came out of the kitchen with a tray of ham and cheese sandwiches and crackers and Cokes. She walked out to the barn and disappeared up the stairs. In a minute she came out and returned to the house and passed the men as if they weren't there. Russell thought of telling his father who the woman was but decided to keep it to himself. Then he stood up and went across the yard and up the stairs and he found them sitting on the bed together. Shoes off, mouths chewing.

'When you get done with that, I want you to wrap that thing up and come with me. Annalee can go in the house and watch TV.'

Maben nodded. Swallowed hard from a full mouth. Russell looked around the room. He and his dad had put it together when he turned seventeen against his mother's wishes. His own place out of the house but within reach. He thought of the girls he had snuck across the backyard in the middle of the night. He thought of shooting at deer across the pasture from the window. He thought of sitting and drinking with his buddies until they passed out. He thought of how he had joked with Sarah that this would be where they would live once they were married and no it wasn't Sarah and no he wasn't married but he had accidentally been right as here he was with a woman and a child to try to take care of. At least for now. Annalee coughed and the sound shook him free and he again told Maben to come down when she was done. With that, he said and pointed. She stopped chewing and said I know it's a gun and she knows it's a gun so why don't you call it a gun?

35

WHEN THE SUNDAY NEWSPAPER CAME OUT with the details it was all anyone could talk about. Deputy murdered sometime in the middle of Thursday night. With his own pistol, which was not at the scene. No witnesses. No trace of evidence. No idea what he was doing where they found him. Nothing certain but that he was dead. They talked about it over coffee and they talked about it in the grocery store aisles and they talked about it in the waiting room in the hospital and they talked about it while they pumped gasoline. During the morning church services the Baptists and the Methodists and the Catholics and the Episcopalians and everyone in between had moments of silence. Said prayers for the fallen deputy. Prayed for his soul. Prayed for his family. Prayed for justice and for mercy on the wandering evil that was capable of such godless violence. Women in dresses cried that there were such monsters alive in their community and men in suits shook their heads that there seemed to be no clue as to what had actually happened. When the amens were said across the town and the congregations poured out and onto the front steps some people said that they were amazed that something like this could happen around here. And some people said they weren't.

36

ANNALEE FOLLOWED CONSUELA INTO THE HOUSE and Russell and Maben got in the truck with Maben carrying the pistol wrapped in a pair of socks. Mitchell stood in the yard and watched them drive away but he didn't wave back when Russell waved to him.

'He don't want us out here either,' Maben said when they hit the highway.

'He don't care.'

'Looks like he does.'

'He doesn't.'

She held the pistol between her legs and she kept her legs closed. Russell drove through town and passed over the interstate and in a few miles he left the highway and turned onto a road that was something between asphalt and gravel. The windows were down and Maben's hair was wild in the wind and Russell reached behind the seat and grabbed a Peterbilt cap and handed it to her. She put it on and pushed her hair behind her ears. Away from town and away from other cars she took the pistol from underneath her legs and set it on the seat between them. At a stop sign he looked over the weeds growing headhigh along the fence line on each side of the road and turned left. Maben rode along without talking, tapping her fingers on her leg to the song in her head. There were more twists and turns and then the road wasn't much more than a sidewalk and the trees thickened and reached over the road to one another and it seemed as if they had driven into a tunnel. The air was cooler beneath the trees and flowery vines of something purple grew thick in the shade and ran along with the road. The road turned left into a wide and looping curve and then it straightened and went uphill and Russell slowed down as he got closer to the top of the hill. Maben sat up and leaned toward the dashboard. When the truck reached the top Russell stopped. At the bottom of the hill sat Walker's Bridge.

The truck idled roughly. An afternoon breeze gave a rustle through the trees. She stared. Russell stared. Waited to see if she would say something.

She pushed back the bill of the cap. Her lips parted.

But she didn't say anything.

He eased on. Rolled down the hill. Stopped in the middle of the bridge. Metal rails had replaced the rotted wooden rails. Initials and hearts and a smiley face and a pentagram had been spray-painted on the rails.

'You need to get rid of that thing,' he said.

She looked out her window and across the creek. Sunlight glared across the wet rocks and ripples. The banks were overgrown with heavy green brush and on down a little ways a tree had fallen across.

'I'm not throwing it out here,' she said. A tremble in her voice.

He got out of the truck and walked around to her side and opened the door. Get on out he said and he turned to look at the water. She took off the cap and set it on the seat. Dropped her head and when she raised it she wiped her eyes. And then she stepped onto the bridge. They stood at the rail, looking down into the water and across into the woods. The hole created by the crashing vehicles had long since been filled in with new growth.

'What made you think to come out here?' she asked.

'Nothing,' he said.

She looked him up and down.

'Am I supposed to know you?'

Russell pointed toward the hilltop and said a few years back or more than a few years back I didn't have nothing else to do one night so I started riding around. Ended up drinking some. Met this girl in town and we messed around for a little while and that got me to feeling even better. So after I dropped her off at her car I kept on riding and kept on drinking. By myself. Killing a night. That was all. Somehow though I ended up pretty drunk. Ended up coming over that hill. Ended up in a bad wreck right here.

He pushed his hands into his pockets.

'You're lying,' she said.

'No.'

'There ain't no way.'

'That's what I been telling myself since I found you.'

'You didn't find me. I found you.'

She turned her back to the water and sat down on the rail. 'Jesus. I wish I knew what made the world turn like it does. Spins strange sometimes. Spins stranger for some people anyhow.'

He picked up a rock and tossed it into the creek.

'I thought you was in jail,' she said.

'I was. Got home about three days ago. Right on time.'

'How long has it been?'

'Long time. Eleven years.'

'Russell. Is that right?'

'That's right.'

She stood up from the rail and walked a lap around the truck. When she came back around she said I hated your guts. Used to pray every night that somebody was beating the shit out of you or holding you down. Used to pray for that. Dear God I'd say and then the rest with the bad words and everything. Bet He couldn't wait every night to hear that one. She looked back across the water and into the woods. Then I got tired of it. Just like that. Woke up one morning and I was too tired to hate you anymore. Too tired to hate what happened. By then I was a long ways from home and running on fumes and you didn't matter no more.

'I'm sorry,' he said.

'Don't. Don't start that up. Don't come out here with that. That was eleven years ago. That shit don't matter no more. Ain't you listening?' She bent over and grabbed her hair with both hands. Mumbled and grunted. Raised up and pressed the heels of her hands into her eyes.

'I never said it then so I thought I'd say it now.'

'Why? Don't change nothing,' she said and she slapped her hands by her sides. 'Might make you feel better but it don't change nothing.'

'Don't really make me feel better.'

'Then shut the hell up.'

She took another lap. Let it go let it go she repeated as she walked. Rubbed her temples with her index fingers. She then stood in front of him. Took two deep breaths and nodded toward the creek.

'I ain't throwing that gun in there.'

'You got to throw it somewhere. In about the next fifteen minutes. I'm not riding around with it anymore.'

'Shit. Guess not. You're guilty as I am right now.'

'Not right. You pointed it at me and told me to drive. I did. Otherwise I ain't seen it. Your word on mine.'

'That should make for some fine damn discussion seeing how upstanding we both are.'

'Just throw it.'

'And then what? Then you take me home. Wanna make it all right. Wanna pay for it all in one big splash.'

'I already paid for it. You can look at this however you want. The way I see it once that gun is gone that's it. That's it between you and what you did and between you and me and whatever I'm doing standing here. Thing is, I've ended up believing everything you said and if it's true then I'm glad you shot that asshole. I don't even know who he was but I can see him in my head. If you're lying then I'm the dumbass. But many times I wish I would've had a gun to shoot whoever had ahold of me. Been many times God heard what you were praying and He damn sure answered. So you can believe He's up there.'

'He heard me then. Not no other times.'

'I don't care about when He heard you and when He didn't. It didn't exactly work out for nobody.'

Maben sat down in the road. 'No. It didn't,' she said. 'But I don't feel right throwing the gun here. It don't work that way. Seems like something is going to creep up. And that creek ain't deep enough. You knew that.'

He nodded.

'Then why'd you bring me out here?' she asked.

But he didn't bother to answer and she didn't ask again.

She leaned back her head and looked toward the pale and empty sky. She had wanted somebody to blame for a long time and now here he was but she couldn't do it. Seemed like everything had paused. Like they would get in the truck and drive back into something different from what was waiting.

'Answer me something,' he said. 'I always wondered why you weren't in the truck with that boy. Why it was only him.'

With the question she stood. Russell sat on the bridge rail and waited to see if she would answer.

She could see him there in the truck bed. Lying flat like she had asked him to. Lying still like she had asked him to. Young and strong and darkskinned from long summer days. She could see him there waiting for her. Waiting like she had asked him to once they had begun to feel one another under the full moon. Wait, she had said. Lay down. Sure it was what she wanted to do but unsure about the best way to go about it. She had told him to lay down and don't look. Maben looked toward the grass at the end of the bridge. Where she had stood and taken off her shorts and T-shirt and bra and flip-flops and set them in a pile on the ground. Certain that if she were to go back to him this way she wouldn't turn back. That she would do what she wanted to do and what he wanted to do. She stared at that spot at the end of the bridge where she had taken off her clothes, remembering how she had looked at herself in the moonlight and assured herself in the moonlight. Naked and young and that beautiful boy lying in the back of the truck waiting for her. She could see herself standing there and she wanted to see herself coming toward the truck. Wanted to see herself climb on top of the boy. Wanted to see the boy's hands on her hips and across her back and shoulders and down her legs. Wanted to see what they were going to do but it had all ended with her standing naked in that spot, interrupted by the hum of an approaching car and the glow of headlights that had appeared over the hill, headlights that came on fast and exposed themselves in two bright bursts before she had time to call out to Jason. Before she had time to pick up her clothes and the car had never slowed down. What she saw now as she stared at the spot at the edge of the bridge was a young girl terrified and ducking with the roar of the crash and she looked back across to the other side of the bridge where his suntanned body disappeared into the dark.

'Maben?' Russell asked.

'I just wasn't in it,' she said. Her eyes still in the trees. 'That's all. Don't remember why.'

He wanted to push her. To get the real answer. But he

didn't. He wanted to make a crack about what the hell was she doing with one of them Tisdale boys anyway? But he didn't. Recognized in her look that she had said all that she was able to say. She then opened the truck door and sat down and she told him to take her to the lake. The gun will sink in the lake.

He put the truck in gear and they drove on. The fields were showing signs of drying out, being fed with only scattered rain instead of a soaking storm. A kid sat on a four-wheeler at the edge of the road and checked the mailbox though it was Sunday. More graffiti on bridge rails and on the road itself. Once they were back in town he told Maben to stick the gun under the seat and he stopped to use a pay phone at a gas station. He called his father and told him they would be back after dark. Feed Annalee. Mitchell said she wanted to try to fish if that was all right. He hung up the phone and he went in and bought beer and then they spent the afternoon riding and drinking, riding along roads and passing houses that triggered memories for each of them, things they thought they had forgotten. When they got hungry they bought chicken in a drive-through. Russell bought more beer and they rode around until it finally got dark and then they drove on out to the lake.

He had not set out for redemption. Not once thought about it in the years and months and weeks and days that led up to the moment he would be free. But he seemed to have stumbled upon its possibility in the thin cheeks of the woman and the sunburned scalp of the child and he kept saying and kept thinking that he had paid and paid some more and he was free and clear but there was something uncomfortable in his gut now that made that sentiment feel less and less like a conclusion. As they rode he set his mind on what he knew. His mother was gone and Sarah was gone. His dad had a different life and the town had taken on a different life. He was sitting next to someone he had no business sitting next to but here they were. He only thought about the things that he knew. The concrete. What he could put his hands on. And the things that he could put his hands on needed someone to put out those hands. To hold out those hands and pull. He thought again about the preacher and how the conversation had only enhanced his confusion about the here and now and the later on but as they drove on and the day became the night he began to understand that his concern lay with right now. His concern was with the woman and the child and what they had gotten themselves into and his role in it all and what the hell else am I waiting on and it was then that any doubts he harbored about helping her were carried away with the evening wind coming in the rolled-down windows.

Do what you want to do and don't look back, he told himself. Like everybody else.

37

H E TOOK HER TO THE SPOT where he had parked and slept two nights before. They got out of the truck. Both a little drunk now. Behind the seat of the truck he found a rag. He slid the pistol from the sock and wiped it down. Then he wrapped and tied the pistol with the rag and it sat on the hood of the truck in a small knotted bundle. They milled around looking at the sky and listening to the water slap against the bank. Drinking. And when it was time to get rid of it he asked her to let him do it. Because I can throw it out farther than you. They couldn't see the splash but they heard it. Deep and certain. And she didn't know why but it was at that moment of the splash that she wanted to tell him about her life. To talk to him and tell him how one day she had left the girl sitting on a bare twin mattress in a back room in a falling down house somewhere on the outskirts of some nameless town. To get cigarettes or chocolate milk or something and how when she came back a man had wandered in from another room and was going for the girl, her small wrists held together with his one hand and with his other hand unbuckling and unzipping and going after this small, helpless thing. This small thing who had a paralyzed look on her face. Maben wanted to tell him how she dropped the brown bag holding whatever it was she thought she had

to fucking have and she climbed onto his back, clawing and
scratching at his eyes and trying to stab her fingers into his
brain, trying to bring blood, and then how he was able to spin
her and slam her against the wall and then she was going for
him again and he got her by the throat and slammed her again,
the air going out of her and the child screaming huddled in the
corner and how he had turned again toward the child while she
lay breathless. A groaning sound coming from her but no air.

He went again for the child but the rhythm of her breathing
came back as if God had put His mouth to hers and then she
stripped off her belt and jumped on his back again, the belt tight
around his neck and she held on as he swung her around and
pulled at her hair and then he was on his knees and then he was
out. A red face and a white liquid running down the corners of
his mouth and she grabbed the child and they were down the
street going who the hell knows where but they weren't there
anymore and they wouldn't be there when he woke up or if
he did. She didn't know why this was the memory that came
with the splash of the pistol into the lake. She didn't know why
this is what she almost told him about or why she wanted to
talk about such things. He turned and said I can tell you one
damn thing. They'll kill me before I go back to prison. Kill me.
You understand? And I'll do the same to keep from going. You
understand? She said yes and she understood. The dropdead
tone in his voice and she understood the look that she imagined
on his face that was hidden with the dark and she wanted to
tell him about her life but she let it go and instead she closed
her eyes and imagined herself floating down with the pistol.
Settling on a soft, muddy bottom. The cool at the bottom of the
lake holding her in a way that she had never been held before.

38

A T HIS FATHER'S PLACE THEY WENT in the back door. They
found the girl asleep on the couch half covered by a
blanket. Consuela was stretched out on the recliner with her
mouth open. The television was on but turned down low.
Mitchell had gone to bed. Russell reached down and put one
arm under the child's legs and the other under her neck and he
lifted her. Maben softly shook Consuela's arm to wake her and
then she pointed at Russell holding Annalee. Consuela nodded
and closed her eyes again. Maben turned off the television
with the remote and then she opened the door for Russell. He
stepped through with the child, careful not to knock her head,
and then Maben walked with him across the yard and to the
barn. They went up the stairs and Russell took the child to
the bed and laid her head on the pillow and she turned and
mumbled something but she never woke. Maben covered her
legs with the blanket and then when she turned around to
say something to Russell he was already out of the room and
heading down the stairs. From the window she watched him
walk to his truck. He paused when he was there and looked at
the barn and she stepped out of view. When she looked back
again he was heading down the driveway.

As he drove toward the house his body told him to lie down

and sleep. He turned onto his street and drove in front of the house. No lights on. Blue tarp still there. Nothing moving inside or out. Seemingly. He drove around the block and when he returned all appeared the same so he pulled under the carport and turned off the truck. Then he walked to the front door and he went inside and turned on lights as he moved from room to room. He moved hesitantly. Thought he was alone but couldn't let himself believe it fully.

Once he had turned on all the lights and checked behind every door and inside every closet he sat down on the sofa. Satisfied. He kicked off his boots and unbuckled his belt. He turned on the television and watched baseball highlights but the sleep came on him and he couldn't put it off any longer. He took off his socks and he walked into the bedroom and then he took off his shirt. He was unzipping his pants when he stopped. Thought for a second. Then he walked back out of the house and to the truck, where he lifted the seat and he grabbed the shotgun and then he went back inside and locked the door behind him. He left the light on in the kitchen and the living room and he closed his bedroom door. He set the shotgun on the floor, parallel with the edge of the bed. And then he turned off the bedroom light and there was plenty of light on the other side. Plenty enough to see footsteps if they were there.

Maben opened the curtains and the moonlight fell through the window. She paced back and forth across the room barefoot so not to wake Annalee. The red tip of her cigarette floated in the dark like a fairy.

She paused at the window and looked out across the quiet land and up into the starred sky. The chirping and croaking and a distant howl.

I gotta get the fuck out of here, she thought. And she paced again.

It was too much. The clean, air-conditioned room for them to sleep in. The Mexican woman bringing them food from a kitchen. The old man's way with Annalee and the worry drained from Annalee's face. The man who seemed to be doing whatever he could to help them for nothing in return. It wasn't the way she had been accustomed to doing things. Something for nothing. Not in her world. And in this still and hollow night she was deciding to beat it out of there before the tide shifted. No matter what they feed you and how sweet they smile and no matter how many times he sticks his neck out to help you it ain't gonna last and you know it. Don't sit here like a dumbass and wait for the bottom to fall out.

She turned from the window and walked across the room and grabbed a cigarette and lighter from the bedside table. She then walked out the door and down the steps. The dew wet her feet as she walked out into the yard and she smoked down her cigarette and tossed the butt. After she had lit the new one she bent down and picked up the butt and stabbed it out and stuck it in her pocket.

She tilted back her head and gazed at the vast night sky. The white moon and a panorama of stars and she found the Big Dipper and maybe the Little Dipper but there were so damn many tiny lights that the clusters ran together and seemed to wash out the constellations. It seemed to her almost false. Like the heavens were only pretending to be this striking and the curtain would be pulled back and unveil a deeper and dulled shade of black.

She turned and looked at the window of the room above the barn. Annalee was so clean. So fed. So asleep. Maben then looked around and there was the Virgin, standing tall and basking in the moonlight. She walked over to her.

There wasn't much she knew from the Bible but she knew about Mary because Maben had always wondered how she did it. Yes the angel came and explained it but Maben had gotten lost in enough of her own strange dreams to believe that Mary could have easily dismissed it. Woke up the next day and told her momma about the crazy shit that filled her head. An angel with great big wings and golden hair and the air of God came to me and told me that I'm about to be pregnant with a holy seed. And not just any holy seed but *the* holy seed. Crazy shit. But Mary had listened and believed and heard the whispers and saw them looking at her as her belly grew and Joseph hadn't asked her to marry him yet. And then Maben had wondered how the hell Joseph did it too. Mary told him I'm still a virgin and this child is not of another man but of God and the good and faithful and maybe naive Joseph said okay. Maybe he was naive or maybe he was something else that Maben knew she wasn't.

She stared up at the concrete statue and then she reached out and touched her hand to Mary's robe.

'It ain't that easy,' Maben whispered.

Maben then tossed her cigarette and she leaned into the statue. Mary's arms above Maben's head and Maben slowly wrapped her arms around the Virgin's waist and hugged. She closed her eyes and let her weight fall against the statue and in this brilliant and anxious night she halfway expected her own miracle. Halfway expected Mary's arms to return her embrace. And then to hear her voice rise above the sounds of the natural world and sing to her some beautiful lullaby that Maben had never heard before. A melodic, spiritual song that would seep into her soul and tenderly set it free.

39

ON MONDAY MORNING HE WAS AWAKENED by a knock on the door. He sat up straight in the bed as if startled from an anxious dream. The light came full in the windows and he could tell that he had slept well into the morning. He put on his shirt and jeans and he opened the bedroom door and walked toward the front door where the knocking continued. He reached through the broken window and peeked around the blue tarp and saw the sheriff's department cruiser parked in the driveway. He walked back into the bedroom and with his foot pushed the shotgun under the bed and then he unlocked the front door and Boyd was standing there.

'Hey there,' Boyd said.

Russell squinted at the sunshine. Moved his head around to stretch his neck and then he stepped back and told Boyd to come in. Boyd stepped into the living room and he walked around the sofa. Russell asked him if he wanted some coffee and he said no but Russell went into the kitchen to make some anyway. As he made the coffee he could hear Boyd walking around with lazy steps. He left the coffee to drip and when he walked back into the living room Boyd was looking at the *Playboy*.

'Shit,' Boyd said. 'Been a while since I looked at one of these. Is it me or have they got better?'

'Hard to tell,' Russell said.

He tossed the magazine onto the couch. 'Don't guess pretty girls are any prettier now than they used to be.'

Russell rubbed at his eyes. His neck. His forearms. He was sore all over. Felt like he could lie back down and sleep the rest of the day. He sat down on the couch and stretched out his legs and Boyd leaned against the wall.

'What is it?' Russell asked. 'You got a shitty poker face.'

Boyd laughed a little nervous laugh. 'I was just wondering where you been.'

'I been right here.'

'Not yesterday. Or Saturday.'

Russell shrugged. 'Wherever, Boyd. It's not a big place.'

'Your daddy tell you I went out there looking for you?'

'I got an idea, Boyd. We can play grabass for a while or you can tell me what you really want.'

Boyd moved over to the couch and sat on the other end. 'Thing is we got a dead man and we got only one thing to go on. I'm telling you what I've been told and not what I think and I probably ain't supposed to tell you that but I am. But when you rode up that night in the middle of nowhere and you had that shotgun in the truck we had to look at you. I know it's not the gun that did it but you're still riding around with a loaded twenty-gauge for whatever reason. A fact that I have kept to myself so your ass isn't on the first bus back to Parchman. So that's what I'm doing now. I told the sheriff I wanted to come over here. Not him. Told him I'd find out. Then it took me a day and a half to find you. I guess you can see why I got to ask you about some things. And one of them is where the hell you been?'

Russell sat still and listened. The coffee seemed to have stopped. So he got up and went into the kitchen and brought back two cups.

'If you got to know I met this woman down at the Armadillo. Caroline, I think. Don't know. I was pretty drunk. Ended up over at her house and you know the rest. It's been a while, Boyd. I wasn't in a rush to get out of there the next morning. And that's why my daddy didn't know where I was.'

'Hot damn. That didn't take long. I know boys down at the office who ain't got lucky in a couple of years.'

'Right place right time.'

'I guess it'd check out, huh?'

'Don't see why not.'

'Now what about the other night at the scene?'

'Like I told you then, I was riding around. Got nothing else to do. You know how it is. Go out riding and end up God knows where. I've been locked up for eleven years.'

'I know it.'

'And that's all. I don't have nothing else to give you. I hate y'all are so stuck.'

'Stuck ain't the word. If we had the pistol I'd swear he shot himself. But we got nothing. Only thing in the ballpark is some woman from the shelter downtown called the cops the other night about a woman staying there who had a gun with her and she took off with it. But we hear shit like that all the time. I don't even think the sheriff wrote down the woman's name. Might end up chasing after that one some, though. He don't want us to look bad but it's heading that way.'

'You still think he was doing something he shouldn't have been doing?'

'Considering there was no call and no reason for him to be out there and he's filled up with bullets from his own gun, I'd say yeah.'

'Everybody think that?'

'Mostly. Still, somebody did the shooting. Don't matter if he was screwing around or not. I don't guess you saw anything that night that might be worth mentioning. A car or motorbike or something.'

Russell shook his head. 'Wish I did.'

Boyd took a few quick sips of the coffee and then he set the mug on the floor. Russell leaned back on the sofa. Stared at the spot on the mantel where the picture of Sarah had been.

'What happened to your windows?' Boyd asked.

'Tornado.'

'Your dad told me the brothers been having a go at you.'

'I told you the same thing already.'

'How serious you think they are?'

Russell sat up. 'Don't know how serious they are together. But I think Larry is pretty serious on his own.'

'He's always been the crazy one. He went nuts on his wife a few times. Ex-wife now. Stupid shit. Knocked her around good with the kid in the house over next to nothing. Can't even see them no more, I don't think. Now he's married to some looker but word is she'll pass it around. She'd better be careful is all I know.'

'I'm not too worried about him.'

'I'd say riding around with a loaded twenty-gauge is a fair sign you are.'

'That's the reason I'm not worried. If I didn't have it and it wasn't loaded then I'd be worried.'

'I got you,' Boyd said and he stood up. 'I hated asking all this. You know that.'

'I know it.'

'And you know I believe every word you say.'

'I know it,' Russell said and he stood and they shook hands.

'It was good to see your daddy. And I was sorry about your momma.'

'Yeah.'

Boyd walked to the front door and let himself out and Russell stood in the window and watched him walk to the cruiser.

Boyd sat down behind the wheel and glanced at himself in the rearview mirror and ran his fingers across the top of his thin hair. Then he backed out and he was gone.

Russell stood in the window like a store mannequin. Maben and the child will have to leave, he thought. There's no way around it.

He walked back to the sofa and drank his coffee and when he was done he went into the kitchen for another cup. He poured it and stood at the kitchen window this time. Across the street a woman dragged a sprinkler into the front yard and she turned it on and then a small child just old enough to run came out from under the carport wearing only a diaper. He walked into the yard and when the water hit him he squealed and he ran away and then he kept running in and out of the water and kept on squealing and his mother laughed and laughed and laughed.

God only knows what might happen if they find her out at Dad's place, he thought. What she'll say to stay free. She's already killed one man when cornered and I'm not going back. Goddamn fingers are already pointing at me and I didn't even do nothing.

He poured the coffee down the drain and stood there watching the boy in the sprinkler and he knew that rough lives got rougher and he hated it for the girl and he hated it for Maben. And he hated that there wasn't going to be a happy ending and then he wondered how much longer he was going to have to keep that shotgun loaded.

He took a shower and then he drove out to his dad's place to see about them. He got out of the truck and as he walked around the house he saw them out by the pond. His father and Consuela and Annalee. No Maben. The Virgin Mary with the sun on her face. His father waved to him and he walked out. It seemed to be getting hotter and brighter every day and he had broken a sweat by the time he reached the pond. The three of them wore fishing caps to keep the glare from their eyes, the child's hat too big and hanging down across her eyebrows.

'Catching anything?' Russell asked.

Annalee peeped out from under the hat. 'I got two. One big one.'

'Nearly dragged her in,' Mitchell said.

'And you,' said Consuela.

'I was wondering when she was gonna say something,' Russell said.

'She can say a lot. She likes to listen mostly,' Mitchell answered.

'Where's your mom?' Russell asked.

'Up there.'

'Still sleeping, I reckon,' Mitchell said.

Russell left them and walked to the barn and up into the room. The room was cold after a full day of air-conditioning and Maben was asleep with a blanket pulled up to her chin. Russell sat down in a chair across the room and watched her. Trying to figure out what to say. How to say it. From outside he heard the child cheer at having caught another fish. A half hour passed and he sat and waited. Crossed and uncrossed his legs. Finally she stirred. First turning over and then sitting up and yawning and stretching and the blanket falling to her waist. She looked over and saw Russell sitting in the chair.

'I'm so tired,' she said.

'I thought you'd be.'

'Tired like I can't do no more. You ever been tired like that?'

'Sometimes.'

'Where's Annalee?'

'Out at the pond.'

'With who?'

'My dad and Consuela.'

She stretched again. Yawned again.

'Why didn't you tell me about the shelter?' he asked.

She licked at her lips. Dry and chapped. 'How you know about that?'

'A friend of mine. A deputy. Came to see me this morning.'

'For what?'

'I was riding around out there the night it happened. Figured they had to come and ask me about it. Told me they got nothing. But the shelter lady had called the cops about some woman with a gun who had run out of there.'

'They got nothing?'

'They got nothing. Right now anyhow. Said they might start looking you up if nothing else comes along. How much did you tell them at the shelter?'

'I told them Maben and then I made up a last name and whatever else they asked me.'

Russell scratched at his chin.

'What you think?' she asked.

'Probably about the same thing you do.'

He took a cigarette and lighter from his shirt pocket. She got up from the bed and he gave her one. She walked over to the window and looked at Annalee. She was standing on the bank, a catfish hopping on the end of her line and the old man trying to unhook it.

'Lot of fish out there?' Maben asked.

'A shitload.'

'I think she likes it.'

'It's a lot more fun when you catch something.'

She turned away from the window. 'When you want us to leave?'

'I don't want you to,' he said. 'But you're gonna have to.'

She walked back to the bed and sat down on the edge.

'I'll take you wherever you want,' he said.

She began to nod. Not only with her head but from the waist up she rocked back and forth. A steady rhythm. A faraway look in her eyes as if she were looking across to the other side of a canyon that was miles and miles away.

'I'm so tired,' she said again and she kept rocking. Her cigarette burned down and a long gray ash hung and waited to fall.

'They don't have nothing and they don't have a gun. You won't have to stay low forever. But I can't let you stay out here with them looking at me.' His words held no meaning for either of them. As if they hadn't been spoken. The ash from her cigarette fell onto the top of her bare foot and she stopped rocking. Lost her faraway stare. She looked at him. Wiped at her forehead with the palm of her hand. Began to smoke again. When she was done with the cigarette she rolled over and stubbed it out in an ashtray on the bedside table.

'I almost left out of here last night. Probably should have.'

'No, you probably shouldn't have. Don't start walking to nowhere with nothing. That's how you got here in the first place.'

'That's how I got damn near everywhere,' she said. 'I just didn't want to leave her but I don't know how much more she can take.'

'Don't you have anywhere you can go?'

She shook her head. 'If I did I'd be there already.'

Outside the child shrieked again.

'Maybe she could . . .' Maben started.

'Maybe she could,' Russell said.

'Let her rest some. Eat some.'

'If you think so.'

Maben then fell back on the bed. Held her hands up toward the ceiling. Traced the circling fan with her index fingers, making quick circles. Then she paused and let her arms fall out to the side and she made a T. 'I don't know how much more she can take,' she said again.

'She'll be fine. A week or two and you'll be back and maybe y'all can start over.'

'I heard that one before,' she said and she turned on her side. Closed her eyes.

Sleep as long as you want, he told her. He left and she pulled the blanket over her and she closed her eyes and she listened to the sound of the child's voice every few minutes whenever she reeled in another fish. The voice seemed to leap across the quiet country and it was the sound of happiness and as she listened to it Maben wasn't sure that it could be the voice of something that belonged to her.

40

RUSSELL WALKED OUT TO THE POND. Mitchell was unhooking a catfish from Annalee's line and her eyes danced with the jerks of the struggling fish. Mitchell pried it free and dropped the fish into a cooler where several more catfish flopped and sucked their last breaths. Consuela stood on the other side of the pond with her own pole and her line was straight and still.

'You're gonna catch them all if you don't slow up,' Russell said to the girl. She smiled at him and asked if she could do it again. Mitchell said sure but then picked up a cardboard box from the ground and opened it and saw they were out of worms.

'We gotta get some more bait. Wanna ride to town?' he asked her.

'Yeah,' she said and she handed him the cane pole.

'Run up there and wash your hands off with the hose and head on to my truck. Meet you there,' Mitchell said and he set the pole and empty bait box on top of the cooler.

Maybe that's not such a good idea, Russell wanted to say. She can't be seen with you. With us. But that would mean letting Mitchell in and he didn't want to do that. So he said I'll ride with you.

'Good,' his father answered and he slapped his son's arm. Then he turned and yelled across the pond to Consuela. Voy a la tienda.

Russell looked at him sideways and said I bet you think you're pretty damn smart and the two men walked together toward the house. Annalee held the hose and sprayed one hand and then she swapped hands and did the same. She turned off the nozzle and ran across the yard to Mitchell's pickup and climbed in without waiting. Mitchell stopped at the hose and got a drink and then they got in the truck with Annalee sitting between them on the bench seat and ready for a ride.

Boyd walked into the sheriff's department just as Gina was yelling at Harvey Dennis to put out that damn cigar. Smells like ass and you ain't supposed to smoke in here.

'Shut the hell up,' the sheriff yelled back.

Boyd stopped at her desk as she spun around in her chair, a feisty little woman with glasses on her head and a small mouth seemingly stuck in the smirk she had worn every day of her twenty-five years at the department. 'Not again,' Boyd said.

'You can tell when the shit hits the fan around here cause he starts puffing on them things,' she said and she opened a desk drawer and pulled out a can of air freshener. She sprayed a circle around her desk as if to form some sort of meadow-scented force field.

'I'm guessing I can go on in,' Boyd said.

'I'm guessing you can.'

The small office building was square and built for function with linoleum floors and cinderblock walls and industrial lighting. Every wall was painted the same shade of vanilla and metal file cabinets lined the hallways and most of them needed a hammer or at least a screwdriver to get into. Harvey's door was open. Boyd tapped his knuckles on the wooden frame.

'Got a minute?'

The sheriff was sitting with his feet propped on the desk and a cigar between his fingers. A cloud of smoke engulfed him.

His hair was thick and gray and combed in an arrow-straight part. 'You can have as many minutes as you want if you can fill them up with something I wanna hear. But I'm going to say you're about to tell me Russell Gaines didn't do a damn thing and don't know a damn thing.'

Boyd walked into the office and sat down in a chair across from Harvey's desk. He started to cross his legs but he was too big for the chair and they wouldn't cross so he slouched instead.

'This air freshener don't do nothing,' Gina griped.

'Go to lunch,' Harvey called to her.

'It's ten thirty.'

'Then go to brunch. Go somewhere. Leave me alone,' he said and he brought the cigar to his mouth and puffed again. He blew the smoke straight up and then said by God she's bound to retire one day.

'I ain't deaf,' she yelled and they heard her desk drawer and then the office door slam.

'Hallelujah,' Harvey said. 'So I'm right. You got no news.'

'No news,' Boyd said. 'Not that I wanted any from Russell anyhow.'

'I bet Mitchell Gaines is cussing my ass right about now but we ain't exactly dripping with leads. I know it ain't in Russell to do something like that but you never know how a fellow comes out of prison. Sometimes for the better and sometimes for the worse.'

'Sometimes the same.'

'Not the same. God, it don't seem like it's been that long since he killed that Tisdale boy. I remember it, though. Russell's damn neck was split wide open and both those vehicles were twisted up like tin foil. I wanted to puke when that boy was dead cause I knew what was coming for Russell. Especially when I found that empty whiskey bottle up under his seat. I wanted to die riding out there and waking up Mitchell and telling him what happened.'

The phone rang and Harvey looked at it. 'I bet you it's that peckerhead from the newspaper. He's called about twenty times already and he can't figure out why the sheriff's department don't have nothing to say. We don't got nothing to say cause there ain't shit to say and when there is he'll be the last to know anyway. Little son of a bitch.'

They both stared at the phone until it stopped ringing and then the sheriff smoked again.

'Did we find out anything about that woman at the shelter?' Boyd asked.

'I sent Watkins over there. Got a name but it brought up next to nothing.'

'What was it?'

Harvey moved around a couple of papers on his deck. He picked up a sticky note and read it. 'Maben. Maben Jones.'

'What?' Boyd asked. He sat up a little in the chair.

'Maben Jones.'

Boyd rolled his eyes up at the flickering fluorescent light.

'Ring a bell?' the sheriff asked.

'I'm thinking that was the name of the girl who was left standing the night of Russell's wreck. The girl out there with Jason Tisdale. The one who ran up the road and called it in.'

The sheriff took his feet down from the desk and took a long drag of the cigar and examined the sticky note that read maben jones. 'That's a helluva memory,' he said.

'What happened when you checked it?'

'Nothing. Apparently there's no such thing as a Maben Jones. Jones part could be made up.'

'Could be,' Boyd said. 'Ain't many Mabens.'

Harvey blew out a stream of smoke and turned in the chair and bent over and let out a gruff cough.

'You ain't supposed to smoke that in here.'

The sheriff raised up. 'Put on a khaki skirt and cop the

attitude of a rattlesnake and I got a secretary's job ready for you.'

Boyd waved at the smoke cloud. 'What now?'

'Why don't you ride back over to the shelter and talk to them? See what she looked like. Any tattoos or anything. If she had a car and what kind was it and whatever else.'

'All right,' Boyd said and he stood up and walked around behind his chair. He paused and looked around the sheriff's office. Framed newspaper clippings and certificates of duty and pictures of grandchildren were hung without pattern. A hat rack stood in the corner and held Harvey's gun belt and a green John Deere hat and a full-length raincoat with pike county sheriff's department in block letters across the back.

'I swear to God I should just pack up and go home,' Harvey said. 'Hard to believe I gave up being a park ranger for this headache of a life.'

'How many times you gonna tell me that?'

'Gets harder to believe, though. Don't it? I don't even understand it myself. All I had to do all day was ride around and wave to men in boats across the dam. Watch kids play on the sandbanks and watch their mommas in their bathing suits with their pretty legs stretched out. Talk to campers, take a beer if offered. Traded all that for car wrecks and wife beaters and fools with guns. And now this crazy meth shit on top of all else. Teeth rotting and brain eating itself. Why the hell would I trade sunrises and sunsets for this?'

Boyd didn't answer. He then asked Harvey if he could have a cigar. 'Didn't I just tell you to go and do something?'

'Yeah, but I'm gonna need a couple of minutes to recover.'

The sheriff pulled open a drawer and took out a cigar and handed it to him across the desk. 'From what?'

Boyd reached down and took a lighter that was sitting on a pile of papers. 'You tell such gutwrenching sad stories I got to cope somehow. I swear to God I'm gonna bust out crying like a little girl next time you start talking about sunsets.'

The sheriff leaned back in his chair and crossed his heels on the edge of the desk and said I wish to God you'd go do something. Boyd flicked the lighter and huffed and puffed until the end of the cigar glowed orange and the fog in the room spread into all corners.

'Maben,' Harvey said.

'Yep.'

'Maybe I knew her momma.'

'She still around?'

'Nah. She wasn't no good. If it's the woman I'm thinking about.'

'This Maben had a kid with her,' Boyd said.

'And that is the beginning and the end of what we know?'

'That's it.'

'Then take your free cigar and go find out something else.'

41

BOYD HADN'T TOLD THE SHERIFF THE part about Russell and the woman at the Armadillo. Caroline. Wasn't much to go on but he figured it was worth riding by the bar and asking, deciding to wait until later to go visit the shelter. The Armadillo didn't open until around one so he lost a couple of hours riding the highways. He dragged a dead deer out of the middle of the road. Ate lunch at the truck stop so that he could look around. See if maybe they were missing something.

He finally drove downtown to the bar and he walked in. It was dark even in midday, lit only by a row of lights that shined on the liquor shelves behind the bar. He heard a clamor and he called out and then a man in a sleeveless shirt came through the swinging door behind the bar. He held a case of beer and he set it on top of one of the coolers and looked at the deputy and hoped he hadn't done anything wrong.

'How you doing?' Boyd asked and he sat down on a bar stool.

'Fine. You?'

'Not complaining. Not right now.'

The bartender's tattoos covered most of his arms and he wore a silver earring in each ear.

'Mind if I ask you a thing or two?' Boyd asked.

'Nope.'

'You don't happen to know a woman named Caroline. Comes in here from time to time.'

The bartender opened the case of beer. Pressed his lips together. Seemed to be thinking. Boyd knew the look. The look of someone trying to figure out how to answer.

'She's in no trouble,' he said. 'None at all. Nobody is.'

'Nobody?'

'Nobody mentioned so far. You know her or not?'

He slid open a cooler and took beers from the box and placed them in and the bottles tapped against one another in small clangs. 'I think I know who you're talking about,' he said.

'What's she look like?'

'Not too damn bad,' he said.

'Come on. Gimme something.'

The bartender shrugged. 'Brown hair. Some freckles.'

'How old?'

'Depends on the light.'

'Ballpark.'

'Thirtysomething. Fortysomething?'

'Don't know a last name, do you?'

'Caroline. Caroline.' He closed his eyes. Trying to see the name on the credit card. 'Caroline Pitts. Caroline Pitts,' he said and he opened his eyes. 'No. Potts. Caroline Potts.'

'Caroline Potts?'

'Think so.'

'All right. That's a big help,' Boyd said and he stood.

The bartender held a beer toward him. 'One for the road?'

'Good one,' Boyd said and he nodded and left.

Back in the cruiser he radioed the dispatcher and asked for an address on a Caroline Potts. He cranked the engine and turned up the air conditioner and waited. A minute later he had what he needed and he drove on toward the address of Caroline

Potts, telling himself that this was a waste of time. That Russell had told him the truth.

The four houses sat in a rectangle and they looked identical. White siding. Green shutters. Red front door. He looked around for number 12. A gray four-door was parked in front and he parked next to it. He walked along the skinny sidewalk that led to the front door and he knocked. He could hear a television. He waited and when no one came he knocked again and the sound of the television went down. Then the door opened and a woman stood there wearing a robe and a towel wrapped around her head. The hair that stuck out from under the towel was wet and there were beads of water on her neck. She seemed a little out of breath and she looked at the sheriff as if he were a strange animal.

'Sorry to bother you,' he said.

She tugged at the robe and tightened it across her chest and neck. 'What is it?' she asked.

'Are you Caroline Potts?'

'What's wrong?'

'Nothing's wrong. Are you Caroline?'

'Yes.'

'Caroline Potts?'

'I said yes.'

'I need to ask you a couple of questions if you got time. Real quick, I promise.'

She opened the door farther and moved back and he walked inside. She left the door open and she wiped at her neck. With her face freshly clean and free of disguise the freckles were more abundant across her nose and cheeks.

'What's this about?' she asked.

'I got two questions and I'm done. If you shoot me straight.'

'Fine.'

'First one is do you know a man named Russell Gaines? He claimed he met you downtown at the Armadillo.'

She nodded. 'Maybe.'

'Maybe what part?'

'I met a man named Russell. Couldn't tell you his last name.'

'You know what he looks like?'

'Tall, dark, and handsome. Like all of them down there, right? Had a soft little beard, though.'

'That's plenty,' he said. 'Part two. Did he spend the night here with you?'

She gave a cross look. 'Without modesty I say yes. But he didn't stay all night. Got up and left. Can you arrest him for that?'

'If I could arrest people for that I'd stay pretty damn busy,' Boyd said and he tried to imagine what was behind the robe.

'If you ever start I got a few more names for you. Anything else?'

'No. Don't guess there is,' he said and he stepped through the doorway. She was about to close the door but then he turned around and he reached out and stopped the door with his hand. 'One more thing,' he said. 'What night was that?'

She rolled her eyes. 'Thursday. Or maybe Friday.'

'Thursday or Friday?'

'That's right. Runs together sometimes.'

'I need you to think a little harder.'

She pursed her lips. Then she said Thursday.

'You're sure?'

'I told you yeah. Until he decided we were done and then he left out.'

'But not Saturday?'

'Do your ears need cleaning?'

'I don't guess you'd know what time he left out.'

'Maybe one. Maybe two. I told you it runs together,' she said and she pushed the door closed. Boyd backed away from the house. Sat for a moment on the hood of the cruiser. Scratched his head. Scratched his chin. Then he got in the cruiser and as he drove he thought about it all and one word kept jumping in and interrupting.

Maben.

He wished he would have never heard it.

Russell was clear of the shooting. But he was lying about where he said he was Saturday night. And a woman named Maben ended up at the shelter downtown. A pistol found in her things by the girl on the night shift. And then the woman named Maben snatching the pistol and grabbing her child and making a run for it.

Shit, he whispered to himself. He's got some good damn reason for not telling me the truth. He scratched at his neck and stared at the pink flamingos. If he wanted to hide something you know where he'd hide it, he thought. In the same place we hid beer and weed and girls. A pay phone we stole. The principal's dog we borrowed for a while. You don't want to go back out there but you ain't got a choice. He'd hide it in the room above the barn.

He drove out to Mitchell's place and turned onto the gravel driveway. He saw Russell's Ford but Mitchell's truck was not there. He sat parked for a moment and watched for movement and didn't see any and so he drove on to the house. He parked next to the Ford and got out and walked to the back door and knocked.

'Mr. Gaines,' he called. He looked through the door's glass pane and studied the kitchen. The light was off and it was clean. No plates or cups on the table or on the counter or in the sink. Boyd knocked again and called again but nothing. He waited and listened for the sound of a television or a radio or anything but there was only silence.

He turned and walked into the yard. The sun was high and gave him a short shadow as he looked around. He noticed the cooler out by the pond and some rusted aluminum chairs on the back porch. A full ashtray on a table between the chairs. He walked around the side of the house and the yard was cut and trimmed and it was such a quiet place. He had forgotten how nice a quiet place could be.

Then he looked toward the barn. The tractor and riding mower parked underneath. Shovels and rakes hanging on nails and stacks of paint buckets and drop cloths and a pile of rolled extension cords. And standing tall out in front of the barn was a concrete statue.

'What the hell?' he said and he walked toward it. He stopped in front and thought she must have been an angel but there were no wings and she wore drab clothing, even for a concrete statue. Then he figured it out. You never know what's gonna end up where in this world, he thought. He shook his head and looked around again. Decided he didn't want to go up the stairs to that room. Not yet. But when he turned to walk back to the cruiser out of the corner of his eye he saw the curtain fall in the upstairs window. And for the first time he noticed the hum of the air-conditioning unit around on the other side of the room.

He reached to the radio on his belt and turned off the sound. The stairs to the room ran up the outside wall of the barn and he walked over and climbed, taking each step slowly and listening for movement in the room as he eased his way up. He knew he wasn't going to surprise whoever was in there but he remained patient with his steps and held his lips together tightly as he moved. When he reached the top of the stairs he unsnapped the holster and put his hand on his pistol. And then he touched the doorknob and turned it as if it might snap or break and the door made a click and he cracked it open.

He paused. Listened. Moved to open the door wide and a voice behind him yelled, 'Hey! Que tal?'

Boyd jumped and standing a few steps below him was Consuela. She was pointing a finger at him and screaming short phrases that he didn't understand but she was damn serious about whatever she was saying.

'Holy shit, you need a damn bell around your neck,' he said.

'Pare! No suba más!'

'Calm down.'

'Váyase de aquí! Ahora mismo!' She was waving her thick arms now and had moved a step closer and looked like she might tear him up if he didn't do what she wanted.

'All right, all right. Calm the hell down. I'm going.'

'Voy a llamar a la policía!'

'I am the damn police,' he said and he pointed at his badge. She shouted and waved and he came down the stairs and slid by her and she paused the animation long enough to let him get past and then she cranked it up again. She followed him down the stairs and stalked him across the yard as he walked quickly to the cruiser, looking over his shoulder every couple of steps to make sure she didn't hop on his back or worse.

'Eres un rata!' she yelled. 'Un rata!'

He hurried into the car and cranked it and quickly turned around. She marched toward him as he backed up and then when he pulled forward she stomped along the driveway, raising her arms and yelling in the trailing dust with a watchdog tenacity.

She chased him along the gravel road until he was onto the highway and out of sight and then she turned and waved at Maben, who was watching from the window.

42

AFTER THEY RETURNED WITH THE FRESH bait Russell left them to it and he got in his truck and headed to his house. He sat now on the front steps and held Sarah's ring in his fingertips. Held it up to the sun and watched the tiny spots of light dance inside the diamond. Then he stuck the ring back into the pocket where he had kept it since Sarah had given it back. Inside he took a beer from the refrigerator and he sat down on the sofa and stared at the blank television screen. He picked up the remote but before he had the chance to turn on the television a car pulled into the driveway. He stood and looked out the window and he saw Boyd walking toward the front door. Goddamn it, he said. Russell opened the door and then he sat again on the sofa and waited.

Boyd plopped down in a chair at the end of the sofa. Didn't say anything. Looked at the television. Looked at Russell. Russell didn't look at him. Sipped on his beer and waited for what was next.

'Rode out to your daddy's a little bit ago. That woman's quite the barracuda.'

'I don't know nothing about that.'

'Well. She is.'

'Good for Mitchell.'

'Yep.'

'That it?'

'No. It ain't. I talked to Caroline,' Boyd said. He leaned forward and dangled his hands between his knees.

Russell nodded. Remained fixed on the blank television.

'Said you was over there, all right.'

Russell picked up the remote from the sofa cushion and set it on his knee.

'Said it was Thursday night. Didn't say nothing about the night you told me. Said you left out in the middle of the night when you were there.'

'How else do you think I could ride up on your little accident?' Russell set his beer down on the floor between his feet. Turned and stared at Boyd, who stared back. He seemed to have become more serious. Less old buddy and more lawman.

'You're not saying the right things.'

'You come over here to arrest me, Boyd? That it?'

'I came over here to tell you what she said.'

'So. You told me.'

'And now I'm gonna ask you again. Where were you *Saturday* night?'

'Don't matter what I tell you. You got a big idea.'

Boyd shook his head. 'I got a wife and a family and a house. And when I get back to the office I'm gonna tell the sheriff what Caroline told me. What you told me. How it don't add up. That's what I do and that's what I've been doing and that's how it's gonna keep on being. Call it a big idea. Call it whatever. I'm trying to let you talk to me without talking to nobody else but you ain't making it easy.'

'I was here. Asleep.'

'No. We already been there.'

'I told you I was around. That means I finally had to lay down somewhere. Just because you didn't see me in my bed don't mean I wasn't in it.'

'Next morning you wasn't here.'

'Read the paper, Boyd. Paper said you don't have a gun. If you don't have a gun I might as well have been sitting on the hood of the cruiser when you got there.'

'There's ways of getting there.'

'Then take me down. Arrest me,' Russell said and he held out his wrists.

'I don't know why you got to make this hard.'

'I'm not making it hard. I'm home and I didn't do nothing and you and your buddies can move in here for all I care. Might as well blame it on Babe fucking Ruth if you're gonna blame it on me cause neither one of us did it.'

Boyd sat back and slapped his hands on his thighs. 'You remember that girl's name who was out there the night of the wreck?'

'What?'

'The girl who was out there with Larry's brother that night.'

'No, Boyd. I don't. I didn't get any love letters from her.'

Boyd propped his hands on his hips. He wanted to walk over to Russell and hit him on the side of the head but instead he said don't lie to me no more on his way out the door.

Russell waited until Boyd disappeared and then he got in the truck and drove downtown to the station. He bought a bus ticket that would take her as far north as Memphis if she wanted. No ticket for the child.

He left the station and he walked a few blocks to the café and sat down at the counter with his back to the tables. He stuck the bus ticket in his back pocket and reached over and took an ashtray from a couple of seats away and he lit a cigarette. A woman with glasses on the end of her nose came out of the kitchen and over to him and asked what he wanted. Without looking at the menu he asked for whatever the special was and some coffee. He smoked and drank his coffee and listened to the clatter of the kitchen coming from behind the swinging door. Merle Haggard played on a clock radio sitting next to the cash register. The café door opened, followed by the voices of children and a father calling for them to slow down before they knocked something over. It was the voices of boys and then the shrill of a girl and then a threat from the father and Russell turned and looked over his shoulder and saw the twins climbing into a booth and their smaller sister following them. Then Sarah sat down facing them in the booth and her husband took a high chair from a stack of high chairs against the wall and he put the little girl in it as she protested that she was big enough to sit with the boys. Russell tried not to look too long but he couldn't help it and before he could turn his head around Sarah looked over and noticed him there. Her eyes went from him down to the table and then over to the boys and her husband sat down on the seat beside her and again told the twins to settle down.

Russell dabbed out his cigarette and asked for a topper on his coffee.

There were few others in the café, so the noise of the family was easily the most notable sound and Russell sat with his shoulders hunched. Sipping and listening to them. Paying special attention when Sarah spoke. The tone she used with the boys more direct than the tone she used with the small girl but everything she said with the special sound of the voice of a mother. Her husband did most of the correcting. Sit up straight. Stop touching him when he says stop it. Don't put your finger in there. Sarah asked the boys what they wanted to eat and if they would share and are you sure you like that and she talked to the little girl about the colors she saw on the wall or what was the shape of the bottom of the salt shaker?

It seemed as though his food would never come and when it finally did he ate with urgency and the mashed potatoes and butter beans and cornbread and chicken strips disappeared so quickly that the waitress asked him if he had dumped his plate in the garbage when she wasn't looking.

As he finished the family's food arrived and that lowered the energy level of the table as the boys paused to eat and the little girl paused to eat and their dad paused to eat but Sarah only paused and moved the food around on her plate with the tip of her fork. Her husband stopped chewing and asked her if she felt all right and she nodded. Said I'm fine. Russell turned on his bar stool and faced them, holding his coffee cup with both hands.

Decent looking guy, he thought. About what I expected.

She said she had to go to the bathroom and she nudged him with her elbow and he scooted off the seat and let her out. She moved between the tables, turning toward Russell one instant and in the next turning away and then she moved into the small hallway at the back of the café where the restrooms were located. Russell looked back at her husband and he had paid no attention to the notice Russell was giving his wife as one of the boys was trying to stick a french fry into the other boy's ear.

So Russell set down his coffee cup and walked to the bathroom. The door to the men's room was on the left and the door to the women's room was on the right and he turned to make sure he was out of view of her husband and everyone else and he quickly opened the door to the women's room and stepped inside and locked it behind him. She was leaning over the sink washing her face and she looked up and saw him in the mirror and she was surprised and not surprised. She took a paper towel from the dispenser and wiped her hands and face and then she turned and faced him. Barely a step separating them in the small space. And then they began to whisper.

'You're in the wrong one,' she said.

'Forgot how to read.'

'Didn't forget how to chase.'

'Don't know if I'm chasing or running away.'

This seemed to hurt her and she looked down.

'It was a joke,' he said.

'I know.'

'I have to tell you something.'

She looked back up at him. Inched closer. He put his hand on her arm and held it lightly as if it were something fragile.

'If something else happens,' he said whispering lower. He squeezed her arm then. Looked at the top of her head as he kept on. 'If something else happens I want you to know that I didn't do anything wrong. A bunch of people might think it after where I've been. But just know.'

She touched his chin and brought his eyes down to hers. 'What are you talking about?'

'That's all.'

'Stay here.'

'What?'

'Stay here. Can we stay here with the door locked? Let everybody go home and turn out the lights and lock the doors? Stay here with me.'

'I'm not the one who can't, Sarah.'

'Stay. We'll stay here,' she said and she put her arms around his waist and her mouth was close to his but she paused there. He felt her breath on his lips as she whispered. Stay. Stay.

'Tomorrow is here,' he said.

'I know. It came so fast. I didn't know it would come so fast.'

'It came slow,' he said. 'It came so slow. Slower than anything.'

'I need it back, Russell.' She leaned her head against him. 'I need it back.'

'Need what back?' he asked and he wanted her to say it. Wanted her to explain and wanted her to say I need you back and I need us back and the years back and there has to be a way there has to be a way. I need it all back. All of it. He waited for her to say it. Had always waited for her to say it and he hoped it would come out the way he had imagined it so many times as he stood in the yard or lay on the thin and musty mattress or as he forced down food he couldn't stand to force down any longer. He had imagined it so many times even after she stopped coming and even after he had gotten the last letter and even though he had known that she led another life. He waited for her to say it and he felt the impulse of hope.

'Need what back?' he asked again. His hand now underneath her hair and across her neck.

She leaned her head off him and looked up. 'The ring. Can I have it back? I just want it back.'

After she said it he began to hear everything again. Everything that had been blocked out by their whispers and her body close to him and the swarm of illusions that had joined them in the small space. He heard the voices of the husband and the twins and the sliding of chairs and the clang of silverware being dropped and the opening and closing of the men's room door on the other side of the hallway. He moved his hand from her neck and touched his fingers to the outside of the front pocket of his jeans. Felt it there. Remembered what he had planned for it and weighed those plans against the voice that had asked for it. Against the voice and the one with the voice and where they had been together and how she smelled against him and what was waiting for her on the other side of the door. He weighed what he had planned for the ring against the moment and then he weighed it against more than the moment. Against tomorrow and the next day and the day after and there was Maben with her shallow cheeks and her thin hands and there was Annalee with her pink forehead and eyes of wonder and there they both were, drifting along on the edge of nothingness. He felt it in his pocket. Realized the possibilities of the ring. Realized that she had not said what he had imagined her saying and realized that she never would. Even if she wanted to.

'I don't have it anymore,' he said. And he eased back away from her and her arms fell at her side.

He could see in her eyes that she didn't believe him but she didn't ask again and she didn't accuse. There was a shriek from the smallest child and Sarah snapped to as if she had been released from a spell. She turned from Russell and took another paper towel and dabbed at her eyes. Dabbed at her nose. She breathed fragmented breaths and then she turned to him again. Managed to pull it together. And then she touched her hand to his chest and she unlocked the door and stepped out.

He locked the door again. Leaned on the sink with his back to the mirror. He hoped that no one would knock on the door and they didn't as he listened and waited until the family was gone. And when they were gone he came out of the bathroom and paid his check and he walked out of the café.

He walked on down the street to a pawn shop and he showed them the ring and he got about a third of what he remembered paying for it and then he walked a couple of blocks to the Armadillo and he sat down and asked for a beer. When he was done he drove back to his house and he put the money from the ring between two plates in the kitchen cabinet and then he drove out to his dad's place. Maben remained sleeping and the rest of them remained fishing though there was not much light left. He sat down on the back porch and lit a cigarette and looked across the place. Wishing for rain. Wishing for something. Trying to believe there'd be an end.

43

He stood in the middle of the road at the precise spot where only four days ago they had found Clint lying facedown in front of his cruiser in a maroon pool of his own blood. Boyd's hands rested on his gun belt as he looked down at the spot and then he looked up and down the road. Across the fields. Into the trees.

Nothing. Which is exactly what he had gotten from the woman at the shelter about Maben. A skinny white girl with a little kid. A girl. But hell we get those in and out of here regularly.

His stomach growled and he patted his belly and shook his head at the girth that kept adding up while he kept swearing to take it off and then he looked at his badge. He unpinned the silver star and he held it out in front of him and examined it as if he were thinking about buying it. The sun was hidden behind a cloud and there was no shine on the badge and he held it to his mouth and breathed hot air onto it and rubbed it on his shirt. Then he pinned it back above his name tag on the left side of his chest and he let out a sigh.

It was a small department and Boyd had heard things. Couldn't help but hear things. Couldn't much tell what was fact and what was fiction and he figured most of it fell somewhere in between but he had heard a lot more about the new guy than he had wanted to hear. Heard he likes the liberty of the badge if you know what I mean. Heard he likes to cross down into Louisiana from time to time to some old house back in some old hills and give his money to halfdressed, halfdrunk women who give him what he's paid for. Heard he likes the late shifts because you can get away with more if you know what I mean. He'd heard it. Nothing that put an X on him for anything in particular. But enough to make Boyd stand there now and ask the question. What the hell was he doing out here in the middle of the night?

And then he applied the same question to Russell.

Boyd knelt down and picked up a pebble from the patchy pavement and he tossed it into the brush off the road. He wondered if their guy had asked for it. Wondered if this was the first or tenth or fiftieth time he'd ended up in this spot. This spot away from everything and everyone and nothing but the sky to see what you're doing.

Don't matter what he was doing, he thought. He's dead and he's one of us. It was hard to get past that one. Hard for Boyd not to imagine himself making the news in the same way someday. Deputy shot and killed. For apparently no good reason. Funeral to be held on Friday. Survived by a wife and two sons.

He walked back to his cruiser and thought about his boys. Thought about Lacey. He got in and called the office. Said he was done for the day. He then took a phone from his shirt pocket and he called Lacey and asked her if she was hungry and when she said yes he told her he'd swing by and pick her up. We're going out.

They lived a couple of streets from the high school and he drove by the football field. His boys were there doing the same summer workouts he had once dreaded. Boyd parked but kept it running and he looked for his boys in the wave of shirtless bodies going up and down and up and down the aluminum bleachers, the clanging of a hundred feet echoing like steel drums. The oldest one had to be there and the youngest one didn't. But he wouldn't be outdone and no coach was going to tell him not to work out if he wanted. Boyd picked them out. Their bodies and heads slick with sweat. All of them slick with sweat. A different set of bodies from the year before and the year before but yet somehow the same. Somehow the same boys running the same bleachers and sweating the same sweat and breathing the same heavy air. It was easy for Boyd to imagine himself running with them. Up and down and up and down until you didn't think you had anything left and then you went up and down again. Feeling the hurt and the exuberance and the strength and the weakness all in the same moment wound together like the spirals of a rope. He sat and watched and it could have been twenty years ago. It could have been twenty years from now. He rubbed at the muscles in his thighs. Could almost feel the burning. Wanted to get out and drop his gun belt and rip off his shirt and head across the field and go up and down and up and down with them. Wanted to but couldn't.

Damn it, Russell, he thought.

He drove on from the football field and he stopped in front of his house and Lacey was outside watering the flowers in her window boxes with the garden hose. Jesus H. if shit don't change, he thought as he looked at her. She turned and smiled and waved and it filled him in such a way that for a moment he felt born again and it made it more difficult to stop thinking about how it would read in the newspaper. Deputy shot and killed. For apparently no good reason. Survived by a wife and two sons.

44

THE WAY LARRY REMEMBERED IT THEY played ball just about every night of the week, so he figured he had a decent chance of seeing him. He hung around at a job site until around five and then he drove over to Buddy's and ate a shrimp poboy and had a few beers. He watched a couple of innings of the ball game and at the end of the fifth inning he left Buddy's and stopped by the liquor store and bought bourbon and then he stopped at a gas station and filled a cup with Coke and ice. He drove down to Kentwood with the stiff drink between his legs and the night falling earlier than usual because of a settling of clouds. He listened to Mötley Crüe as he drove. Turned up loud. The drink and the music getting him going in the direction he liked to go.

He turned off the interstate at the Kentwood exit. Check cashing offices and condemned houses lining the main road. Few signs of progress. Fewer signs of effort. He saw the lights of the ball fields shining over to the right and he drove toward them and turned into the parking lot that sat behind the outfield fence. He circled around the lot and when he couldn't find a space he hopped the curb and parked in the grass. He poured another shot into the cup and then he got out of the truck and he followed the walkway that led to the concession stand and bleachers.

Little brothers and little sisters ran up and down the walkway, faces pink and knees dirty and wet hair matted to their heads. Teenage girls stood along the fence lines with their shorts high and backs arched and they talked to the boys in the field or in the dugout. Mothers sat in the bleachers with magazines or with their hands folded on top of bare knees and fathers and grandfathers stood around the concession stand smoking cigarettes and griping at the umps. He checked the bleachers for Dana and when he didn't see her he sat down and sipped at his drink and tried to remember if his boy was thirteen or fourteen.

After an inning his drink was low and he hadn't seen the boy but he had noticed two more teams warming up behind the outfield fence. The scoreboard said it was the bottom of the sixth. So there was another chance. He figured he had time to mix a drink so he stopped at the concession stand and bought a Coke and then he walked back out to the truck. He poured the ballpark Coke into the big cup and then he poured in what was left of the bourbon and he made his way back toward the bleachers.

He drank. Not paying much attention to the game. Convinced that if his boy was there he would be in the next game. It was hot and the drink made it hotter and he began to look around at the mothers and the teenage girls. Couldn't decide which he liked better. And then he heard someone yell come on Cody. And then somebody else yelled let's go Cody. Start it off Cody. And he looked back to the field and a lanky kid waltzed toward the plate, the tip of the bat dragging on the ground until the third base coach yelled for him to get his ass in gear and the kid put the bat on his shoulder and he stepped into the batter's box.

He took a fastball right down the middle and the ump yelled strike. The voices said come on Cody. That's all right. Ready now. Get your pitch.

He took the second pitch right down the middle. Another

fastball. This time the ump didn't yell and only gave the strike sign.

'Swing the bat for Chrissake,' Larry whispered.

He swung awkwardly at a curve ball and when he walked back to the dugout he threw his bat against the fence and the kid on deck had to jump out of the way. The third base coach ran over to the dugout and let him hear about it and made him come out of the dugout and pick up the bat. Cody came out leisurely and picked up the bat and set it in the rack and then he walked into the dugout and sat down. The women in the stands shook their heads. Larry heard a man standing next to the bleachers say something about attitude.

Larry turned up his drink.

After the third out Cody's team trotted onto the field for the last inning and Larry watched him cross the pitcher's mound and end up at first base. She was right. He was getting tall. He tossed grounders to the infielders as the pitcher warmed up and when the pitcher was done he lobbed the ball toward the dugout, missing the coach who had made him pick up the bat by only a couple of feet.

Larry turned up his drink again. And then he walked down the bleachers and around behind the first base dugout and he leaned against the fence. The first pitch was a grounder and the shortstop picked it up and threw it over to first. Cody tossed the ball to the pitcher and held up one finger and then as he walked back to position he looked at the man leaning on the fence with the big cup.

'Hey,' Larry said.

The boy didn't reply and didn't look at him long. He turned and faced the plate and waited on the pitch.

'Hey,' Larry said again. Louder.

The kids in the first base dugout looked at the man. So did the first base coach.

'I'm playing,' the boy said with his eyes toward home.

Larry sipped on his drink. Watched a few pitches go by.

'You swing at fastballs,' he said. The boy ignored him.

'I said you don't stand there and stare at fastballs.'

Cody reached down and picked up some dirt and rubbed it between his fingers.

'Come on up one day and we'll work on it.'

'I don't need no help.'

'That ain't what it looks like to me.'

The first base coach was some college kid home for the summer and he turned to Larry and said give the kid a break.

'You mind your own goddamn business.'

The kids in the dugout mumbled to one another.

He drank some more. The heat and the liquor getting to him. He wiped at his damp face. Said something to himself.

'Where's your momma?' he asked.

The umpire in the field moved a few steps closer to first base. 'Where's your damn momma?'

'I ain't talking to you.'

'I bet you are.'

'No I ain't.'

'Shit,' Larry said to the dugout. 'Boy won't talk to his own daddy. That's some bullshit.' Half the kids nodded. The other half shied away to the other end of the dugout. And then Larry set his cup on the ground and he opened his wallet and he took out a twenty and he told the dugout that the first one to bring him a bat could have it. The first base coach told them not to move but when he turned again to the game a longhaired kid grabbed a bat and brought it over to the end of the dugout and handed it to him through a space between the roof and fence. Larry stuck the twenty through to him.

He walked back to his drink. Picked it up and finished it and it burned and burned. And then he slammed the bat across the top of the chainlink fence, sending a ping across the ballpark and the umpire and the coaches and the kids in the field and the kids in the dugout and the people in the stands and the men smoking all looked down the right field line at the man with the bat. He raised the bat and hit the fence again and then he yelled I bet you'll talk to me now goddamn it.

Everyone stood still. Then the field umpire began to walk across the infield toward Larry and Larry waved the bat at him and said come on over here and see. He brought the bat down again across the top of the fence and he called out for any of them to come on over here and see. Come on and take it from me if you want it. Come on over here and fucking find out. Play fucking ball. The pitcher looked at the umpire and the umpire told him to go ahead and they started again.

When the cops arrived five minutes later he was standing in the same place. The game had gone on and he hadn't made another sound but he held the bat in his sweaty hands. Ready. He felt their eyes heavy on him and the kids had kept to the far end of the dugout. Away from the man with the bat. The longhaired kid had split with his twenty bucks before the coach could get his hands on him. They arrived in two cars and there were three of them and they approached in the way that one approaches a wild animal. Hands at their sides. On the tips of their feet. Larry had seen them pull into the parking lot and he thought about what he would do when they got to him. Thought about Cody's momma and what she would say when she heard about this. Two of the cops looked like they might have lived in a weight room. Short but stout as anvils and they didn't look like they were going to take any shit.

'Swing at fastballs,' he yelled across the infield to his son who was sitting in the dugout. And then he turned and swung at the three of them and on the second swing and miss he staggered and one of the stout cops charged before he could gather himself to swing again and then they were on him and they shoved his face in the dirt and their knees in his back as they pulled his arms behind and cuffed him. They yanked him up and his lip was busted and the blood and the dirt and the spit and the sweat ran down his chin and neck. They took him along the walkway with little kids standing off to the side as if they were watching some grotesque parade and when they shoved him into the back of the police car he fell over on his side and he didn't even bother to try to sit up.

45

WALT SAT AT ONE END OF the bar and made damn sure to talk with Earl enough so that Earl would remember him being there. He wanted somebody to see him because later on when he told Larry that he had been out and that's why he didn't get the message and that's why it had taken him so long to get down there he wanted there to be others to back him up. He wanted to stay on the right side of the fight for as long as he could.

He kept one eye on the clock above the bar, trying to decide when it would be safe to go and get Larry.

Not yet.

He hadn't liked the way it felt with the shotgun on him. And he had been shaken by the way Larry talked as they drove away from Russell's house that first night. Point a fucking gun at me, he said. Go ahead and point a fucking gun at me and see what happens. When are they gonna learn? When? You tell me. When are they gonna learn you do not fuck with me? Go ahead and point it. Put it right on my head. Right here. Right here on this spot between my eyes. I swear to God somebody's gonna learn. Point a fucking gun at me. He was all over the road as he went on. Spit coming out of his mouth. Finger pointing at the windshield then at Walt then back at the windshield. Think that shit scares me? That shit don't scare me. Point a fucking gun at me. Go ahead and keep on fucking with me and see what happens. Goddamn everybody thinks they got something. Don't they? Think they got something they just got to do. Got to do or it's gonna goddamn kill them. Got to go fucking drive around fucked up and top a hill and kill somebody. Got to go do it. Ain't worried about what might happen 'til it happens. Got to. Got to fuck around. Don't matter it makes me look like a dumbass. Got to. World might stop spinning if I don't go fuck around. Got to have it oh please God yes right there got to have it. Don't think about shit else but keep on fucking with me. Everybody. Please keep on. You'll find out. Hell yeah you'll find out. I bet he thinks it's funny right now but hell no it ain't gonna be funny next time. Next time I take that gun out of his goddamn hands and shove it down his goddamn throat. Son of a bitch points a fucking gun at me like he rode into town on a white fucking horse. He owes me and you and Jason and he knows it. Goddamn it keep on.

Walt had always been on board with his brother. The bullying. The drinking. He liked the fights. Liked them as a kid. As a teenager. As a younger man. As a man. Particularly liked them when they had the odds like they did most of the time. He had been on board when Larry started talking up Russell's homecoming. About how he'd killed Jason and didn't deserve to be walking around and we'll get even for our little brother who can't get even for himself. Had looked forward to it. Had liked getting his hands on Russell at the bus station. Liked thinking about the next time they would get to drinking and go after him.

But he didn't like that shotgun being pointed at him. Didn't like the stakes that high. Didn't like being scared. Like he'd found himself when he walked into the room and Russell was standing there with the gun. He'd played tough but something inside him had skipped. Never had a gun pointed at him before. All the bar fights and all the parking lot fights and there had never been a gun. And he had seen the look in the man's eye who held it on them and Walt believed he was capable of shooting. He would knock somebody's head against the wall and he missed Jason like any man would miss his brother but he wasn't going to get shot. And he had to figure out how to tell Larry that.

He asked Earl for another one and he lit a cigarette. He had listened to his brother's message four times. I need you down here, Walt. Down at the Kentwood jail. Come on and get me. Don't fuck around. Get on down here. Where the hell you at anyway? Walt knew that if Larry was calling from the Kentwood jail he probably deserved to be there but that didn't stifle the guilt he felt in ignoring his brother.

Earl brought the beer and set it down and then the door opened. Walt looked and there was Heather. Earl said hey to her and she smiled back and then she asked Walt if he had any rules about what she was allowed to drink while sitting there next to him.

'I don't give a shit,' he said.

She asked Earl for a glass of wine and while he poured it she reached over and took a cigarette from Walt's pack that was sitting on the bar.

'Where's your brother?' she asked.

He took a long drag from his cigarette and blew the smoke out his nose. 'Where's your husband?'

'Same place your brother is.'

He nodded. Wondered if she knew what he knew.

Walt kept his eyes ahead on the shelves of liquor bottles. Heather sat sideways and looked around at the empty tables. He drank and then said you are a wonder.

'A wonder? Like how?'

'I'd just as soon not say,' he said. He thought about the conversations he and Larry had about her when Larry was getting ready to marry her. About how leopards don't change their spots and all that shit and hell I know she's fine but something fine walks in the door every night and you don't have to marry it and worry about it like you're gonna worry about her.

'Tell me,' she said and she bumped his leg with her leg. 'How am I a wonder?'

'Not like Wonder Woman. A wonder like goddamn she makes you wonder.'

Heather laughed. She couldn't help but laugh.

'See what I mean?' he said.

'No. Hell no, I don't see what you mean. That doesn't make any sense.'

'Does to me. Does to Larry.'

'Larry doesn't think about me.'

'You don't know what he thinks about,' he said.

'You don't either.'

'I know better than you.'

'You want to call me a wonder and then sit here and tell me you know what Larry thinks about. Nobody knows what Larry thinks about. He don't even know.'

'All I know is you're a wonder.'

She laughed some more. Tossed her head back and tossed her hair around. Smiled at herself in the mirror behind the bar. 'You don't even know what that word means,' she said.

'I'll tell you what it means,' he said. He met her smile with a serious stare and his brow had the same bend of Larry's brow when he meant business. He shifted on his seat. Took a drink from his beer. Looked back to her and said it means that I wonder why the hell you just can't give him a break. I wonder why you gotta do the things you do. Why you gotta shove it in his face. Why you gotta make him a big joke. I wonder why. That's what it means. I wonder why you can't give him a break every now and then. And I'm getting the hell out of here and you can pay Earl. You got Larry's money in your pocket. You got everything. And I'm a son of a bitch for sitting here talking to you when I should be somewhere else.

They had stuck Larry in the holding cell with the rest of the Monday night roundup. There were ten of them. No window and a bench on each wall. The floor slick and stained. The smell of beer and worse. Larry sat with his arms folded, furious that no one had answered his calls. Furious that it was damn near midnight and he was still sitting there. Three guys in the corner across from him had begun to watch him. Everyone else kept to themselves. Cigarettes and anxious feet tapping and faces in hands.

There were two big ones and one little one. The little guy did the talking and pointed at Larry while the two big ones nodded and grinned. Larry sat with his elbows on his knees but when the two big men walked over to him he sat up straight. There was more girth than muscle on the two men and one of them had his head shaved while the other wore pigtails and it looked as if he might have been wearing a soft shade of lipstick. They both wore overalls. Shirtless underneath. The little guy stayed across the room with his legs crossed and his hands folded on top of his knee as if he were posing for a portrait.

'My friend over there likes your boots,' said the big one with the shaved head. The one with the pigtails pointed at Larry's feet as if to clarify.

Larry leaned around the men and looked at the little man. Eye shadow and mascara and his jeans were rolled to his knees and he wore sandals.

'Good for her,' Larry said.

'What size are they?'

'They're my size.'

The man with the pigtails began to rub his hands together.

'Maybe you could let him try them on.'

Larry looked around the cell. Thought that some of the others might come over and even the odds but he was on his own.

'How about twenty bucks instead?' Larry said.

The big man with the pigtails sat down next to Larry and put his arm around him and said how about I give you a big juicy kiss right on that pretty mouth of yours. Then the other man sat down on his other side and Larry tried to hop up but they pulled him back down. He wondered if it'd matter if he yelled for someone. They squeezed him like he was their favorite doll.

'You want me to take them off for you or you want to do it?' said the shaved head.

'Let me go and I'll take them off.'

'Take them off and we'll let you go.'

'Let's take him home,' said the pigtails and he blew into Larry's ear. 'I been thinking we need a cowboy around.'

Larry kicked off the boots.

'Socks, too.'

Larry pulled off his socks and tucked them into the boots.

'That's some ugly ass feet,' said the shaved head.

'They ain't that bad,' the other one said.

'Let me fucking go,' Larry said.

'You better be nice now,' said the pigtails. 'We might end up spending the whole night together.'

The big one with the shaved head stood up and took the boots and told the other one to come on. They left Larry and went over to their friend and their friend gave a playful wave to Larry and then he sat still while they put the shoes and boots on his feet.

Larry stood up and grabbed the jail bars. 'Walt, you son of

a bitch! You son of a bitch! Take me to the telephone! Hey! Somebody take me back to the goddamn telephone!'

Half an hour later the jailer opened the door and motioned for Larry and he followed him down the hallway and into an office where he signed some papers and was given back his keys and wallet. They took him out the door and down another hallway and then through another door and there stood Walt.

Walt looked down at Larry's feet. 'Where the hell are your boots?' Larry walked past him and out the door. Walt followed and asked twice more about the boots but quit when they reached his truck and Larry still hadn't answered.

They left the station and drove through Kentwood and to the interstate. When Walt turned north Larry said my truck is at the ballpark you dumb shit.

'Don't call me a dumb shit,' Walt said. He didn't wait for the next exit but cut across the median, the headlights bouncing across the night and Walt gunning it to beat an oncoming car. He turned onto the ramp and Larry said I'll call you what I want. Neither made another sound until they stopped at the ballpark at Larry's truck.

When Larry reached for the door Walt said hold on. You gotta know something and I don't want you to go flying off the handle when I say this. You and me both know Russell has got to pay for what he did but I'm drawing the line at shotguns and pistols. I ain't looking to die and you shouldn't be neither. And if we push that hard then that's what is gonna happen and I ain't ready to be buried. That wouldn't do me or you or Jason no good. I'll do whatever else.

Larry opened the truck door and stepped out. Stared at Walt. 'What?' Walt said.

'So. You're one of them,' Larry said.

'One of them what?'

He glared at Walt and felt his blood rising as if he were beginning to melt on the inside, his rage stoking the heat in his veins until he became nothing more than some torrid and molten puddle of flesh and bone. He glared and didn't answer and then he slammed the door. Walt didn't wait around for a convoy back to McComb and he stomped the gas and his back tires spun on the rough pavement. Larry walked around to the back of his truck and let down his tailgate and sat and stared at the empty ball fields. At the empty bleachers and walkways. He then walked barefoot along the walkway and he entered the gate at the first base dugout and he ran. He ran and slid headfirst into second base and then got up and went for third and slid headfirst again. Red dirt streaked down his shirt and jeans and arms and neck. Heart racing and breathing hard and he took off his shirt and ran and slid. Ran and slid. His chest and arms scraped and bleeding and the dirt in his nose and ears and under his fingernails and the raging eyes of hate.

46

T HE NEXT MORNING RUSSELL AND MABEN stood by the pond
and talked it out. The last bus of the day would leave at
ten o'clock that night. Nice and dark, he said. Kill the day out
here and then I'll take you to the station. Not much chance of
running into anybody or of me and you being seen together.
Even if Boyd comes this way we'll see it coming along the
highway and tuck you and her away. Bus heads north but
Memphis is as far as you can go. Get off wherever looks good
to you. Maben smoked and nodded, watched a cloud of gnats
hovering above the surface of the pond.

Annalee spent the day feeding the fish and then catching
them. Tossing bread to the ducks. Climbing up on the tractor
and pretending to drive. Throwing rocks into the pond or at
trees or whatever.

Maben was not so easy. Anxious. Jumpy. Ready to go.
Overcome by her nomadic nature. She smoked a pack and
asked for more. Russell fed them to her like they were french
fries. Didn't matter to him what she did as long as she stayed
put and then got on that bus. Once the afternoon passed and
the evening came on he figured they were safe. That ten o'clock
was going to arrive and she would leave town under the cover
of stars and in a few weeks or a month she would be back and

then they could go from there. No need to try to figure it all out in one day.

They finished eating a late dinner after it had been difficult to get Annalee to put away her fishing pole and Mitchell and Russell sat outside with coffee while the women sat in the living room watching television. Only the light from the window above the barn interrupted the dark.

'She's going tonight,' Russell said.

'Going where?'

'She's not sure.'

'Just she?'

'Yeah. Only the big one.'

'What you gonna do with the little one?'

'Watch her. Give her something to eat every now and then. Can you do that?'

'For how long?'

'Not long.'

'And what are we going to say if someone asks about her?'

'We'll say she's visiting Consuela. She's her niece or something.'

'That don't sound so great.'

'Well. That's all I got right now.'

The back door opened and Maben came outside to join the men. She sat down in a rocking chair next to Mitchell.

'We'll let it get a little darker and then I need to stop by the house before we go to the station,' Russell said to her. 'Got some stuff you might need.'

'Fine,' she said.

'When I finish my coffee,' he said.

'Anything you can get here?' Mitchell asked.

Russell shook his head.

The evening sky stretched out in lavenders and pinks. Wisps of bluegray clouds settled along the horizon and the weight of night began to drape the twilight. Mitchell stood and patted

Maben's shoulder and then he left them and took his worry out to the pond.

'So what is it I need exactly?' Maben asked.

'How much money you got?'

'Don't know. I've had less, though.'

'Then that's what you need. I got some at the house. Not much. Some.'

'You don't have to give me no money.'

'I know I don't have to.'

'You don't have to do none of this.'

'I know,' he said again. 'We better go.'

Consuela had packed Maben a bag of clean clothes and a toothbrush and hairbrush. And at Russell's instruction she had tucked away a pencil and paper and several stamped envelopes. A scrap of paper with Russell's address paper-clipped to the top envelope. The bag sat at the edge of the porch and Maben rose from the rocker and slung it over her arm. Then she stood in the open door and stared inside at Annalee.

'Do you want to tell her bye?' Russell asked.

'I did. Before I came out here.'

'Do you want to tell her again?'

Maben watched her child. Took one step toward her and stopped. Then she turned and walked past Russell and across the yard to the truck.

Driving through town they crossed the arching bridge that stretched over the railroad tracks and at the height of the bridge she took a quick look down the tracks. 'There's something pretty about that,' she said.

'About what?'

'About the railroad tracks at night. How they go on and on and you can't see where. But they're so straight and perfect. Like there's no way to get lost.'

'There ain't no way to get lost on a train.'

'You know what I mean,' she said. 'Maybe pretty ain't the word.'

'Maybe.'

'But what if you get on the wrong one?'

'What about it?'

'You'd be lost then.'

'You got me there.'

'Don't go to your house yet. Let's ride some,' she said. 'We got time?'

'Some.'

She turned on the radio and she didn't talk anymore. When they passed through town Russell told her to duck down and she kept her head below the dashboard until the lights of town were behind them. They moved along the winding, dark roads. Shades of black through the trees and across the pastures in a moonlit night and then he asked if that was enough and she said no. Keep riding some more.

Later she said if you don't have to then I don't understand why you are doing all this. Nobody never helped me or her. They were deep in the country when she asked. Only able to see what the headlights would give them. He didn't know how to answer. But she waited.

'You're the one who picked me,' he finally said. He looked at her. At the dim light on her face from the dashboard lights. Her tired face. Her old face. Not yet thirty but the face of the defeated. The face of holding on. 'It's like you got an invisible collar around your neck and so do I. And there's an invisible rope pulling us together.'

'That might be a fair way to put it. Like soul mates. But between bad souls.'

'Bad?'

'Maybe bad ain't the right word. Sometimes I don't know what word is right.'

They drove on. The back roads like a shelter.

'Even if they figure it out I won't say nothing about you helping me.'

He shifted in his seat. 'You'll do whatever you got to do.'

'I mean it. I won't say nothing.'

'Okay.'

'I won't. I just wanted you to know.'

'Okay.'

He stayed out among the stars for a little longer and then he drove back into town. She didn't talk anymore. And neither did he.

47

WHEN LARRY TURNED ONTO RUSSELL'S STREET he didn't see the Ford and that was what he wanted. He parked a block away and then he walked to the house with a beer in one hand and a crowbar in the other. He stumbled with the uneven sidewalk. Stumbled off the curb and dropped the beer and he kicked it across the street. But then he gathered himself and he walked on carefully. When he reached Russell's house he went around to the back door and turned the knob. It was locked and then he pushed at the bedroom window and it seemed to give. He wedged the end of the crowbar underneath and he lifted and the window raised. One leg in the window and then the rest of him and he sat down on the bed. He didn't turn on any lights and he sat still with the crowbar across his lap. If he would have slid the heel of his new boots back six inches he would have bumped the barrel of the shotgun.

The longer he sat still the more he realized he was alone. For whatever reason he was alone and he didn't envision a future that would be any different and then the booze and the emptiness bled together and he began to cry. And as he cried his thoughts weren't filled with faces or voices or any of the memories of a life but with the image of sitting at the bottom of an empty well and looking up at the circle of light. Reaching for a rope that was out of reach. He cried like a man who was out of faith and he didn't try to stop himself and he was glad that there was no one to see him or to hear him. He laid the crowbar on the bed and he walked around in the dark bedroom, pulling at his hair and crying like the forsaken and stomping in a circle and kicking at anything that interrupted his pacing and in the streaks that ran from his face and down his neck he began to feel a cleansing, a release, an answer, a promise and he raged on and on, crying and wailing and stomping. Forcing it out of his body as if there were a holiness to be achieved. He stomped around the room and heaved and then he clenched his jaw and growled and raised both fists and shook them at the God he didn't want to know.

He then opened his hands. Touched his fingertips to his damp cheeks and his damp neck. He bent over and felt as if he might vomit and thought how good that might feel but he raised back up and he extended his arms and palms toward the ceiling and screamed a muffled scream with his teeth clenched as if not quite ready to fully release the hell burning inside.

He walked back over to the bed and picked up the crowbar and sat down. A loaded Beretta was underneath the passenger seat of his truck but he did not want the power of the clean and the crisp. He stared at the wall and his blood surged and in the shadows he felt it all. His young brother Jason ripped away from him and the son he could not see and his ex-wife dismissing him with a wave of a hand. The joke he had become to Heather and everyone who knew the shit that she did and even now Walt turning his back on him. The final betrayal. And that motherfucker Russell free and clear. His hands sweating around the iron bar and his jaw clamped tight and then he heard the Ford pull into the driveway and he knew that he was ready and he was going to make it hurt and hurt and hurt.

He stood and moved into the small hallway and then slid into the bathroom doorway as he heard the front door unlocking. The door opened and a light came on in the living room and he couldn't tell if they were the steps of one or the steps of two but he heard something coming his way and he squeezed the crowbar and he imagined right where Russell's forehead would be. And when the steps made it to the edge of the bathroom he was already beginning to swing and he saw that it wasn't what he was after but it was too late and he hit a woman in the side of the head and she dropped.

He paused drunk and confused and Russell flew at him as Larry stood over the fallen body. Russell tackled him back toward the bedroom and the crowbar clanged on the floor as the two men went flying. Russell got his hands around his throat but Larry was able to pry them away and Russell took a head butt to the nose and then another and they rolled across the room, hands clawing at the eyes and mouth and throat of the other and Larry was able to get to his knees first and he got Russell by the hair and thrust his head back against the wall in three quick knocks but Russell sent a sharp elbow into his stomach and pulled away from him and they hurried to their feet. Larry went for the crowbar and expected to be grabbed or pulled but he made it to the hallway and picked it up and then turned around to see Russell lying on the floor next to the bed. Reaching underneath and snatching out the shotgun and Larry had only half a second to be surprised before he heard the blast and felt the sting and the searing hot pain in his chest. He stumbled back, falling over the motionless woman and dropping the crowbar and then getting to his knees and crawling for the door as another blast sounded and splintered his hand reaching to open the door.

He screamed and dropped to his elbows but he kept on, getting the door open and falling out and then looking over his shoulder anticipating the next blast but it never came as

Russell was bending over the woman with his hands waving in confusion. Larry crawled across the yard and then got to his feet at the sidewalk. He made his way toward his truck like some broken puppet and as he opened the truck door with his good hand he heard the sirens. He fumbled with his keys and screamed again at the heat shooting through his chest. He got the keys in the ignition and the sound of the sirens grew louder and he was able to get the truck cranked and he put it into drive. As he moved away he noticed lights coming on in the houses that lined the street and he squeezed his mangled hand between his legs and he wondered whose head he had cracked as he cried out in pain and fury and raced into the night.

48

T HEY FIRST SPOTTED HIM TEN MILES down into Louisiana
driving a hundred miles an hour. Passing cars on the left or
the right and running down into the median and back up again
like a maniac off the leash. He held his busted hand under his
armpit to try to stop the throbbing and the bleeding but there
was nothing he could do about his chest except pretend there
wasn't a hole in it. The blood was down his stomach and into
his lap. He was sweating and had somehow managed to get a
lit cigarette into his mouth and he ignored the flashing lights
of first one and then two and then three Louisiana highway
patrol cars. He charged on, driving hard and driving fast and he
was nearly to Hammond when he saw them up ahead. Highway
patrol cars lined across the road with their lights circling into
the trees and he stomped the gas pedal to the floor and as he
got closer he saw them standing in front of their vehicles with
their rifles ready and he laughed at the thought of this. At how
fucking stupid they must be to think that he gave a damn and
they scattered like roaches as the truck laid on its horn and if
they could have seen the man behind the wheel they would
have seen him laughing at them as he jettisoned himself into
their wall.

49

HE STOOD OUTSIDE THE EMERGENCY ROOM doors smoking a cigarette. Pacing. Talking to himself. Russell wondered where that son of a bitch had gone and if he had bled to death yet and he hated that he hadn't fired on him until Larry had to be carried out of the house in pieces. He smoked the cigarette down and tossed it and lit another. There was blood on the shoulder of his shirt where he had picked Maben up and carried her, a trickle coming from her ear as her head fell against him. He had laid her across the seat of the truck and driven like hell, nearly causing pileups as he ignored the red lights of at least three intersections. Two young men in scrubs had come through the automatic glass doors and taken her from the truck and laid her on a stretcher and he told them she got hit in the head as they wheeled her out of sight. He couldn't take it in there so he went back out and he had been pacing and smoking and waiting. A woman behind the desk kept waving to him from inside and shaking a clipboard at him, wanting him to come in and tell her what he knew. But he shook his cigarette back at her and ignored her.

It was about that time when the cruiser pulled into the emergency room driveway. Boyd saw Russell and so he looped around and parked and then he met Russell on the sidewalk.

'Heard it over the wire,' Boyd said. 'Heard your address. You okay?'

'Do I look okay?'

Boyd tapped the tip of his index finger on the blood on Russell's shoulder. 'Who does that belong to?'

Russell flicked away his cigarette. Stood up straight and looked out across the parking lot. He felt Boyd's eyes on him. Knew that he was running out of things to say to him. Running out of alleys to hide in. Running out of excuses to make. Knew that the next thing Boyd would do was to go inside and find out what happened. Find out it was Maben in there. Then he'd wait until she could make a sentence. Whether it was an hour or a day or a week he would be the first person she'd see when she opened her eyes and then she'd have to answer and there was no way to know how she'd answer after the whack she'd taken on the side of the head. Or if she would be able to answer at all. Maybe she'd forget everything. Maybe she'd forget just enough. No telling what was going to come out of her mouth if she ever started talking again. No telling what might be left in her head.

'What happened, Russell? You can either tell me now or tell me later.'

Russell lit another cigarette. 'Went to my house and Larry was in there. Had a woman with me and he hit her with a crowbar or something. Thinking it was me. Then me and him got into it and I got hold of my gun and shot his ass.'

'Cops been here yet?'

'Not yet.'

Boyd walked a small circle. Hands on his hips. 'So. Who was she?'

'Just a woman.'

'It bad?'

'Guess so. Fucking crowbar to the side of the head.'

Boyd walked another circle. Wanted Russell to come out and

say who she was without having to ask again but it didn't seem to be coming.

'Who was it?' he asked in a dead tone.

Russell held his head back and blew smoke into the air. Wiped at the blood on his shirt. Then he pointed at the cruiser and said, 'You got some gas in that thing?'

'I got some.'

'Then come on. Let's go for a ride.'

Russell started for the car and Boyd followed him and they got in and left the hospital parking lot, passing a police car pulling in. Boyd said which way and Russell told him to go out to the lake. They rode through and out of town in silence. The radio called out a wreck on the highway but they didn't need everybody and Boyd told them he was checking on something at a tractor place out near Pricedale. At the lake Boyd drove slowly and waited on Russell to give him another direction and finally Russell did as he guided him to his favorite spot. The cruiser eased down the dirt road and squeezed between the trees. They stopped at the water's edge.

'Kill it,' Russell said. Boyd turned off the lights and the ignition. Russell got out of the car and sat on the hood and Boyd sat down next to him. He folded his arms and waited. Russell finished his cigarette and he stepped to the water and tossed it into the lake. He didn't want to go back. He could still smell it. He could hear the shouts and threats and promises that would come his way when he returned. There were so many fights left to fight but he knew that he could take it better than she could.

He turned and faced Boyd.

'Got to trust each other. Told us that every day for four years, didn't he?' Russell said. 'I bet Coach Noland's still saying it to whoever will listen. Got to trust each other.'

'Got sick of hearing it,' Boyd said.

'Everybody can tackle. Everybody can run fast. Everybody lifts weights. Everybody works hard. That ain't it. Got to trust each other. Got to do your job. Do your shit. Let the other ten guys believe you're there doing it. Believe they're doing their job while you're doing yours. That's the difference.'

'Seemed like it worked. Won a helluva lot more than we lost. And we weren't the biggest and strongest most times.'

'Nope.'

'But we gave a damn. Probably more than most.'

'Probably.'

'But I'm guessing we ain't out here to tell war stories.'

'No,' Russell said. 'We ain't.'

'Then what are we out here for?'

Russell sat down again on the hood. Crossed his legs. Pointed out toward the water. 'Right out there,' he said. 'Your boy's pistol is right out there.'

'What you mean my boy's pistol?'

'You know what I mean, Boyd.'

Boyd wiped at his mouth. Rubbed his eyes. 'Shit, Russell,' he said.

'Yeah. Shit.'

The water lapped lazily against the bank. Boyd slapped away a mosquito. An owl hooted and something screeched.

'And now it's your turn,' Russell finally said.

'How so?'

'It's your turn. To trust me.'

'Don't start with that.'

'I'm not starting anything. I want you to listen. I mean it. Listen. You got to trust that I'm telling you the truth.'

'I'm gonna try.'

'Not try,' Russell said.

'I ain't giving you some bullshit oath, Russell. I can't do that. You know it and I know it.'

'Fine. Just do your best and let me finish. And don't listen like a lawman.'

'Then what you want me to listen like?'

'Listen like you're you and I'm me and that's it.'

'You got a shitload of rules for somebody who just pointed out where the one damn thing is that everybody in this county is looking for.'

'You know I didn't kill him. Damn well better know.'

'Then who did?'

'Nobody who shouldn't have.'

Russell stood again. Walked out in front of Boyd. Looked at him in the dark, at the wide silhouette of what he hoped was still a friend.

And then he started talking.

He told Boyd that the woman in the hospital was Maben but I'm guessing you got that figured out. Yeah the same Maben. And then he told him how he came across her. How Maben had held the pistol on him as he came out of the Armadillo and told him to drive. How she hurried the child into the truck and how shaky she was with the pistol in her hand. So shaky that I reached right over and took it away. How they had driven through the night and that was where I was on the night you kept on asking me about. Then he told him how the deputy had taken Maben from the truck stop and driven her out away from everything and what he had made her do. How when she thought it was finally over he told her it wasn't over. Company was coming and keep your damn mouth shut. And how she panicked about Annalee left behind in the motel room and how she wasn't going to let it end this way for them and the next thing she knew she had the pistol pointed at him and then he was down and dead and she was running.

And then he told Boyd that she was convinced nobody would believe her and that's why she was running and I told her she was right. Nobody would believe her. Except that he believed her and he didn't know why or maybe he did know why but he felt like he was supposed to help her. I brought us here. All of us. Maben to running with that pistol and me and you sitting here right now. My road is the road that brought us all here led by what hand I don't know. But here we are and I can't let this go. It's just her and the child and it'll get worse and worse and some of us can take it but some of us can't and some aren't supposed to have to. She's a small child. But got a long look. Like Maben. They've been up and down the road, Boyd. God knows where and back again. If you heard her tell it you couldn't help but believe her either. And so I took them out to my daddy's place and let them get some food and some rest and Sunday night we rode out here right to this spot and I took the pistol and threw it right out there. Far as I could. And I hoped that was that. But apparently it ain't. I was putting her on a bus tonight and we were going over to my house to get her some money and that crazy motherfucker might have killed her. She's had it, Boyd. She's had it. And I'm telling you all this so you'll understand right now when I ask you to leave her alone. I ain't telling you. I'm asking you. Leave her alone. He got what he got. Let it fall.

Boyd had sat still and quiet as he listened to Russell. And he sat still and quiet as he thought about what Russell had asked him to do.

'It's not so simple,' Boyd said.

'Yeah. It is.'

'No. It's not. Not even. You know who's sleeping in my house right this damn minute? A wife and two damn kids. That's who.'

'I know.'

'Then don't tell me it's simple.'

Boyd stood up from the hood and walked to the edge of the water. He bent down and picked up a stick and tossed it out into the lake. 'I imagine there's some people want to talk to you about now,' he said.

'I imagine so,' Russell said.

'How far out there is it?' Boyd asked.

'Far enough.'

Boyd tugged at his gun belt. Adjusted his pants. 'Come on,' he said and he turned and walked to the cruiser. Russell followed him and got in.

'Say something,' Russell said. 'I know you got something else to say.'

'Not right now,' he answered without looking at him and he shifted the cruiser into reverse. He backed up carefully, cutting it between two trees and then putting it in drive and they moved off the dirt road and looped back around the lake. Lights from the cabins shined on the far shore and a houseboat sat still in the middle of the lake in the windless night. They drove back to the hospital without talking and Boyd didn't pull into the parking lot but instead stopped at the curb. Two police cars were parked next to the emergency room entrance.

'Go on,' Boyd said. 'But you listen to me now. I ain't making you no promises and I ain't making no deal. I heard you and that's all. I heard you. Wish to God I hadn't.'

'That's all I want. You to hear.'

'That's not all you want. Jesus. You got no idea what you're asking me to do. I know you been living by a different set of rules for a while and I get it but goddamn. You got the easy part now.'

'There's no easy part.'

'There might not be an easy part but I'll be damned if we both don't have a lot to lose. I'm thinking I got more.'

'You might be right.'

'I know I'm right. You think it was hell on you in Parchman? Let them throw a deputy sheriff out in that yard and see how nasty it gets. I'm guessing it'd make your time look like a cakewalk at a junior high fundraiser. Guessing you wouldn't wish it on nobody. And that's what's out there at the end of all this.'

Russell sat still and didn't answer. He looked over at Boyd who stared at the top of the steering wheel. He didn't know what else to say. Didn't want to push anymore. It was out there and whatever was going to happen was going to happen.

'Go on in there,' Boyd said.

Russell nodded and then he got out and walked toward the emergency room. Tired now and dragging. Tender in the places where Larry had gotten him. Behind him he heard the cruiser shift into gear and drive away. He wished for a place to sit down and be alone though he knew that wasn't going to happen. He entered the emergency room and standing at the desk were two policemen. They greeted him with the news that Larry was dead and that Maben was alive. And then they turned him around and cuffed his wrists and marched him outside. They stuffed him into the back of one of the cop cars and drove him to the station where he sat in a room with a square table and hard chairs and a cigarette and an ashtray and explained how he'd come to shoot Larry.

50

B OYD DROVE PAST HIS HOUSE AND all the lights were off except
for the floodlight on the corner of the garage which shined
onto the driveway and Lacey's car. The small pickup that he had
bought for the boys to get around in was parked along the street
in front of the house. A trailer hitched to the pickup carried a
riding mower and a push mower and a weed eater and a rake.

He drove on by the house and along the street. A sprinkler
left running in a front yard. A tricycle on the sidewalk and trash
cans next to the curb and the feeling that there was peace in all
their dreams.

In his fifteen years as a deputy he had come to accept the
fact that people did filthy, unspeakable things to one another.
To those weaker than them. Smaller than them. Defenseless
against them. Unspeakable things that made him sit next to the
beds of his boys when they were small children. Home late and
them already asleep and the knowledge of these things on his
mind and sitting there in the dark listening to them breathe.
Their bodies and their minds at the mercy of what was outside
the door and the fact that he couldn't walk with them every
step of the way gnawing at him as he watched them sleep.
Sitting there in the dark and praying that the things he had seen
wouldn't find his children and trying hard to understand a God

that would allow the weakness of innocence and the strength of evil. He kept the ugliest of what he knew to himself. Unwilling to tell Lacey because he did not want her to lie awake at night and share his fears. There in the dark as he sat next to the beds of his children he could only hope and he had continued to hope over the course of the years and as the cruiser passed through the sleeping streets of his neighborhood he was reminded of this hope. The hope that there was a good out there and that it quietly protected when no one else was around to help. He was reminded of this undetectable good and how much was left to its mercy and he wondered if perhaps that mercy hadn't presented itself on the night that the deputy was murdered. If there really was such a thing that he had always imagined there to be.

He drove out of his neighborhood and along Delaware Avenue and he crossed over the interstate and drove out into the emptiness of those beloved back roads where so much happened. There was beauty in the depth of the sky and the black of the trees and the stillness of the empty acres. He turned off his radio and unbuckled his gun belt. Unsnapped the holster and pulled out the pistol and set it on the seat next to him. He pushed a button on the armrest and his seat leaned back and he turned off the air conditioner and rolled down the windows and the warm wind wrapped around him like the arms of a good friend. He drove farther and farther out until the random lights were gone and there was only the man and the land and the night. Safe from any approaching cars he slowed down and turned off his headlights and coasted along with only the orange glow of the parking lights leading him as if the cruiser were some alien craft examining a foreign terrain.

He thought again of his sons. Thought of how quickly they were becoming men and he hoped they would become good ones and he wished that he had a better understanding of what that meant. He thought he had that understanding until tonight. Thought he could sit down with them in the living room and tell them what a good man was and how to become one and maybe he still could but he knew that whatever he decided to do about that pistol and that murder would somehow taint his definition of a good man. Knew that whatever he decided to do there would remain an uncertainty that would walk with him and sleep with him and go with him to ball games and cook out with him in the backyard and grow old with him.

He had always liked the badge and the law because it gave him what was right and what was wrong and he was adrift between that by no fault of his own but it didn't matter. He was there anyway. He held his arm out the window with his palm facing forward and he felt the wind through his fingers, hoping to get a grasp of that undetectable thing that would give him an answer and then protect him from the things that came with that answer but nothing wrapped itself around his fingers and nothing crept out of the darkness and past the orange glow and into the cruiser and nestled beside him. He held his arm out and he held his hand open and then he slowed and came to a stop. He turned off the ignition. Turned off the orange lights. Silent black in front of him and behind him and all around him. He rubbed his hands together. Rubbed them on his face. Lay his head back on the headrest. And he sat there in a daze under the weight of the crown that had been given to him.

51

OCTOBER. THE THICKNESS OF SUMMER GONE and replaced with the relief of the autumn air. Russell sat in his truck in the parking lot across the street from the elementary school and watched the first falling leaves spin and scatter across the playground. He rubbed at his face and felt the softness of his beard. Thicker and fuller as if it could soften a blow if it had to. He looked in the rearview mirror and picked specks of paint out of it and then he picked at the paint on his hands and fingernails and he tried to figure out how much longer it would take him to get done with the house he was working on so that he could get paid. He needed to line up another job soon. In a couple of short months the easy fall weather would be gone and he needed to find as much work as he could before the cold and rain of winter. A child's workbook sat on the seat next to him and he opened it and looked at her capital letters. Some of them were successes. Some had a ways to go. She has a lot of catching up to do they kept saying and he knew that even by saying this they were being nice.

The bell rang and the double doors opened and children filed out in lines with teachers leading the way and some loaded onto buses and others crossed the street and made their way home along the sidewalks. Other children walked to the end of the breezeway to where the cars were lined up and one by one they disappeared into backseats. Every day he had to wait for Annalee to appear. She told him that she didn't like going out with everyone else. That she wanted to wait until they were gone. When the crowd thinned and the cars and buses moved out into the street the double doors opened again and a woman with glasses held the door while Annalee walked out with her arms folded and her steps careful. She looked up and down the breezeway and when she was satisfied she looked across the street and Russell waved to her and then he cranked the truck and drove over to pick her up.

She tossed her backpack in first and then she climbed in and he said hey and she asked if they could go get a milk shake. They drove down Delaware Avenue and stopped at the Star Drive-In and she got banana and he got chocolate and then they drove out to Mitchell's where he planned to let her out and then use every minute of daylight to paint as much as he could. Mitchell and Consuela and Maben were sitting in chairs in the backyard shucking corn and dropping the husks into silver bins. He looked out into the backyard and noticed that the statue of the Virgin Mary was draped in a white sheet and he asked her what that was about. It's a ghost, she said. A big white ghost. For Halloween. Consuela tied two sheets together. You mean sewed two sheets together, he said. Sewed, she repeated. He nodded and told her he'd be back later and she got out of the truck with her milk shake and she shut the door. She ran a few steps but then she stopped and turned around and waved at Russell.

He had hoped that his father would understand in the way that his father had asked him to understand Consuela and he had. I want them to stay out here over the barn but I'll pay the bills, he'd said. Fine, Mitchell answered. But it ain't gonna be easy. I know, he'd said. But she'll be up and going good before long. And then it'll be better. And that was as much as they had talked about it. Mitchell fished with Annalee and drove her around the place on the tractor and Consuela had tried to make her a dress once or twice though success was still on hold. Maben moved from chair to chair. Dizzy often. But not as often as before. Beginning to help in the kitchen. Learning from Consuela. They all ate dinner most nights out at his father's place and then they would sit on the back porch and take turns reading with the child while the nights fell cool around them. After the reading and the sitting were done Maben and Annalee would say good night and walk out to the barn and up the stairs and Consuela would take her slow, melodic walk out into the backyard and around the Virgin Mary and out to the pond. She would touch Mitchell on the shoulder as she would return and then she would go inside and Russell and Mitchell would have a bourbon or two before calling it a night. If someone were watching them from the road there would seem nothing peculiar about this collection of people.

He finished the milk shake as he drove back to town. The house he was painting was in his neighborhood and he stopped in front and admired his work. A little sloppy on the window frames but nothing that couldn't be scraped. Solid work on the trim. Nothing splattered on the roof as far as he could tell. He had planned to come back and put in another hour or two but the milk shake had weighed him down and he decided it could wait. He needed to stall some anyway until he could find another house to start on.

He put the truck in drive and he rode around town and like he did in nearly every empty moment he thought about Boyd. He had passed him on the road a couple of times and they had exchanged waves but that had been it. Sometimes at night as he lay awake he felt guilty over what he had asked Boyd to do. That if anything ever came about all the risk belonged to his old friend. But then he thought of Maben out in that black and silent country with her eyes shut and there was nothing to do but hope there would never be another word about it. He had heard something about the sheriff winding up retired after frustration with the case had reached beyond his limits and that seemed as good an omen as there was.

Still, something remained unsettled within him. As if it would be lazy and irresponsible to have a day pass without uncertainty. He only slept in intervals and when he did sleep his dreams put him back into that cell and some nights the visions were so real that when he woke he felt the same anxiety he had felt every morning when the sounds of men and steel had awakened him. But in his dreams he never left his cell and he was alone in the prison and the light was always gray and there was always the sound of a woman's voice calling out for him and he was never able to determine the direction that it came from. A woman's voice filled with anguish and calling his name on some nights but on the worst nights of the dream the voice was ghostly. A moaning in the dark. Echoing through the walls of an empty prison and he never knew if she was there to help him or if he was supposed to be helping her and then he would wake in a panic.

As he moved along the familiar streets he thought about the dream and he thought about Boyd and he imagined a day when they would all be sitting together at his father's place and a row of cars with sirens on the top would come up the driveway. He lit a cigarette and propped his arm in the open window. Thought maybe he'd drive back out to his dad's and get an early start on the bourbon this evening. Sit on the porch and watch the day die away and watch the evening fall across the land like a blanket covering it for the night. Minutes later he turned into his father's driveway and let off the gas and rolled across the gravel, hoping to see what they were doing before they noticed him.

He rolled on to the house and he found the four of them together in the backyard. Annalee and Mitchell and Consuela standing. Maben sitting in the chair next to them. The sheet was gone from the statue and they each held a corner end of it, flapping the sheet up and down and making a white wave. Russell got out of the truck and walked toward them and stopped. Annalee saw him and called out to him. Come on, she said. We got room for you. He stood still and watched them and then he noticed the Virgin Mary. The sun was low in the reddening sky behind her and her shadow stretched toward them. He thought that she seemed to be leaning their way, her outstretched arms wide enough for them all. As if to say, Come here and let me hold you.

About Us

In addition to No Exit Press, Oldcastle Books has a number of
other imprints, including Kamera Books, Creative Essentials,
Pulp! The Classics, Pocket Essentials and High Stakes
Publishing > oldcastlebooks.co.uk

For more information about Crime Books go to
> crimetime.co.uk

Check out the kamera film salon for independent, arthouse
and world cinema > kamera.co.uk

For more information, media enquiries and review copies
please contact marketing > marketing@oldcastlebooks.co.uk